Summer at Sea

Beth Labonte

Love comes to some gently, imperceptibly, creeping in as the tide, through unsuspected creeks and inlets, creeping on a sleeping man, until he wakes to find himself surrounded.

P.G. Wodehouse, *The Prince and Betty*

1

Just kill me. Somebody, right now, kill me. Please. If somebody doesn't hurry up and put me out of my misery, I cannot be held responsible for the words that come out of my mouth.

I mean, have *you* ever helped your parents pack for a weeklong cruise?

No? I didn't think so. So shut it. You have no idea the torture that is engulfing every fiber of my being. There is underwear all over the bed. Literally everywhere. My parents' underwear is everywhere—like ninety-seven pairs between the two of them—for an eight-day cruise. I tried to talk them into narrowing it down to maybe sixteen pairs each. I thought that was pretty reasonable. If they are both suddenly unable to control their bodily functions, sixteen pairs will still leave them with one fresh pair to change into daily. Reasonable enough.

"But what if something *happens?*" Mom asks, clutching six pairs in each hand, like underwear pom-poms. "What if something happens to the boat and we can't get home? What will we wear?"

"You realize you could always re-wear a pair, right? You could even rinse them out if they got dirty." I'm trying to ignore the underlying grossness of this conversation and just keep it together. My parents somehow lived through multiple wars, and *this* is the kind of stuff that they find to worry about. "I bet you could even get by with bringing only five pairs for the entire week." I throw that last bit in just to be a jerk.

Mom laughs maniacally, as if I told her she should try out for the Dallas Cowboy cheerleaders, or eat sushi. Then she gathers up the massive collection of underwear and shoves all of them into her suitcase. Subject closed.

"How many pairs of slacks do you think your father will need?" She shuffles over to the closet and starts rifling through pairs of corduroy pants. We're cruising to Bermuda, in August, and she's packing corduroy pants. I sink into a rocking chair in the corner of the bedroom and bury my head in my cell phone. While Mom is engrossed in determining whether or not a pair of pants is navy blue or black—why does this even matter?—I covertly snap a photo of all the junk on the bed. Four jackets of varying weights, enough socks for the entire Confederate Army, three umbrellas, most of the antacid aisle from the local pharmacy, and six pairs of old people sneakers that all look exactly the same. My parents don't pack six pairs of sneakers for style purposes. It's not like "This pair of plain white sneakers look better with these navy blue corduroys than this pair." No way. They're all being packed out of sheer terror that one of them might step into a puddle while walking across the pool deck.

Not only might they walk through a puddle, but also some force of nature—perhaps the Bermuda Triangle itself—might prevent them from lifting their feet from the puddle in a timely manner, thus soaking them through all the way to the skin. And if that were to happen, mixed with the ultimate threat of getting "a chill" from the air conditioning, you may as well just accept that your death is imminent and you will never again set eyes on dry land. I can't even imagine how Mom sleeps at night with the possibility of wet feet looming in the air.

And then there are the umbrellas. I mean really, are umbrellas even allowed on a cruise ship? I'm not sure that anybody has ever attempted to bring one aboard before. If it rains, wouldn't you just move along to one of the covered areas? I'm pretty sure they don't want thousands of people roaming around with open umbrellas, poking each other's eyes out. I would love to throw all of them overboard. The umbrellas, I mean. Right.

Packing for the Umbrella Apocalypse.

I punch the words into Twitter, attach the photo, and off it goes. I still can't even believe we are going on this trip. My parents never travel. There are too many possibilities of death and destruction involved with every mode of available transportation. Ironically, they love to travel by car—the only mode of transportation that literally has a crash rate of *every minute of every day.* But for some reason they feel safer with my dad behind the wheel, driving forty-five miles per hour down the interstate, than on a cruise ship full of lifeboats going eleven miles per hour through a totally empty Atlantic Ocean.

I sigh more loudly than necessary, and look up to see how Mom is doing. She's moved to the other end of the closet—the part where Dad keeps the suits that he used to wear to work before he retired. Mom and Dad had me when they were in their early forties, which was unusual at the time. Some of my friends' parents are in their forties *now*, while my parents are already in their sixties and retired.

The age gap tends to make things a bit…difficult.

"Uh, Mom," I ask, putting away my phone. "What are you doing in the suit section?" She's just kind of standing there, staring up at the suits. Maybe she's having a nervous breakdown. Mom is always claiming to be having nervous breakdowns. It's taken me twenty-six years to figure it out, but I think my mother announcing that she's having a nervous breakdown is the equivalent of a regular person saying, *I could really use a drink.*

"I was just thinking that your father might need a few suits," she says. "I mean, what if we're asked to dine with the captain?"

I pick the cruise brochure up off the bed and stare at the cover. Two casually dressed twenty-somethings are laughing it up over dinner. They're both wearing head to toe white linen outfits, and eating at a table practically on the prow of the ship. A pair of dolphins leaps gleefully in the background. *Freestyle Cruising* it reads across the top. I know there's nothing realistic about the photo, but I am still unbelievably jealous of them. The young couple, I mean. Not the dolphins. I can't even imagine the freedom of going on a vacation not only without your parents, but also with a boyfriend. Going to dinner, sightseeing, doing anything you want at any time. Not having to wear a sweater.

I hold the cruise brochure up for Mom to see.

"I think this cruise line's different," I say. "You can wear whatever you want. Look, Dad can wear an unbuttoned white linen shirt with his chest hairs showing."

"But I saw a show on television once," says Mom, totally

missing the humor. "The people on the boat were *all* dressed up. They had on sequins and these big shoulder pads." Mom makes *big shoulder pad* motions with her hands.

The Loveboat. She's talking about *The Loveboat.* She's been basing her entire wardrobe around a television show from the nineteen-eighties. I take a deep breath and toss the brochure back onto the bed. The white linen couple lands facedown on a stray pair of Dad's underwear. Serves them right.

"Look, Mom. Why don't you just work on fitting all of *this* stuff into the suitcase? If you have any room left we can do some more packing after dinner."

Hopefully by that point she will have forgotten about the fancy clothes and moved on to a more manageable category such as toiletries or motion sickness remedies. Besides, the chances that the captain is going to decide that he simply must have dinner with the umbrella-wielding elderly couple are basically slim to none. Dad could pack nothing but snorkel gear and an inner tube and everything would turn out just fine. I walk over and shut the closet door, and then gently lead my mother back over to the bed.

"How many suitcases did you say we could bring?" she asks.

"Two each, Mom. Plus a carry-on."

Her eyes light up at the mention of a carry-on. "Do you think we should bring The Duffle?"

The Duffle is the largest duffle bag ever created. It is six-feet long by three-feet wide, and was most likely manufactured for use by the mafia. Mom likes to stuff it full of socks and underwear. I shudder at the thought of them carrying The Duffle through the cruise terminal, one at each end, like they're moving a bureau. But there is no sense in trying to talk her out of it. The day she found The Duffle laying in the middle of the luggage aisle at Wal-Mart was one of the best days of her life, right up there with the birth of her children. And when you think about how many pairs of socks and underwear The Duffle can hold, compared to how many pairs of socks and underwear her children can hold, well, I think we have a clear winner.

"Totally up to you," I say.

I leave my mother to decide the fate of The Duffle, and retreat to the safety of my bedroom in the basement. My own suitcase sits unpacked on the floor. I suppose that it's at this point—just in case I don't make it back from this vacation alive and need somebody to jot down my meager memoirs—that I should tell you my name. It's Summer. Summer Hartwell. Okay, Summer *Eve* Hartwell. My parents, in their attempt at giving their little girl a cute name, accidentally named me after a line of feminine hygiene products. At least I assume that it was accidental. Whatever the case, it certainly did nothing to alleviate the self-consciousness that has plagued me for most of my life. It also did not help that in the sixth grade, six seconds after Mrs. O'Neil did the unforgivable and read off my full name during roll call, that Alex Sanderson nicknamed me Summer Douchewell. He called me that up until the very last second that I saw him after our high school graduation ceremony.

"Cheers, Douchewell!" he'd yelled across the parking lot—his graduation gown hanging open, his mortarboard long gone since he tossed it into the air. I had hung onto mine just as my mother advised. "Only idiots toss their hats," she'd said. Alex was getting into a car with some other kids, probably headed to a drunken orgy, while I climbed into the back seat of my parents' Hyundai Excel.

I remember watching Alex peel out of the parking lot as Dad checked his pants pockets for his wallet. I remember unzipping and removing my graduation gown as Dad went back into the auditorium to retrieve his forgotten jacket. I remember closing my eyes while my parents discussed where we would go for lunch. I remember rolling my eyes as I pictured them sipping their coffee while I sat in the booth bored out of my mind, waiting for them to pay the bill. I remember the car finally beginning to move, and at sixteen miles per hour, pulling out of my high school for the last time. It was nothing like it is in the movies. Nobody's hair was blowing. The top wasn't down. No horns were tooting. It was just me and my parents, putt-putting off to the Outback Steakhouse.

And now, eight years later, we're preparing to putt-putt across the Atlantic Ocean.

Smooth move, Douchewell.

2

Last night, in a fit of passive aggressive rebellion, I attempted to pack nothing but dresses, shorts, and t-shirts. I waited until eleven o'clock, when I was sure that both of my parents would be asleep, before hauling my suitcase upstairs. That's when Mom popped up from the living room couch and scared the living daylights out of me. Apparently she'd been lying there all evening with the television turned off, just waiting to catch me in the act. She marched me back downstairs and began examining the contents of my suitcase.

I'll spare you the details of the apoplectic fit that followed when she found it completely devoid of sweaters. I tried my best to defend my decision, but there is no argument that can win against the fact that *there will be air-conditioning on the ship.* And so I stood silently by while she went into my closet, pulled down the last two sweaters that I ever would have chosen, and stuffed them into my suitcase.

Said suitcase is now standing by the front door along with the others, including The Duffle, ready to be loaded into the limousine that my brother Eric is sending to pick us up. At least

I assume it's a limousine. He said that *the car* would be here at ten o'clock. I glance nervously out of the living room window, but it still hasn't arrived yet. I can't take this much longer. The longer it takes for the limo to get here, the more stuff Mom and Dad keep remembering that they need to pack.

Watching Dad is giving me anxiety. He's been in and out of the bathroom incessantly since we finished breakfast, and he keeps checking and re-checking all of the pockets of his cargo pants. He wears these insane pants that have more pockets than they do surface area. They're like some kind of miracle of physics that he thinks help keep him organized. In reality they just give him more places to lose things.

"Joan?" Dad shouts into the center of the living room. "Did you pack the hand sanitizer?"

"Right here!" Mom pops out of the hall closet, and in a move that would have impressed David Blaine, produces two small bottles from the palms of her hands. Dad slips one into each of his pockets, never to be seen again.

"Do you think we need these?" Mom holds up a pair of black rubber overshoes with dust bunnies dangling from the heels.

The room begins to swirl. Umbrellas I can deal with, but rubber overshoes are an entirely different kind of crazy.

This entire trip is Eric's fault. He's rich. Well, up until a couple of years ago he was an immature twenty-eight year old who I only saw during the major holidays. Then he went and invented an iPhone app that makes fart sounds and became a millionaire. Here's how it works: you push a button and it farts. That's it. What sets it apart from all of the other fart apps on the market is that it doesn't just make the same sound over and over again. My brother's stellar attention to detail has led him to replicate over fifty different tones—everything from a low foghorn to a high-pitched air-coming-out-of-a-balloon sound.

Gross, right?

It was particularly gross when he debuted it in front of the entire family over Christmas dinner. Especially after he told everyone that he had recorded all of the sound effects in my bedroom while I was asleep.

By the time I saw him again at Easter dinner, his creation was the top seller in the app store. He partnered up with his best friend, Graham Blenderman, and together they added several more apps to their portfolio. A couple of months later they sold their empire of flatulence to a major gaming company, and now my brother drives an Audi. I'm happy for them, and at the same time very sad that there are so many people willing to pay ninety-nine cents for a whoopee cushion.

Long story short, Eric decided to take us all on a cruise in order to celebrate his success. I'm not exactly sure why he decided to make us wait two years for it, but a free vacation is a free vacation. Mom and Dad agreed to it because it sails out of our home state of Massachusetts and there will be no air travel required. Meanwhile, Eric's spent the past week relaxing in his luxury condo in the city while I try to fit my parents' entire existence into four suitcases.

When the doorbell finally rings, I fling open the front door expecting to find whichever unfortunate limo driver was assigned to our case—sometimes I find myself referring to my family as a case—but instead find myself face to face with Graham Blenderman. Before I can even say hello, Mom has hip-checked me out of the way.

"It's so wonderful to see you!" she cries, wrapping her arms around his neck.

I roll my eyes. Mom is in love with Graham. Well, not in *love* love. But she thinks he's God's gift to the world, second only to my brother. She's always going on and on about how smart he is and how fabulously he played "Fur Elise" at this piano recital that was literally seventeen years ago. When she's not trying to fix me up with one of her old lady friends' awful sons, she's asking me why I don't "get together" with Graham. As if you can just make a man become interested in you. As if you can just make *Graham* become interested in you.

Graham Blenderman.

If his name doesn't throw you immediately off guard, the rest of him will. He's got this dirty blonde hair that spikes up in every direction, and a penchant for clothes that were destined to be the last color left on the clearance rack. I'm not being a snob against clearance racks or anything; I'm just saying that he sometimes goes a little overboard with the chartreuse. He's like the guy at the resort who's always trying to get people together for a game of pool volleyball. He'll come barging up to your lounge chair, nose slathered in zinc oxide, while all you want to do is disappear behind a book. He has more personality than I'm comfortable with is all I'm saying.

Not that he's terrible on the eyes or anything. To be honest, if anybody can pull off a tangerine colored cardigan, it's him. I wouldn't say that he's drop dead teen romance vampire hot—you know, when it takes every ounce of willpower to refrain from tearing his clothes off in the middle of chemistry lab. No, he's more Goofy than he is Casanova. But there has always been something about his unique combination of height, humor, and complete disregard for fashion norms that has rendered him quite intimidating to me.

"Hello, Joan," says Graham, extracting himself from her tentacles, and tipping an imaginary hat in my direction. "Summer." His eyes linger on me for a few seconds, moving from my face down the entire length of my body, and back up again.

I shift uncomfortably, wishing that I had chosen to wear something other than my travel sweats. Graham is wearing a polo shirt in the shade of blue that they dye children's breakfast cereal. Blue Dye #1.

"We weren't expecting to see you until later!" gushes Mom, squeezing the side of Graham's face in her hand. "What are you doing here?"

"Joan!" interrupts Dad, shouting from…the basement? What could he possibly be doing in the basement?

"Oy," says Mom. "Let me go see what he wants."

"What *are* you doing here?" I ask, as soon as she's gone. I smooth out my hair, which I threw into a who-cares-I'm-traveling-with-my-parents sort of ponytail this morning. It goes well with my travel sweats.

"Eric sent me to pick you guys up," says Graham, still surveying me.

"What are you looking at?"

He shrugs. "I like the outfit."

"Sorry I'm not wearing a mini-dress and stilettos."

"Why are you apologizing? I said I liked it."

"I assumed you were joking."

"Nope. It'd be a little strange if you had stilettos on right now, don't you think? You're traveling with your parents. No, I just meant that you look cute with the yoga pants and the —" he twirls his hand around the top of his head, referring to my ponytail.

12

"Oh," I say, a bit thrown. "Thanks."

I suppose that now is a good time to tell you that there was a short time, in my teen years, when I did actually think that Graham might be interested in me. He and Eric had gone off to college in Boston, and often times they would come home together for the weekend. That's when Graham would do the strangest things.

For example, one time he stood in the driveway shouting my name through a bullhorn until I came out of the house. When I finally came out, all he did was smile, say hi, and then walk inside to see my brother. Another time he wrapped my entire car in toilet paper. He wrapped it up so much that I had to cut my way in with scissors. Once I got in I found a note on the driver's seat that said *Hi*.

I knew that both of these occurrences could have been attributed to Graham being a lunatic. But there were other things. Like if I were sitting in my room doing my homework, he would knock on the door, sit down on my bed and just start talking. He'd talk about college, or living in the city, or the books he was being forced to read in English Lit. Usually it was just until Eric was ready to go wherever they were going, but still. Nobody had forced him to come in.

One time, when we were having one of these little chats, he went so far as to offer to take me to my prom. It was kind of out of the blue, and I found it to be a bit of an insulting offer—I mean, I was perfectly capable of finding a date to the prom—but still. Nobody had *forced* him to make the offer. So when it was one week before the prom and I still hadn't managed to scour up a date (completely beyond my control), I thought that maybe I would actually take him up on it.

Okay, fine—I was excited to take him up on it. I'd lain awake in bed quite a few nights imagining what it would be like to spend prom night with him, all dressed up and in a limousine. It was so surreal and terrifying. Graham to me was a *man,* while I still felt like an awkward little girl—especially when I was in his presence. But I had the crazy idea knocking around my head that maybe the bullhorn and the toilet paper and the cozy little chats weren't just Graham being goofy and silly. I had the crazy idea knocking around that maybe he actually liked me.

Hey, it was a nice thought.

By the time I had the guts to take him up on the offer, he'd started dating a twenty-five year old cocktail waitress. The worst part is that I didn't *know* he'd started dating a twenty-five year old cocktail waitress until I called him on the phone and asked if the offer still stood. There was this horrifyingly awkward silence on the other end while he came up with the words to tell me that he'd started seeing someone. He said that since it was such a new relationship it might be weird if he took me to the prom. He apologized a lot, and I said *no that's okay* a lot, until finally I hung up the phone, flopped face first into my pillow, and didn't breathe for the next two hours. That's when I realized he'd just been goofing around and teasing me, and all the stuff with the bullhorn and the toilet paper were simply because Graham is a raving lunatic.

Lesson learned.

In case you were wondering, I did find a date to the prom—my platonic friend Barry from marching band. It was a very pleasant evening.

Anyway, now that Graham and my brother are business

partners, he remains a constant in my life. We are graced by his presence on all of the major holidays, typically accompanied by his gorgeous girlfriend of the week. (Information that I provide solely so that you may form a more complete picture of the man that is standing in my living room and not because I take any interest in his love life. Like I said, lesson learned.)

Neither one of us has ever brought up the prom incident. Thank God.

"You were saying that Eric sent you to pick us up?" I ask. "What happened to the limo?"

"Limo?" Graham glances at our pile of suitcases, his eyes focusing on The Duffle, and then looks nervously back at me. "Didn't you know that he was sending me to pick you up?"

I look at him dumbly and walk over to the living room window to look outside. There is a yellow Camaro parked at the curb—a yellow Camaro with about six inches of trunk space. Graham shrugs helplessly as a small trace of amusement passes across his face. He would find this funny.

Of course Eric didn't book us a limo. One teensy little expense that would have made this vacation less of a living nightmare for me, and he decides to cheap out and send Graham in his little shoebox car. I'm about to screech all of this at Graham, when I snap my mouth shut. It's not his fault. I should just handle this matter like a mature adult.

"Mom! Dad!" I shriek in the direction of the basement stairs. "You're going to have to unpack a whole lot of your crap!" I motion to Graham to come further into the house and close the door behind him. This could take a while.

"What are you talking about?" Mom asks. She's emerged

15

from the basement carrying a roll of toilet paper and is unzipping one of the suitcases.

"You can't bring toilet paper!" I cry. "This is a cruise ship. They will *have* toilet paper!"

Dad comes upstairs behind her, carrying a hammer. "There's no toilet paper on the ship?" He looks desperately at Mom before heading towards the bathroom.

"THERE WILL BE TOILET PAPER ON THE SHIP!" I shout. I am heading for a full-on meltdown, when the soothing shade of Blue Dye #1 sidles up beside me.

"Mr. and Mrs. Hartwell," says Graham, "there is absolutely nothing to worry about. Eric sent me over to drive you into Boston. That's all."

"Because Eric was too cheap to book us a limo," I chime in. Mom should know that her perfect son isn't always so perfect.

"How fabulous!" says Mom, clasping her hands in front of her chest.

I should have known that any crisis resulting in additional time spent with Graham would seem fabulous to her.

"It's not *that* fabulous," I say, walking to the living room window and pulling back the curtains. "Graham's car is a little on the small side." Mom's face melts into panic-stricken horror as she pushes past me to see for herself.

"I'm having a nervous breakdown," she declares. She slumps back into an armchair, the toilet paper falling from her fingertips and unraveling across the floor. Dad is just kind of frozen in place, overwhelmed by the news, and stuck between revisiting the bathroom and joining my mother in her nervous breakdown.

The trouble is that Mom and Dad, under my advisement,

dropped their only car off yesterday for repairs. I thought that they wouldn't need it for the week. Not that either Mom or Dad would have been able to drive us into Boston with the pressure of the upcoming cruise bouncing around in their heads. We may as well drive ourselves straight off the Zakim Bridge.

"What if we take my car?" I suggest.

"What do you know about driving into Boston?" asks Mom.

"What's the big deal about driving into Boston?"

"Oy, please," says Mom, dismissing me with a wave of her hand.

Oy please is Mom's way of saying *You've got to be fucking kidding me.* It's a very versatile phrase, as it can be used at the grocery store to acknowledge an increase in the price of canned corn, or after being diagnosed with Type 2 Diabetes. If aliens suddenly invaded Earth and were systematically blasting apart all of the houses on our street, Mom would look out the front door, say *Oy please* and then go back inside.

"What do you mean 'Oy, please'? I've had my license for ten years now." I glance over at Graham, embarrassed, but he's once again staring quizzically at The Duffle and doesn't seem to hear.

"Listen to her, Richard!" says Mom. "Driving into Boston!"

"Okay, forget it. What if Graham drives my car?" I hate myself for conceding that I don't have the wherewithal to drive into the city. I mean, it's their fault that I wasn't allowed to drive on a highway until I was twenty-two, not mine.

"No," says Mom. "We don't do that kind of thing."

"Okay, how about *you* drive my car?"

"We're not driving your car. It's unreliable."

"How come you let me drive it then?"

Mom is about to defy all logic in order to answer my question, when Graham interrupts us.

"Have you got any bungee cords, Mr. Hartwell?" he asks. "Because I think that we can manage to make everything fit. You've just got to think outside the box. Or in this case, outside the Camaro." He winks at Mom who recovers from her nervous breakdown long enough to beam back at him.

Yeah, great joke. Bungee cords? This should all go swimmingly. The request propels Dad into motion and he heads back down to the basement. I grab my suitcase and head out the door, ignoring my mother's frantic pleas to let Graham carry it lest I strain myself.

Graham follows me out carrying The Duffle with one hand, which I didn't even know was possible.

"You're going to strain yourself," I say.

Graham laughs and jiggles The Duffle. "What's in here anyway? A couple dozen severed heads?"

"Four million dollars cash. Dad's got a meth lab in the basement."

"I knew it."

Graham pops open the trunk and I see that it is already half-filled to capacity with his lone suitcase. He puts The Duffle on the ground and heaves my suitcase in next to his. Full.

"This one might have to go up top," says Graham, nodding toward The Duffle.

Of course it does. The one time I get to ride in a cool car, there's going to be a duffle bag full of my parents' underwear strapped to the roof.

3

"I'm sorry you got stuck dealing with this," I mumble, more to myself than to Graham.

"With what?"

"Um, this." I motion toward The Duffle, and then toward the house. I thought it was obvious.

"I love your parents," says Graham. "They're cute."

"Cute, right. I suppose that's one way to describe them."

"How come you haven't moved out yet?" Graham asks, as if it were just the simplest thing in the world to do. As if it wouldn't go completely against The Prophecy.

Let me explain.

We live in a college town. By living at home and going to college close by, Mom and Dad saved a ton of money on room and board and never had to worry about me drinking or partying too much because I was always right here.

Always.

Right.

Here.

It made financial sense. I couldn't argue with my parents in that regard. And it alleviated their anxiety—well, some of their anxiety. The only thing that will alleviate all of their anxiety is a visit from the Grim Reaper. But I digress. Had I lived in the dorms, I would have had to deal with frantic phone calls from my mother and nightly video chats to make sure I wasn't lying about having eaten enough. Most of the time I convinced myself that it was worth it.

Most of the time.

Then there were the other times when I felt so smothered that it was all I could do not to run screaming from the house. But did I? No. Even after graduating from college, I stayed put. Five years later, I continue to stay put. The tiny seed of regret that was planted the moment I agreed to go to school close to home was growing into a blistering resentment. No, I take that back. It has already grown into a blistering resentment. I feel trapped, and I have nobody to blame but my parents.

You thought I was going to say that I have nobody to blame but myself, right?

Wrong.

My brother Eric went away to college with no argument from our parents, and he never looked back. I, on the other hand, was made to feel as if I were personally digging my parents' graves if I made the choice to move out. There were so many guilt-driven reasons to stay and so many self-centered reasons to leave, what was I to do?

It was during one of these moments of extreme frustration that my mother chose to say—and I always imagine that she said it in a booming clairvoyant voice while wearing lots of jangly jewelry— "You'll live here until you get married!"

Fuck.

That's what I call The Prophecy—Mom's antiquated idea that girls should live at home until they're married. And after all these years, I've come to believe that it's my destiny. I honestly don't see another way out. As much as my parents drive me crazy, I don't want to be the one who pushes them over the edge—and I feel like packing my things and moving out on my own would do just that. So here I stay—the good daughter—biding my time and biting my tongue until I find a husband to whisk me away into the world of the sane.

I like to blame my situation on the Universe and the idea of everything happening for a reason. Like perhaps the love of my life is scheduled to get a flat tire in front of my parents' house a week from Tuesday, and had I been living in an apartment downtown we never would have met. It appears that the Universe and my mother are similar influences on the trajectory of my life.

"It just makes more sense to live here and save money until I get married," I say, flinching at the sound of my mother's words being parroted out of my mouth.

"Are you engaged?" asks Graham. I do not appreciate the look of confusion on his face.

"You know I'm not engaged."

"Are you seeing somebody?"

"Not at the moment." I avoid eye contact.

"Horny?"

"No!" I laugh. "I don't remember this being any of your business, Blenderman."

"It just sounds like you might be living here for a while." He slams the trunk shut and leans against the car, arms folded across his chest. He looks me slowly up and down again.

"I've done the calculations, thank you. And why do you keep looking at me like that?" I turn away and stare at the speed limit sign across the street. "It's disturbing."

Graham laughs. "That's exactly why I keep looking at you like that."

I continue to avoid eye contact and busy myself with plucking cat hair off of my yoga pants.

"Maybe you should learn some stress reduction techniques, if you know what I mean."

"Excuse me?" I look up, eyebrows raised.

"Meditation." He gives me a wink.

"Right. Meditation." I air quote the word. "And who's going to teach me these techniques? Let me guess." I look him critically up and down, attempting to make him as uncomfortable as he's been making me. But all I succeed in doing is noticing that he's gotten himself a rather nice tan.

"I'm just saying that you're an adult, and if you're not happy, you should do something about it," says Graham, seemingly unfazed by my perusal of his body. In fact, he seems rather pleased with himself. "You don't have to wait around for a man to rescue you. You do know what year it is, right?"

"It's not that simple," I say.

This is humiliating. I mull over his words as we stand in silence waiting for Dad to appear with the bungee cords. *I am an adult.* I imagine—and only for a mere millisecond—that it is only our two suitcases that need to be loaded up. Perhaps we are off to Bermuda on our honeymoon. Mom and Dad, relaxing from having just planned our lavish wedding, are staying home, on a planet far, far, away. I stifle a laugh at the thought of Graham and I on our honeymoon. I would be hiding behind a newspaper while he organized a Zumba class on the beach.

It just sounds like you might be living here for a while. His words have really struck a nerve. As you can imagine, things are getting a bit desperate for me in the man department. I'm not admitting to being some sort of basement dwelling psychopath that fantasizes about marrying every man she comes into contact with in order to escape from her parents' house. It's not like I'm going to drug Graham, put on a flea market wedding dress, and have my cat perform the nuptials in order to fulfill The Prophecy. It's just that the thought of freedom from my parents has really started to take up a lot of my time.

On any given day, the following guidelines are generally in place:

1. If I come home after midnight, Mom and Dad freak out.
2. If I come home smelling like alcohol, Mom and Dad attempt to admit me to rehab.

I committed these offenses a handful of times with a few girls from school. But after walking into the house and experiencing Mom's histrionics, it just wasn't worth keeping up. I also couldn't help feeling a bit sorry for her, sitting up all night worrying about me. Imagining me kidnapped or dead in a ditch. After a while, my two girlfriends ended up in serious relationships and didn't want to go out to the bars much anyway. So it all kind of worked out.

Sort of.

Online dating is out of the question because Mom has established that I should never, ever, go out with anybody *from the Internet*—as if the Internet is its own planet inhabited by murderers and rapists. And even if I did manage to go out on a blind date, Mom would probably have Dad follow us to the restaurant and sit a few tables away, hiding behind a menu like Hercule Poirot. And when I say "probably" I mean that she has suggested it in the not so distant past.

Basically, if I don't meet a guy at the school where I work, it's just never going to happen. I'm a middle school librarian, and since my adolescent students are out of the question, that leaves two male teachers—one of which is retiring next year, the other of which is dating our gym teacher, Mr. Wilbur. The Prophecy could quite possibly remain unfulfilled indefinitely.

Not acceptable.

And so, I've been secretly devising a little plan. Our cruise ship leaves out of Massachusetts. I live in Massachusetts. The ship holds two thousand two hundred and twenty-four passengers, half of which are probably men, a quarter of which are probably single. My totally arbitrary calculations lead me to believe that I'll have a fairly large captive audience of eligible bachelors from my local area, and that a good portion of my female competition will be over the age of sixty.

"Summer?" Mom yells from the house. "Did you remember to take the fanny pack that I bought you?"

"Yes, Mom!" I shout back, shuddering at the thought of actually wearing that thing. It's made out of stonewashed denim, and she thinks that I'm going to keep tissues in it. I take a deep breath. It will all be okay. I'm in the home stretch now.

This is the week that I land myself a husband.

It's not like we need to get engaged before the week is over, or anything crazy like that. The magic of the cruise will simply set the foundation for our relationship—the slow dancing under the stars, the wine, the spray of the ocean, the dolphins leaping gleefully in the background. In a few short days it will feel as if we've known each other for years. Once we've gotten the initial sparks underway, we'll exchange contact information and meet up a couple of times after returning home. Then comes the engagement, the wedding, and voila! Prophecy fulfilled.

Look, I know it's a stupid idea. *Of course* it's a stupid idea. Don't flatter yourself with the thought that I didn't realize this myself. I know it's exceedingly dumb. But as dumb as it is, there's still a chance of it working. You know the old saying *it's so crazy it just might work.*

That phrase is what I'm counting on.

It takes another half an hour before all of us and our belongings are squeezed into every available crevice of Graham's car. The trunk, secured with bungee cords, looks like a hippopotamus vomiting Samsonite. The Duffle is strapped to the roof. My parents are strapped into the backseat surrounded by carry-on bags. I know I should have let Dad have the front seat since he is a slightly larger person, but I allow myself this one luxury.

I cringe every time Mom and Dad try to speak, as I am convinced that they are going to ask Graham to turn around so they can get something they forgot—cell phone charger, Rolaids, extra pair of water shoes. I say, "try to speak" because Graham's got this crazy Latin hip-hop/techno album going at full blast and all of the windows are rolled down. Mom and Dad look pretty frazzled, which I have to admit, is awesome.

Don't stop the paaaarty!

Graham drums on the steering wheel while I stare out the passenger window.

"Loosen up, Sum! You're on vacation!" He glances into the rearview mirror at Mom and Dad. "You guys are going to have a blast this week!"

Mom, who most likely can't hear a word he's saying, smiles and nods. Dad's face has collapsed into a slack-jawed zombie kind of appearance.

'You're crazy," I say, shaking my head.

"Why?"

"You just are, trust me. I know crazy."

"No, *you* trust *me*," says Graham. "You're going to have a great time. It all starts with a positive attitude." He reaches over and slaps me on the thigh, then gives it a firm squeeze. I stare down at my leg, eyebrows raised. I'm somewhat taken aback, and somewhat wishing that he would do it again. I'm undoubtedly uncomfortable.

Maybe he's right, though.

I can't act like an old stick-in-the-mud and expect to attract a husband, can I? Even with my parents in the backseat—and they're going to be in my metaphorical backseat for this entire trip—I'm going to need to loosen up. There's no time like the present.

I smile over at Graham and lean my head back against the front seat. I drum my fingers to the music.

You can do it, Douchewell. You're in the front seat of a good-

looking car, next to a good-looking guy, even if it does happen to be Blenderman.

The wind is in my hair and an inkling of excitement begins to make its way into my soul.

"You know what I forgot?" asks Dad, his head appearing between the two front seats.

And just like that, it's gone.

4

Graham drops us off in front of Black Falcon Terminal and drives away to park the car. As much as he gives me a headache, I kind of wish he was going to be there while we check in and go through security. Against all logic, he seems to have the same calming effect on my mother as a shot of brandy. But Eric and his girlfriend are probably waiting for us inside, so we load The Duffle—which looks alarmingly similar to a body bag—onto a luggage cart, and proceed to the check-in desk.

Check-in goes about as smoothly as one can expect when assisting your parents with international travel documents. I've had this fear for the past few weeks that the agent will tell me there's been a screw up and I have to stay in a cabin with my parents. It's totally irrational since I have the travel documents that clearly show my room number, and my parents have their own documents that show their room number. But still. What if they overbooked the boat or something? What if they're keeping an eye out for family members to squash together? The agent doesn't know that the sound of my father scratching his big toe with his other big toe will make me dive head first into the ship's propellers.

I breathe a bit easier once the agent has handed us our keys and confirmed that our cabins are on separate decks. I don't know if Eric did that as a favor to me; it's more likely that he booked me into a room directly over the bowling alley.

We've just gone through security, and I am gathering up my things on the other side of the metal detector, when I realize that Mom and Dad are no longer behind me. I turn around to find the two of them pulled off to the side, speaking to a security guard. Now they're pointing at me. *Crap.*

"Hi," I say, walking over. "Is there a problem?"

"Are you travelling with these folks?" He nods towards my parents. I suppose now is my chance to either admit that they are my parents, or leave them to fend for themselves and actually enjoy my cruise.

"Yes, they're my parents," I admit. "Is something wrong?"

"I'd like to take your father aside for some questions. Please follow me."

Questions?

We follow the security guard to a small room containing a metal table, four chairs, and a water cooler. There is a poster on the wall detailing items not allowed onboard. Weapons. Illegal Drugs. Firearms.

"Passport please," says the security guard. Dad pulls a wad of papers out of his pocket, sprinkling receipts all over the table. From pocket number two come three small bottles of hand sanitizer and a sugar packet from McDonald's.

I glance nervously at the security guard, but he remains stone-faced. Dad finally locates his passport in his left knee pocket, and hands it over. The security guard reads it intently and studies

Dad's face, looking back and forth between him and the photo.

Is that Richard P. Hartwell or Osama bin Laden? I joke to myself. Then it hits me. Dad's hair is standing on end from the ride in the Camaro. He's agitated from dodging the crowds of people and going through security. His pants pockets are filled with enough bottles of suspicious liquids to blow us all out of the water. And The Duffle. My God, The Duffle.

They think Dad is a terrorist.

Like, they *seriously* think Dad is a terrorist. Even if he doesn't turn out to be one himself, he could very well be hiding one inside The Duffle. Despite the circumstances, a snort of laughter escapes me.

"Is something funny, Miss?"

"No, I'm sorry." I clamp my mouth shut and look over at Dad. If only he had combed his hair down, we could be getting on the ship right now.

"Have you left your luggage unattended at any point today, sir?"

Dad stares at the security guard, speechless and frozen in panic. "Sir?"

"Dad," I mutter. "Just answer the question."

"Um. Well, we, we uh, we came from the car and then we put the bags on, on the…what do you call that thing?"

"The luggage cart," says Mom.

"The luggage cart, right. Then I went to the, uh, the men's room. So, they may have been unattended, I believe. Is that right?" He looks to Mom and me for support.

"Of course we didn't leave them unattended!" I snap. "Mom and I were standing there with them!"

"Oh, right."

"You seem nervous," says the security guard.

"He's *always* nervous," I mumble.

"I'd like for your father to answer his own questions."

I stop talking and bury my face in my hands.

"Sir, have you any reason to be nervous about boarding the vessel today?"

"Do I have any reason to be nervous?" repeats Dad. My face is still buried in my hands but I can tell from the silence that he is looking to me and Mom for an answer. I try to shake my head inconspicuously. "Of course I have a reason to be nervous."

"What reason is that, sir?"

I raise my head and look over at Dad. *Yes, what reason is that?* Maybe he actually is a terrorist. That would be something. Maybe he's been such a nervous wreck all these years because he's been plotting how to bring down the United States government. Even the security guard seems to be holding his breath in anticipation of the big reveal.

"Well, I wasn't able to receive final confirmation from my contact before arriving here today," says Dad. His face suddenly looks quite grave.

Oh my God. What is he talking about?

"Final confirmation of what?"

"Of whether or not I would be able to acquire the um, the necessary materials once I had made it onboard."

The security guard reaches for his holster and glances quickly from me to Mom. Holy shit. This is really happening. We're going to jail.

"What contact, sir? Exactly what type of materials are we talking about? Chemical? Biological?" He reaches for his radio.

31

"I'm going to need backup in holding room one."

"Antibacterial," says Dad. "My cousin Morty came on this cruise last year, but he couldn't remember if they sold Purell in the gift shop."

"Cancel request for backup." The security guard puts his radio back down on the table. "Purell?"

"Yes, hand sanitizer. I'm not sure if I brought enough. I also may have forgotten my fanny pack and an extra pair of reading glasses."

"Not wearing a fanny pack is not a federal offense, sir."

"What about the hand sanitizer?"

"I think you'll be pleasantly surprised once you get onboard" says the security guard, who I imagine is quite looking forward to ushering us out of his office. "You three are free to go."

"What a relief," says Dad. "For a minute I thought you were accusing me of trying to blow up the ship!"

And we're still going to jail.

"Richard!" Mom snaps. "That's not funny! My husband doesn't know what he's talking about!"

"He really doesn't," I say. "Look at him." Mom and I both motion to Dad like he's Exhibit A in the People Who Could Never Coordinate a Terrorist Act display.

The security guard apparently agrees, because he pushes back his chair and stands up.

"Please refrain from making jokes of that nature. We take them very seriously around here." He hands the passport back to Dad, clearly not taking the joke seriously at all, and ushers us out of the office. "Enjoy your vacation."

We thank him profusely, as that's what you do when you've

narrowly escaped life in federal prison. Our bags, which have clearly been searched for weapons of mass destruction, are waiting for us outside the room. The Duffle has been carelessly repacked so that there is a series of odd lumps and protrusions along the sides—making it look even more like it's filled with dead bodies. One of my nicer shirts is hanging out of my suitcase, caught between the zippers. I yank open the zipper, tearing a hole in the fabric of the shirt. If only I could tear a hole in the fabric of the Universe, I could travel a week into the future when this ridiculous vacation would already be over.

Okay, maybe I've been reading too much science fiction lately. But I work in a middle school library, so give me a break. I'm just saying, how handy would it be if you could shoot into the future and see how everything turns out? I could see if The Prophecy is ever fulfilled, or if I'm still forty-seven years old and living in my parents' basement. Then I could pop back into present day and go about my business with a bit more peace of mind. I suppose one might also find out a lot of awful stuff, like when Ebenezer Scrooge travels into the future and finds out that everybody's glad he's dead. But even that story had a happy ending, right? I'm telling you, time travel could change my life.

As the three of us arrive in the waiting area, I scan the crowd looking for my brother. I'm sure he assumes that I will be entertaining Mom and Dad for the entire week, and I am eager to inform him that I will be doing no such thing. This vacation was *his* idea and he's going to do his part to spend some quality time with them—preferably starting within the next five minutes.

Since Eric's become rich he's been growing his hair long, like he's in a boy band, and wearing a lot of linen pants and Hawaiian shirts. He should be fairly easy to spot, but I don't see him anywhere. I'm starting to get nervous when a flash of Blue Dye #1 catches my attention from the far side of the room. It's Graham, waving to us. As we head over, I check to his left and right for either Eric or Eric's girlfriend Tanya, but he appears to be sitting alone.

"Hey," I say, setting down my bags. "Where's Eric?"

Graham rubs the back of his neck and stares down at the floor.

"Hello? Where's Eric?" I ask again.

Graham stretches and yawns. I whack him on the shoulder.

"What's wrong with you? Where's Eric?"

"Rich! Joan!" Graham exclaims, jumping up and greeting my parents as if he hasn't seen them in years. "How'd everything go at check-in?"

"Wonderfully!" says Mom.

Wonderfully? Sure. I guess the interrogation by Jack Bauer was no biggie.

"Graham, look at me." I wave my hand in his face. "Where is Eric? The ship is boarding in like fifteen minutes."

When we finally make eye contact, I don't like what I see. Graham gives me an unnaturally large and guilty-looking smile. Uh oh.

"What is it? What happened?"

"Well, see, the thing is…"

"WHAT?"

"Eric's not coming."

"Excuse me?"

"He texted me a few minutes ago saying that something came up. Tanya's sister invited them out to San Diego for the week."

"WHAT?"

"You know how spontaneous Eric can be."

"WHAT?"

"Don't worry, the cruise line let him cancel his suite. He'll get a full refund."

The room starts to spin. Is this some kind of elaborate prank? Are there hidden cameras? That would help to explain the terrorist investigation we just went through. I take a deep breath and count to ten in my head, but it doesn't change a thing. By this point the hidden camera people should have come out. I mean, it doesn't make for good television to just sit there and watch a person suffering indefinitely. After a reasonable amount of time it's customary to jump out from behind the potted plants, say *Gotcha!* and then ask the poor fool to sign a bunch of release waivers. But nobody's coming. This isn't a joke. Eric has booked me onto a cruise ship with my parents, and then ditched me.

"You think I care about his *money?*" I say, sinking down onto the bench. "Eric's ditched me for a week with *them.* What am I supposed to do?"

Yes, I know, I live with my parents on a daily basis. But I go to work during the day, and Mom and Dad have their normal routines, however weird they are, that don't typically involve me. That time and space apart, it makes life relatively tolerable. But eight days and seven nights trapped aboard a sea-faring vessel with Mom and Dad and motion sickness pills and fanny packs, without a sibling along to share the burden? I mean, that's the reason Mom and Dad had two children, wasn't it? So that Eric and I could share the burden. There is no way that I can be expected to go this alone.

"What's the matter?" asks Mom. She didn't hear a word of what just happened as she was fussing around inside Dad's fanny pack the whole time. It looked a bit perverse, if you must know.

"Eric's not coming," I say.

"What?"

"He ditched us to go to San Diego."

"Oy! Richard!" Mom grabs Dad by the fanny pack. "Are you hearing this? He's not coming!"

"Who's not coming?"

"Eric!"

"What do you mean he's not coming?"

"I mean, *he's not coming*," I say, just to clarify.

"Are you sure?" asks Dad.

"Well he's in California and we're about to get on a boat in Boston Harbor," I say. "It doesn't get much more *not coming* than that."

"WHAT ARE WE GOING TO DO?" Mom shrieks. She is yelling at the top of her lungs while squeezing Dad's fanny pack between her fists. Other guests are eyeing us in concern, because, well, it looks as if she's got him by the—

"It's okay, Mrs. Hartwell," interrupts Graham, standing up and draping his arm across her shoulders. "You guys have still got me."

"Are you insane?" I ask. "Why would you possibly still want to go on this trip?"

"Why not?"

I don't exactly have the eternity that I would need in order to answer that question.

"What do you mean why not?" I ask.

"I mean, why shouldn't we still go?" repeats Graham. "Eric was going to be hanging out with Tanya all week anyway. It's not going to be that different."

"Of course it's going to be different!" I protest. I grab him by the arm and drag him over behind a pillar, out of Mom and Dad's earshot. "It's just going to be me and—" I jerk my head in their direction.

"No, it's going to be you, and—" Graham jerks his head in the direction of my parents, "and *me*."

I raise my eyebrows. "One big happy family, huh?"

He shrugs. "Hey, why not?"

"Why not? Maybe because the second we step onboard you're going to ditch us in search of cocktail waitresses and showgirls. And then what? Then it's just *me* trapped for eight days with—" I jerk my head in their direction again.

"You think I would ditch you for a cocktail waitress?"

I have to bite my tongue to keep from replying to that one. I take a deep breath, although my lungs suddenly feel two sizes too small, and answer his question with a question.

"You're going to just hang out with me and my parents, for a week, on a cruise ship? This is your idea of a good time?"

Graham looks at me as if the TARDIS is growing out of my forehead.

"Well, it's not exactly Mardi Gras, but yeah. I think it could be fun."

"I'm having a nervous breakdown!" Mom cries.

"It's your funeral," I mutter, throwing my hands up into the air. I walk out from behind the pillar and over to my parents. If Mom doesn't stop screaming we're going to end up back in the interrogation chamber.

"Joan, Richard," says Graham, calmly rejoining us. "Everything is fine. We're going to go on a lovely cruise, and we're going to have a lovely time, and the only one who's going to have any regrets, is Eric. Can I get a one-two-three, Bermuda?"

He's got to be kidding. He sticks one arm out in front of my parents who look extremely confused.

"Come on, everybody puts their hands in the middle. You too, Sum."

I arrange my face into the most unenthusiastic expression possible, before piling my hand on top of Mom's. Graham doesn't seem to notice.

"Come on Rich, right there on top of mine. That's it. On three. One…two…three…"

"Bermuda!"

"Bermuda," says Dad.

5

I've retired to a bench to await the boarding call. There's not much else to do. I mean, we've already shouted *one, two, three, Bermuda!* We're kind of required to head out now. And if we don't take the trip, Eric will lose a whole lot of money. In my opinion, it would serve him right, but Mom and Dad won't hear of it. They haven't said a word about what an inconsiderate jerk he is for ditching us, only that it would be a shame for all of his hard earned money to go to waste. Oh please. Eric's fart app will have earned back the cost of this cruise in an hour, with absolutely no effort on his part.

But still, it's a free cruise to Bermuda and we're already packed and here at the terminal. So we're going, and that's that.

Since we're going, I may as well start checking out the situation in regard to fulfillment of The Prophecy. I glance to my right at a guy my age making out with his girlfriend. Strike one. I glance behind me at a group of senior citizens. Strike two. Although, there are three old men and two old ladies, so one of them might be available. I shake my head and glance to my left. Graham is sitting a few seats away smiling at me.

"Can I help you?" I ask.

"Nope. Just watching you."

"Did you pop a Viagra this morning? You're acting even creepier than usual."

"I'm just excited to be on vacation. And I've been looking forward to spending some time with you."

I raise my eyebrows. "Now I know for sure that you're on some kind of drug."

"What are you talking about?"

"Why would you be looking forward to spending time with *me*?"

Graham looks all around the terminal. "Do you see anyone else here for me to hang out with?"

"Ah, so that's why. I'm flattered."

"Now you're insulted? You confuse me."

"We're just different people, Blenderman. I thrive in solitude. You're a people person. I don't really see it working out."

"I didn't ask you to marry me. We're just going to be on the same boat for a week. It might be fun to hang out." He stands up and heads in the direction of the restroom. Then he looks back at me with a crooked smile and a wink. "I really do like the outfit."

Black yoga pants from Target. Who knew they'd be such a sensation? I watch Graham walk away before I resume checking out my surroundings. There is a group of young people milling around a few aisles over. They're all carrying garment bags and seem to have already started drinking. A wedding party. Ugh. Good for them. Embarking on their new life together must be *so* joyous. Why do they have to celebrate so publicly? There's a lot to be said for a private ceremony at city hall.

On the other hand, wedding parties are good because they tend to include a variety of single groomsmen. I take my cell phone out of my purse, shield it between my legs, and open up the notepad.

Prospects:

1. Groomsmen

2. Widowers

3. Graham

No, stop it. This is humiliating. What kind of a loser makes a list of men she intends to hit on? Never mind that the man I'm basing my second entry on is probably on furlough from an assisted living facility. And the third one is just out of the question; I don't even know why I put him on there. I get one compliment on my yoga pants and suddenly I'm making lists with Graham on them. No. The list is a bad idea anyway. I'll just keep everything safely in my head so there is no hard evidence of my ridiculous plan. As I've said before, I am well aware that it is a ridiculous plan. But everything about my current living situation is ridiculous, so why shouldn't my exit plan follow suit? I'm not ashamed. I would just prefer that nobody ever find out about it.

"Looking for somebody?" asks Graham, his head appearing over my shoulder.

I jump about a foot and shove my phone back into my purse. I can't believe I almost blew it already. I hope he didn't see anything.

"No, who would I be looking for?"

"I don't know. You just looked like you were looking around

and taking notes." He climbs over the back of the seats and plops down next to me. The smell of freshly applied Axe body spray hits me like a brick.

"I wasn't taking notes," I lie. "I was just updating Facebook."

To my horror, Graham whips out his phone and opens up the Facebook app.

"Nope, no updates from you since yesterday. Nice *Doctor Who* quote, by the way."

"Thanks," I say, staring at him for a few seconds. "They don't always show up right away, you know."

"Oh really?" He reloads the page. "Still nothing."

"Maybe you don't have any service in here."

"No, I have service." He holds his phone up so I can see all the bars.

"Maybe you should stop being a creep."

We stare at each other for a few seconds before Graham bursts out laughing.

"Okay fine. I'll drop it for now, Sum. But I do believe you're up to something. And before this week is out, I'm going to find out what it is."

Fat chance, Blenderman.

Before I can make my sentiments known, a voice comes over the loudspeaker announcing that group number twenty-seven may board the ship. Graham stands up and holds out his elbow.

"Shall we?"

Ugh. This is it. I want to say no. I want to just abandon all of my bags and jump through a plate glass window; yet I still have the rebellious desire to look calm and collected in the face of my parents' unbridled panic. And so I paste a smile on my face and reluctantly hook my arm through his.

"Okay fine," I say. "Let's get this fucking trip over with."

Let's get this fucking trip over with is probably not the most jovial phrase to mutter as one steps onto a luxury ocean liner—though I like to imagine it was muttered by some upon boarding the Titanic. And they were right, were they not? They had a feeling that their trip was going to be bad news, and so do I.

Well, whatever. If we go down, we go down. There's not much I can do about it.

As we make our way up the gangway, smiling crewmembers dance to Calypso music and spray everybody's hands with sanitizer. Dad should be in his glory. Mom clutches the handrail as if we're extras in the *Poseidon Adventure*.

"Is the ship moving? It feels like we're moving!" she yells to nobody in particular.

"We're not moving until four o'clock, Mom." I'm actually surprised that my mother doesn't claim motion sickness from the Earth's orbit around the sun.

"I can still feel it moving. I hope it doesn't get any worse than this or I'm going to have to leave."

"Of course it's going to get worse than this, we're still *docked*. And what do you mean you're going to leave? You do know that you can't go anywhere until we reach Bermuda, right?"

"I can leave if they take me away in a helicopter," says Mom. She has a disturbing sort of triumphant gleam in her eye.

"A *helicopter?*" I whack Graham on the arm. "Are you listening to this?"

"Listening to what?" He peels his eyes away from the back of the blonde walking in front of us.

I knew it. I knew that as soon as we set foot on this ship he would stop being our attentive little tour guide and start ogling all of the female passengers.

"Nothing. Forget it. You know, I knew that as soon—"

"Hold that thought," says Graham. He jogs forward a few steps and taps the blonde woman on the shoulder. "Excuse me? You dropped this." He hands her a twenty-dollar bill.

Oh. Right.

"Sorry," says Graham, falling into step beside me. "I saw her drop that a little ways back. What is it that you were saying?"

"I was saying that my mother thinks they're going to *airlift* her out of here just because she's seasick!"

"And dizzy!" Mom staggers, panic-stricken, toward the wall with one hand on her chest, and slumps against the handrail. "And having heart palpitations!"

About forty people begin piling up behind the luggage that she abandoned in the middle of the walkway. Some of them glance at Mom, mildly concerned. Most just look inconvenienced.

"Joan," says Graham, putting his arm around her shoulders and gently guiding her back onto the walkway. "I want you to let go of all your negative thoughts about seasickness and heart palpitations."

"And nervous breakdowns," I chime in.

"And nervous breakdowns," adds Graham. "You're going to be so busy having fun this week that you won't even have time to notice the extremely slight rocking motion of the ship." He gives Mom a wink.

Mom exhales dramatically and smiles up at him. For a split second I see a flash of a rational, sane person.

"You're such a comfort," she says. "Richard, isn't Graham such a comfort?"

Dad doesn't answer as he's having his hands sanitized for the umpteenth time. I roll my eyes and quicken my pace. How does Graham get labeled *a comfort*, when all I manage to do is send her careening into the walls with heart palpitations? It's not fair.

When we finally emerge into the ship's atrium, I waste no time pulling out my boarding pass and searching for my cabin number.

"If you guys don't need me, I'm going to find my room. I'll catch up with you later, probably at the…" I mumble something unintelligible and head for the elevators. I feel a bit bad about leaving Graham behind with my parents, but not bad enough to actually go back. I've managed to survive the morning and am now officially on the ship—it's time for a break.

The corridor leading to my cabin is endless. I'm not even using hyperbole. I honestly feel like if I walk much further I may pop out of a manhole cover in Piccadilly Circus. I finally arrive outside my door and mentally prepare myself for the telephone booth-sized room that awaits me. I swing open the door.

Oh. My. God.

My cabin is gorgeous.

No, let me rephrase that. My *suite* is gorgeous.

I have a *suite*!

A couch, chairs, and coffee table sit across from a large flat panel television. Straight ahead is a sliding glass door that leads onto a balcony. I immediately check outside and find two deck chairs and a hot tub.

A hot tub!

I head back inside and walk into the bedroom. I can't believe that I have a bedroom separate from the living room. I mean, I thought there was a chance I'd have to pull my bed down out of the wall.

The bed is loaded with pillows and faces a wall of curved windows. In front of the windows, another flat panel television is perched on a pedestal. On the other side of the bedroom is the door to the bathroom. I drop my bags onto the bed and wander back out to the living area. A door on the far side of the suite catches my eye. Curious, I walk over and push it open. It's another bedroom. I have a two-bedroom suite? Eric is not that generous.

And then it hits me. Somehow, someway, my worst fear has come true. Even though I checked and double-checked those boarding passes, it's still managed to happen. How could it be? I suppose it doesn't matter how it could be, it just is.

I will be sharing this unbelievable suite with my parents.

I jump at the sound of somebody unlocking the cabin door. Here they come. I take a deep breath, roll my eyes upward toward the heavens, and—

"Hey there, roomie," says Graham, dropping his bags onto the floor and letting out a long whistle. "Sweet suite, eh?"

6

Wait. What?

Any relief I felt at not seeing my parents step through that door is negated by the sight of that blindingly blue polo shirt.

I was supposed to have freedom on this vacation. Even with my parents here, I was supposed to have my own cabin. Part of my plan to fulfill The Prophecy involves having the freedom to come and go as I please. I don't care what The Eagles say; freedom is more than just some people talking. Freedom is having your own private cruise cabin, without your brother's hyperactive best friend nosing around in it.

He'll probably have a karaoke machine set up in our living room before I even have my suitcase unpacked. Then there will be loud-mouthed strangers tromping in and out of here all week singing "Hotel California" and "Free Bird." Maybe even women. No, not maybe. There will *definitely* be women. My stomach turns. I may be averse to shacking up with a guy while Graham sleeps in the next room, but he may not be as concerned about my feelings.

Not to mention that this is where I'm going to be walking

around in my pajamas, and where I'm going to be waking up every morning with my hair all over the place and my contact lenses not even in yet. I do a quick mental inventory of the pajamas I packed.

Bad. Worse. Terrible.

I think I'm having a nervous breakdown. Is this how Mom feels all the time?

"I had no idea we were sharing!" I squawk, my voice coming out much louder than intended. I clear my throat before continuing at a normal volume. "I mean, I just kind of assumed that you and I had separate cabins."

"Eric splurged on three deluxe suites so he could get a bunch of onboard credits." Graham opens up the refrigerator and grabs a beer. "Then the only question became, does Summer want to stay with her parents, or does Summer want to stay with her brother's handsome, yet totally approachable best friend? The choice was simple."

"Simple, right." I say. "Although, don't you think maybe you guys should have consulted me first?"

"So you'd rather have stayed with your Mom and Dad?" asks Graham, squinting one eye at me. "Because we can still arrange for that." He picks up the room phone and starts punching in numbers.

"I will kill you." I wrench the receiver out of his hand.

"So you want me to stay?"

"It's not so much that I want you to stay, as that I don't want my parents to arrive. Big difference." I firmly hang up the phone and head into my bedroom. Graham follows me.

"Why can't you just stay in Eric's empty suite?" I ask, the idea suddenly dawning on me.

"Eric canceled, remember? They've probably already given his suite to someone else."

"Oh, right." I let out a disappointed sigh.

"So, we're roomies?" Graham jumps onto the bed and bounces up and down, clapping his hands.

"You're so weird. But yes. Fine. We're roomies. Now don't ever call me that again." I flip open my suitcase, then immediately shut it. Apparently security decided to relocate all of my underwear to the top of the pile.

"I'm just teasing you," says Graham. "You'd better get used to it if we're going to be roomies. Sweet bejesus, this bed is comfortable." He leans back into a mound of pillows, stretching his arms over his head. The bottom of his shirt rises up to reveal an inch or so of tanned stomach and a portion of his canary yellow boxers. They're covered with little hot dogs wearing sunglasses.

"Nice undies," I say as I grab my bag of toiletries and step into the bathroom to avoid staring. Why should an inch of exposed skin suddenly be a big deal? His arms have been sticking out of his sleeves all day and I barely even noticed. I mean, of course I noticed. I am a living, breathing female. It's just that arms are arms, and stomachs are nearer to other regions. Graham's other region.

I should not be having these thoughts.

"You like them? I've got more."

"I should hope so. We're here for eight days."

The phone rings before Graham can reply, and I hear him jump off of my bed to answer it.

"It's your Mom!" he calls from the other room.

Great. Not that I was expecting anything less than constant phone calls and sweater monitoring. I was just hoping to at least be able to unpack first.

"Hello?"

"Summer, it's Mom. Why is there a man answering your phone?"

"That wasn't a man, that was Graham."

"Why is Graham answering your phone?"

"Because it rang,"

"Is that some kind of joke? I'm asking you a serious question."

"Sorry. Graham is answering my phone because Graham and I are sharing a room."

I hadn't set out to give my mother a nervous breakdown; it's all just falling into place so perfectly.

"What do you mean?" she asks.

"I mean Graham and I are sharing a room." I delight in the four seconds of dead air on the other end. "It's got two beds though, so it's no big deal." I fail to mention the fact that it also has two bedrooms.

"Oy! Richard! She's sharing a room with *Graham*!" Mom says his name like he's the only man on Earth in possession of a penis. "I don't want him thinking that he can have his way with you!"

"Have his way with me?"

Graham, who had been staring out the window at the harbor, looks over with raised eyebrows.

"Boys only have one thing on their minds," says Mom.

"Graham's not a boy. He's almost thirty."

It's at that moment that the almost thirty-year-old man moves away from the window and begins to make some very inappropriate gestures to the back of the couch. My eyes widen and I have to clamp a hand over my mouth to keep from laughing. Then he jumps up on the couch, pulls off his shirt, and twirls it over his head. Oh my. Graham's been hiding a six-pack under those hideous shirts.

"*Men* only have one thing on their minds," Mom clarifies.

"What?" To be honest, I haven't heard a word she's said.

"I said that men only have one thing on their minds."

"And what is that, exactly?" I ask. Not that I want to hear my mother say the word *sex*.

"S-e-x," says Mom. Seriously, she spelled it out.

"So you think Graham's going to, like, assault me?"

"No, but he might try to take advantage of you."

"Not likely to happen, Mom. Anyway, I thought you loved Graham? I thought that he could do no wrong? Remember how he played "Fur Elise" at that piano recital seventeen years ago?"

Graham's shirt lands on my head and I whip it back at him.

"He plays the piano like an angel. But he's still a *man*. Maybe you should come and stay in our room," says Mom.

"I've already unpacked!" I lie, glancing back over at Graham. Annoying, goofy Graham who used to yell "Suicide!" while throwing my Barbie dolls off the back porch, is gyrating shirtless on my couch.

"Oy. She won't listen!" Mom's voice fades away as she hands the phone off to Dad.

"I am listening!" I shout, holding the receiver a few inches from my face. "I'm just not going to do what you're asking. There's a big difference!"

As if somebody flipped the off switch, Graham sits down

civilly on the couch. He puts his shirt back on and gives me a thumbs-up.

"Summer?" Dad is now on the line. "Your mother is very concerned."

"I know she is, Dad. But she shouldn't be. Look, is there a reason that you guys called? I'm kind of busy."

"Oh, um. Hang on." An alarming number of noises come from their end of the line—doors shutting and suitcase zippers going back and forth. Finally Mom comes back on the line.

"I called because your father and I are planning to eat in the main dining room tonight. We assume that you'll be joining us?"

And so it begins.

"What about Graham?" I ask. If I'm going down, he's coming with me.

"We would love for him to join us too, of course. Graham is wonderful, just wonderful."

I roll my eyes.

"Let me ask him. Hang on, he's just putting his pants back on."

"What?!"

"I'm kidding. Hang on. Graham, do you want to have dinner with me and my parents?" I form a gun out of my thumb and forefinger and point it to my temple. He laughs.

"Sure, why not."

"Okay, the wonderful man is in," I report back. "We'll meet you outside the restaurant at six."

I hang up and sit down across from Graham. "Have you ever been tested for ADD?"

"I was just trying to make you laugh. You did well, by the

way. Not giving in to your mom, I mean."

"Really? Because I don't think she heard a word I said."

Graham shrugs. "Whether she heard you or not, at least you said it. You need to do that more."

"What?"

"Assert yourself. Stop letting them force their opinions on you."

"Oh." I click my tongue, not in the mood to analyze my relationship with my mother. "Aren't you late for a flash mob or something?"

"Is that how you think of me? As some clown who lives only for the spotlight?"

"Of course that's how I think of you. You know you don't actually have to come to dinner with us, right?"

Graham shrugs. "What other plans do I have?"

Proverbial crickets chirp while I mull this over for a few seconds. It wasn't the most flattering response in the entire world, but he has a point.

"What are you going to do all week without your best friend here?" I ask. "It's going to be lonely for you, isn't it?"

Graham shrugs. "Even if Eric had come, I would have been on my own most of the time since he was bringing his girlfriend. I was prepared for it. What about you? I could ask you the same question."

"I love being alone," I say. "I actually prefer it. If there was one thing I was looking forward to about this trip it was that I might get some time to myself while Eric entertained Mom and Dad. But without him here, that plan is in serious jeopardy."

"Hey, your parents may surprise you. Maybe they're not so keen to hang out with you either."

"I would never be that lucky. I'm surprised that you were okay with being alone all week. Don't you thrive on social interaction?"

"A man can be an island when he needs to. But even an island doesn't necessarily want to eat dinner by himself on vacation."

"Fair enough," I say, thinking that I would much rather order room service and eat it alone on my bed, than join my parents in the dining room. "But if a better offer comes up between now and dinnertime, feel free to bail on us. I'm kind of hoping for a better offer myself."

"You flatter me," says Graham.

"I meant a better offer than my *parents*," I clarify.

"I know what you mean," says Graham. "There are plenty of single guys on this boat that you're dying to get your sticky little paws all over. I'm not offended."

"Who says I was talking about guys?"

"Girls? Even better."

I give Graham a look. "*No*, not girls. Okay maybe I was talking about guys. But my paws are not sticky. Where do you come up with this stuff?"

Graham studies my face in silence for a few seconds. "I'm not here to cramp your style or anything. You just do your thing, and I'll do my thing, and every so often, if you happen to feel like it, we can meet in the middle. Right here."

"Deal," I say, sticking out my sticky little paw. Graham shakes it. "But if you're dancing shirtless on the couch when I meet you here, I'm going to have to ask you to leave."

"And if *you're* dancing shirtless on the couch when I meet you here, I'm going to have to ask you to keep it up." Graham glances down at his watch. "You going to come up on deck when we leave Boston?"

"I think I'll pass." The sky over the harbor is a bit overcast and I have a vision of Mom and Dad standing on either side of me with their umbrellas open. Sure I'd be standing on the top deck of an ocean liner, but I'd still be suffocating.

"You need time to recover from all this," he says, running a hand down his chest. "Understandable."

"I actually need a few hours to repeatedly wash out my eyeballs."

"I like a girl with a sense of humor," says Graham, winking at me as he carries his bags into the bedroom. "I'll catch you later for dinner then. A good time will be had by all."

7

Okay, so the good times haven't exactly started rolling yet.

I'm sitting across the table from my parents waiting for them to finish their salads, which is taking an eternity. I was hoping to get this dinner over with quickly and then start putting my plan into motion; not that I have any idea how to go about doing that. I assume I'll have to hit up one of the bars or nightclubs, but the idea of doing that alone makes me feel a little sick. I had been planning on going out in the evenings with Eric, Graham, and Tanya. But that sure as hell isn't happening now. I mean, Graham is still here, but the last thing that will help me pick up men is to walk into a bar alone with Graham. I take a long sip of wine. Okay, *another* long sip of wine. I told you that this dinner has been taking forever.

Speaking of being alone with Graham, it's totally strange having dinner with just him and my parents. He's been carrying on most of the conversation—asking Mom and Dad about their cabin, telling them about what he wants to do when we reach Bermuda, and other such topics that are of interest to the elderly. He's a natural. He doesn't even look annoyed when Dad tells him about a parasailing accident that he saw on the news. I study his face from the side. How does he control his eyes like that? They're not rolling at all. Not even a little.

Our main courses finally arrive, and it's nothing but oohs and aahs over the quality, and most importantly, the quantity of the food on Mom and Dad's plates. Dad ordered the filet mignon, and Mom the baked haddock. There is a flurry of activity as they both, in perfect synchronization, produce two bottles of hand sanitizer, squirt one glob into each hand, and rub until dry. Then begins the process of trading side dishes back and forth—some of his potatoes for her, some of her asparagus for him. Confirmations are received from both parties that the food is neither too spicy nor too bland. I've seen this routine a thousand times, but Graham watches them with interest.

"You two are adorable," he says, motioning to their plates. "I hope someday that I find a special lady to share my meals with."

I snort.

"Something funny?" asks Graham.

"Don't you have a new special lady every other week?"

He looks at me for a few seconds, slowly biting a baby carrot off of his fork.

"None of them were really the side dish sharing type," he says. Then, without taking his eyes off of me, he reaches his fork onto my plate and steals a piece of broccoli.

Oh. I stare at the empty spot on my plate—the gears in my head turning, trying their damndest to make something out of nothing.

That was nothing, right?

"How can such a wonderful young man not have a special

lady in his life?" asks Mom, steamrolling over my moment of speechlessness. She looks at me with that *look*, the one that means *Summer, there's a man sitting next to you and he's rich and single.* I know that Mom would be ecstatic if Graham and I ever got together, but there's also a part of me that has the feeling Mom thinks I'm not good enough for him.

"It's shocking, I know," says Graham. "But I'm on a bit of a self-imposed relationship hiatus. I'm looking forward to some alone time this week, just me and my thoughts."

I snort again.

"Now what?" he asks.

I shake my head and take a large gulp of wine. Graham is on a relationship hiatus. So when he stole my broccoli, he really just wanted some broccoli. Of *course* he just wanted some broccoli.

"I was just wondering what kind of thoughts you were planning on hanging out with. The dumb ones or the dirty ones?"

That may have been a bit mean, but it really is time to get down to business—and Graham is not my business. I can't let this entire week be a wash. We're only a few hours into the cruise, and broccoli-stealing Graham and his stupid sunglass wearing hot dog undies are already distracting me from my goal.

It's excusable to get distracted once, okay *twice,* but I won't let it happen again. Graham can be a very charming guy, but he's not husband material. Especially since a very important requirement for a man to be husband material is that he not be on a relationship hiatus. And also that he not be Graham Blenderman.

I have one goal—fulfill The Prophecy. Simple.

I turn away from the table in order to start checking out the other guests. It's quite a disappointing lot if you must know—old people and happy couples as far as the eye can see. Anybody single probably isn't going to be dining alone in a fancy restaurant. I'm about to give up when my eyes are drawn to a cute guy in a black button-up shirt on the far side of the dining room. He's seated across from an older couple that could potentially be his parents. That would definitely make for a good icebreaker. *Hey are you on the most stressful and soul-crushing vacation of your life? Me too!* I stare at him until he looks over at me. I maintain eye contact, take a sip of wine, and then look away. *Smooth move, Douchewell.*

Unfortunately, looking away brings me into direct contact with my mother's death stare.

"What?"

"That was very rude what you said to Graham."

"What did I say to Graham?"

"You know, about his thoughts."

"Oh, right. I was just joking. Graham knows that." I look over to see Graham's response, but all he does is silently pluck the wine glass out of my hand and place it on the table.

"Hey!"

"Pace yourself."

"Why?"

"I want you to be able to keep up with me later."

"Later?"

"Yeah, later. We're going dancing."

"Excuse me?" I snatch back my wine glass.

"How much has she been drinking?" interrupts Mom.

"Since you find my being alone with my thoughts such an

amusing concept, you get to hang out with me instead."

"I don't want her drinking too much!" says Mom.

"I already have plans," I say.

"No you don't."

"How do you know?"

"Is she drunk?" asks Mom.

"You haven't left the suite since we got onboard. Who did you make plans with?" asks Graham.

He's got me there. I finally look across the table at Mom who's in the throes of a nervous breakdown.

"Mom, I'm not drunk. I can handle a few glasses of wine." I give her the death stare right back and take another long, spiteful sip.

"Don't worry, Mrs. Hartwell. It's just that the night is young and I don't want her falling asleep on me." He shimmies his shoulders back and forth. Mom's eyes light up.

"Maybe we should all go!" she says. "Oh, Richard. We haven't been dancing in such a long time!"

Oh God. Mom and Dad haven't exactly grasped the concept of modern day nightclubs. They still think that *The Penguins* are going to be onstage singing "Earth Angel" while couples box step around the room.

"We're not going dancing!" I say. "And even if we were, it would be very late. Like after midnight."

I hate to say it, but hanging out with Graham might be my only option for finding some nightlife. And it's not like we'll be joined at the hip or anything. I'm sure Graham will want to mingle with women who aren't his friend's little sister. The only thing that I can't have is Mom and Dad showing up. I'm not able to act normally around them. Never have been.

"Oh," says Mom, a bit crestfallen.

"You guys should go to the casino," I suggest. "That might be more your speed." I feel somewhat bad about crushing my mother's dreams of fast dancing to techno music, but Dad seems a bit giddy at the thought of playing the slot machines.

By the time the check comes, I'm convinced that I have a fifty-fifty chance of an evening of total freedom.

***

After dinner, Mom and Dad head off in one direction and Graham and I in another. It's still too early for any sort of nightlife, so we wander aimlessly. People are dressed up and gravitating toward the theater for the eight o'clock variety show. A piano player is singing "Beyond the Sea" at the atrium bar. I wonder if he just plays that one song in a loop. I don't mind; it's one of my favorites. Occasionally I bump into Graham and convince myself that it's the choppy Atlantic Ocean making it difficult to walk straight.

"So are we really going dancing?" I ask, giving him a sidelong glance and trying to sound indifferent.

"I was just trying to make you uncomfortable in front of your parents," he says. "We don't have to. I know it would go against the whole 'you do your thing and I'll do my thing' agreement we made like two hours ago."

"It does," I agree. "But, you know, I could make an exception for our first night here."

Graham comes to a stop in front of a pink, velvet loveseat and sits down. I sit next to him. "So you want to hang out with me after all?"

I turn sideways and look meaningfully into his eyes. "I don't want to walk into a nightclub all by myself."

Graham laughs. "That's flattering. You should have tacked a 'no offense' onto the end of that statement. It would have taken away the sting."

"Hey, you only came to dinner with me because you didn't want to eat alone," I say, sinking against the back of the loveseat. "Now we're even."

"So we're just using each other? Kinky."

I whack him on the arm. "You're so dirty."

"And that surprises you? I think this is just the most time you've ever spent alone with me. Get used to it. We've got seven days left."

"Oh man." I lean forward and rest my forehead in my hand. "I'm still just a little thrown that you're excited to hang out with me. You realize I'm not very exciting, right?"

"Have we met before?" Graham sticks out his hand. "The name's Blenderman. I make fart apps for iPhones. And you are?"

I laugh. "Come on, the fact that you make fart apps for iPhones is exactly why your life is so amazing. I'm a *librarian*."

"You have a warped image of me."

"No I don't. I've known you forever. You're outgoing. You danced around shirtless in our suite a few hours ago. And you're always dating supermodels."

"I date supermodels?"

"Um, yeah. That Victoria's Secret model that you brought over a couple of Christmases ago?"

Graham whistles. "Oh right. So I dated *one* supermodel. She's married to a football player now. Tom something."

"Tom Brady."

"Right." Graham lets out another long whistle. "Okay, so what else you got?"

"What about all the swanky clubs you and Eric are always at in Boston? I've seen the pictures on Facebook."

"Please tell me you're not basing everything you think you know about me off of what I post on Facebook?"

Busted.

"Well, I spend a lot of time on there. What do you expect?"

"People post the most interesting and exciting aspects of their lives on Facebook, and conveniently leave out the other ninety-eight percent."

"You drive a Camaro."

"I play kickball at the YMCA on Tuesday nights."

"Every time you come to our house you've got a new girlfriend."

"They're only after the fart app fortune."

"That can't possibly bother you very much."

Graham shrugs. "It starts to lose its charm. At some point, even little old me wants more out of my relationships."

"I'm not buying it." I shake my head. "You're a gigolo, and your life is amazing. Why would you want to change anything? It's my life that's pitiful."

"Wow," says Graham. "First my thoughts are dumb and dirty, and now I'm a gigolo? I'm not made of stone, Summer. That hurts. Let's take a little peek at your life, shall we?"

To my horror he pulls his phone out of his pocket and opens up the Facebook app. He starts scrolling through my profile, his face going through a myriad of expressions. "Last week you posted a picture of a bird eating from a birdfeeder. How old are you, eighty-six? And before that you posted a picture of your cat doing—what the heck is he doing?"

"A handstand," I mumble.

"Come again?"

"A *handstand*."

"Really?"

"I had to help him a little bit, with his legs. But yeah."

"That's impressive. But, okay. I agree with you now. Your life is kind of pitiful."

"Hey!"

"I'm not trying to be rude. But if these are the most interesting highlights of your daily life, you should probably do something about it."

"I thought you were trying to make me feel better!" I say, becoming irritated. "I don't need you to rub it in, Blenderman. I live in my parents' basement. You and Eric invite me out to Boston like once a year. I've got two girlfriends who are both married with kids and can't exactly hang out on the weekends. What am I supposed to do about that?"

"You can stop blaming other people, for one. I agree that your life is pretty dull. I don't, however, agree that it's because *you're* dull. And that's exactly why I'm excited to hang out with you."

"I don't see any distinction between the two."

"That's a shame."

"What's your point?"

"When was the last time you really let loose and had a good time?"

I shrug. "High school prom?"

Graham raises his eyebrows. "Jesus, Summer. With that dude from marching band? That was ten years ago. What did you and that trombone genius do that was so fun and exciting anyway?"

"First of all, his name was Barry." I'm annoyed that he would insult the person who spared me from spending prom night with my parents. "Second of all, I didn't exactly have much choice in the matter."

"What do you mean?"

Ugh, he doesn't even remember. One of the most defining moments of my teenage years was nothing but a thirty-second phone call to him.

"Never mind," I say. "Fine. I haven't *let loose* in a long time. What's your point?"

Graham tips his head back and lets out an exaggerated sigh. He stares at the ceiling, his mouth curving into a mischievous smile. Then he looks me in the eyes, and for a few seconds I almost forget that it's Blenderman.

"My point is," he says, "that we go dancing."

8

Graham and I are seated at a small cocktail table at the ship's main nightclub. I've changed into a pair of jeans, heels, and a black tank top. Graham is looking surprisingly subdued in a blue and white plaid button-up shirt and dark jeans. It's like he's channeled all of his vibrancy into the brightly colored shots that he bought us at the bar. It feels strange being here alone with him. Luckily the music is so loud that I don't have to worry very much about making conversation.

The DJ is playing hits from the eighties, and members of the cruise ship staff are out on the dance floor trying to get everybody moving.

"Are you ready?" asks Graham. He slams his shot glass down onto the table and rubs his hands together.

Is he kidding? I need at least thirty minutes to let the shot do its thing. Wide-eyed, I look past him and into the crowd forming on the dance floor. This is all happening way too fast. I mean, everybody is so...so...what's the word that I'm looking for? Loose? And me, I'm so...so...what am I? I'm the uptight librarian with her hair in a bun and her glasses firmly planted on her face. I'm very seldom in this type of environment. As I mentioned earlier, I never go to clubs unless Eric invites me, and that's only happened a handful of times in the past five years. Sure I've been in a few other situations where dancing was involved, but I wouldn't say that attending cousin Janet's wedding last April, where I spent the entire night sitting alone at a table watching Mom and Dad Foxtrot, has prepared me for this. Why did I have to go and push the going-out-dancing issue with Graham? I could have been happily in bed asleep right now.

Before I can form an argument, Graham is out of his seat, grabbing me by the hand, and dragging me onto the dance floor. As soon as he lets go of my hand I'm cut off by a swarm of middle-aged women and pushed to the outskirts of the dance floor. I shuffle awkwardly from side to side, watching in amusement as Graham is mobbed. Did I mention that he's kind of a magnet for the forty-five plus demographic? Well, he is.

Graham looks at me helplessly and shrugs. I shrug back. Then he breaks into a semi-choreographed dance routine, ending with a floor spin and a near perfect Moon Walk. The crowd of cougars goes wild. I continue to shuffle awkwardly from side to side.

After a few minutes of this, I consider sneaking off the dance floor and returning to our table. That's when Graham and I make eye contact again. He beckons me with his finger. I shake my head no. He nods his head yes. He points at me, and then to himself, and then quickly back and forth a few more times. The eyes of a thousand cougars shoot me with daggers.

That would have made a good Agatha Christie mystery—The Eyes of a Thousand Cougars.

I shake my head again, though with slightly less vigor, and

allow Graham to pull me into the center of the circle.

He puts his arm around my waist and pulls me into his chest, tossing my arms up around his shoulders. With heels on, my face is level with his neck and I am immediately aware of the scent of his skin and the feel of his shoulders beneath my hands. It's been a very long time since I've had such close contact with a man. My last boyfriend, Jack, broke up with me two years ago. I had been afraid to tell my parents that we were taking a ski trip to Colorado because of their fear of airplanes, snow, and avalanches. So instead, I just didn't go. Jack went without me and fell in love with his ski instructor.

They're married now.

Anyway, my point is that it's been a while. I've had a handful of dates with the occasional awful son of one of my mother's awful friends—always some sort of heinous bore with bad breath or adult acne. I've also had dates with the occasional substitute teacher from work—the kind that claim to be substitute teachers because they're working on some really awesome side project like farting iPhone apps—but those relationships all fizzled out along with their really awesome side projects.

None of these fine candidates ever advanced past first base. I thought I was okay with that—maybe even that I was starting to come to terms with my new life of celibacy. But now I'm not so sure. That brightly colored shot is starting to take effect, and feelings that I thought were long since dead have started to rematerialize. I have to constantly remind myself of whom it is I'm dancing with so that I don't start running my fingers through his hair. *Think, Douchewell. This is Blenderman—the same man who led you on back in high school. He was only killing time with you waiting for Eric, and right now he's only killing time with you on a boat.*

There was nothing there then, and there is nothing here now.

I pull back a bit and look up, only to have the stubble on Graham's chin brush by my lips. That doesn't help the situation that is developing in certain regions of my anatomy. Neither does the fact that certain regions of our anatomy that have never been in even remote proximity are now shaking hands and making introductions. Dancing with Barry at the prom sure didn't feel like this. Doesn't he realize what this kind of thing does to a woman? Of course he does. He just doesn't care. It's just another day in the fascinating life of Graham Blenderman.

At least I don't need to worry too much about my dance moves. Even if I went completely limp, Graham would most likely keep marionetting me around the floor.

I try to shut up my internal ramblings and just enjoy myself. That was the whole point of this night, anyway—for me to let loose and have a good time. It was Graham's idea to pull me out here and throw my arms around his neck, not mine. As long as I don't completely humiliate myself by suctioning my lips onto his neck, what's the harm? Graham's not the only one killing time on a boat; we're all imprisoned here. I inch back in closer.

I'm starting to relax and enjoy myself when something by the entrance of the club catches my eye. It's like one of those scenes from a horror movie when the psychotic murderer is standing there in silhouette revving his chainsaw in a cloud of smoke. Only instead of a chainsaw murderer—and trust me, I'm keeping my fingers crossed for next time—it's my parents.

***

I detach myself from Graham's neck and come to a complete standstill on the dance floor. No way can I dance like this in front of my parents. My parents don't even know that dancing like this exists. When Mom heard that Graham and I were going dancing she was picturing my right hand on Graham's shoulder, Graham's left hand on my waist, and our free hands clasped beside us while we do some sort of choreographed waltz. The concept of fast dancing, without a specific set of steps, is completely foreign to the both of them.

"I thought they were going to the casino!" The words are barely out of my mouth when Graham actually starts waving them over. "Stop it! Are you nuts?"

I reach up to yank his hand out of the air, but it's too late. Mom and Dad are making their way over. Then Graham does the most disturbing thing yet—he puts his arm around my waist, and pulls me back in.

"What are you doing?" I ask, starting to panic. Not only has he pulled me back in, but something has changed in the way that he's moving. It's like we've become guest performers on the *Sabado Gigante Cinco de Mayo Extravaganza.* His knee is jammed between my legs, not in a good way, and he's tossing me to the left and right with exaggerated hip motions. All that's missing is a spandex tube top and a mariachi band.

"Joan! Rich!" Graham's got this ridiculous smile on his face. "Great that you guys could make it!"

I want to die, but I can't get out of his grip without making a scene. I don't want it to appear like he's attacking me or anything, I just want to stop dancing. I just want to sit down, motionless, and wait for my parents to leave.

"We heard music!" says Mom. "We thought we'd peek in and see where it was…coming…from." Her words slow down as she realizes whose rear end it is that Graham has been tossing around the dance floor. Her faces goes through a rapid succession of changes from delight to disgust to sheer horror as she takes in the rest of her surroundings. Part of said surroundings include a shirtless member of the cruise staff wearing a pair of huge, glittery, angel wings. I choke back a laugh. This place is a bit weird.

I glance down at the floor and notice that both of my parents have changed into their ballroom dance shoes. *Just thought you'd peek in, eh?* Okay, fine. I suppose they have every right to be here. I'm just not going to be here with them.

As if he can read my mind, Graham gives me a push and I find myself freed from his grip. Maybe he's not completely insane after all. Now to just get the heck off of this—

Ah!

He wasn't releasing me at all. He was throwing me to the shirtless, angel-wing-wearing staff member who chest bumps me back into Graham. Then Graham chest bumps me back into the shirtless, angel-wing-wearing staff member. Now I'm being pin-balled back and forth between the two of them at an alarming rate, with Mom and Dad looking on in complete, albeit comical, horror.

"What are they doing to her?" shouts Mom. "Make them stop!"

"Are they twerking?" shouts Dad. "Is that what they call twerking?"

I swear I've never heard anybody say anything louder than my father just said the word *twerking*. How does he even know that word?

Graham, of course, is thoroughly enjoying every miserable second of this. When he and his shirtless angel-wing-wearing friend are done, he pulls me back in for another round of tossing me about.

"What kind of step was that?" Mom shouts, tapping me on the shoulder as Graham dips me almost all the way down to the floor. I look up at my mother's face, surrounded by a background of pulsating strobe lights. God, it's like some sort of nightmare.

"Step?" I ask, as Graham heaves me back up. "What are you talking about?"

"When they were tossing you back and forth." She makes *tossing you back and forth* motions with her hands. "What is that called?"

"I don't know. Chest bumping? Does it matter?"

"Oy, Richard! They were doing chest bumping to her!"

Graham and I look at each other and for a brief moment, I start to laugh. I can't help it. Mom is standing there in an ankle length flowered dress and ballroom dance shoes, saying things like *they were doing chest bumping*. It's too much.

"What's so funny?" asks Mom. "Richard, what are they laughing at?"

Dad doesn't answer. He's just kind of frozen and staring off into space. Maybe the strobe lights are giving him some sort of seizure.

Mom waves her hand at him in disgust. Then she reaches between Graham and me and tugs on the neckline of my tank top, pulling it towards my chin. "What did you need to wear *this* for?"

"What's wrong with this?" I yank the shirt out of her hand, accidentally punching Graham in the jaw. "Sorry."

Mom motions to my chest area, pointing from one boob to the other. "There's no coverage! Have you even got a bra on under that?"

Coverage is one of her favorite terms. That's how we picked out my dress for senior prom—by which one had the most coverage. It's ironic because I have literally no cleavage that needs covering, yet she acts like I'm Anna Nicole Smith.

Before I know what's happening, Mom materializes one of her old lady sweaters out of thin air and tries to forcibly shove it onto my shoulders.

"Get it off!" I yell, flinging the sweater to the floor.

Mom gives me a dirty look as she picks it up and shakes it out.

"Come on Richard," she says. "We're leaving." She motions to Dad to follow, except he doesn't move. He's still staring at something across the dance floor, and this time I see what it is.

There's a woman over there. At least I think it's a woman. She's got this long, dark brown hair streaked with blonde that's sprayed back on the sides and up in the front. Her lips are lined with dark brown pencil, like a kid that ate a box of Oreos. She's all breasts and gauzy turquoise blouse with matching turquoise palazzo pants. She's holding a Cosmo up into the air and rolling her hips like a cement mixer.

Dad is transfixed. I've never seen him like this. I reach over and whack him on the shoulder.

"Dad?"

He looks at me, blinks, and then glances back over at the woman. He snaps his fingers and does a few awkward knee bends.

Oh my God. I think he's doing a mating dance.

"What's happening?" I ask Graham. I step closer to him, seeking shelter. Graham just shakes his head.

"Is this twerking?" shouts Dad. He bends forward, touches the floor, and starts to shake his khaki pants clad butt around in the air.

"Dad!" I scream. "Stop it!"

"Get up off that floor!" yells Mom. She makes *get up off that floor* motions with her hands. But it's too late. The spectacle of my father twerking has done what I suspect was its intention all along—it's attracted some female attention from across the floor. Some gauzy, turquoise, female attention. And suddenly she's here, right in front of us, grinding against my Dad's khaki pants clad butt.

Mom looks completely mortified. I turn and bury my face in Graham's shoulder, laughing.

"Work it, Rich!" says Graham, and suddenly I feel his hand around my waist, pulling me tightly against him. For a second I forget that Dad is twerking with a possible drag queen, and all I can process is the feeling of Graham's hand around my waist. For some reason, this one small act feels more intimate than any of the other dancing we've been doing tonight. It feels protective and intentional.

It doesn't last.

About two seconds later, Graham gives me a light push and

starts twirling me around in front of him. If I had a tiered skirt on he'd probably have slapped the ruffles as I spun. Then he yanks me back into his chest.

"Can you just stop with whatever this is?" I tilt my upper body back and motion to my hips that are being forced to gesticulate against their will. "My *parents* are here."

"So what?"

"My parents do not need to see this!"

"Yes they do. They need to see that you're a woman, not a little girl."

I raise my eyebrows. "You think I'm a woman?"

He doesn't answer. He just gives me a crooked smile.

"We look ridiculous," I say.

Graham leans his face in very close to mine. "Would you rather they have seen the way we were dancing before? Your choice."

I look him in the eyes, two inches away from mine, and feel my cheeks warm.

"Well, *no*. But both ways are completely embarrassing!" I break eye contact and stare into his shoulder.

"Your parents thought we came here to waltz. You were too afraid to show them reality, so I did it for you. I ripped the bandage off, so to speak."

"I never asked you to rip off any bandages!"

Instead of replying, Graham releases me, takes a step back, and starts twirling an invisible lasso over his head. I have the feeling that I'm expected to play the part of some sort of farm animal. I most certainly will not. I shake my head *no* and make a quick exit back to our table.

I'm joined a moment later by the whole hellish gang. Mom and Dad take chairs on either side of me. The possible drag queen sits down across from me and next to Graham.

"What did you bring her over here for?" Mom shouts across my lap at Dad.

"What?" shouts Dad, leaning across my lap the other way.

"I said, what'd you bring *her* over here for?" Mom shouts even louder, leaning across me again.

"What?" shouts Dad.

Oh come on. I'm having flashbacks to being in a movie theater with my parents when I was fifteen. They spent the entire movie leaning across me asking each other who the bad guy was.

"Mom's upset about your new friend," I yell into Dad's ear.

Dad glances sheepishly across the table.

"The name's Angel," the woman says, holding out her hand. Her voice is deep and throaty and not at all angelic. "Angel Cake O'Brien."

Angel Cake O'Brien? I give her a feeble smile and shake her hand, trying desperately not to laugh. I glance over at Graham, wanting to see his reaction, but then I remember that I'm still sort of mad at him.

I've really got to get out of here.

9

I scoot out from between Mom and Dad and head to the ladies' room. The restrooms are located in the corridor outside of the club, and the sudden silence is deafening. I plop down on the toilet and rest my head in my hands. My ears are ringing and I feel a bit dizzy. Just a few minutes ago I was feeling really good. Now I'm embarrassed and annoyed and want to do absolutely anything but go back to that insane asylum of a table. It's amazing how quickly things can change when you're stuck on a cruise ship with your parents, a drag queen, and a psychotic family friend.

I take my time washing my hands and fixing my hair in the mirror, trying to imagine what I looked like out there dancing with Graham. Not the earlier dancing that was, if you must know, *amazing.* But the ridiculous stuff that came later. I wish I could behave normally around Mom and Dad, but I can't. Graham should respect that. Never mind that what he was doing to me was the antithesis of behaving normally. I suppose that's what he meant by ripping off the bandage—embarrass the hell out of me now and whatever happens tomorrow won't be a big deal. Well, maybe *he* can handle acting ridiculous and being in the spotlight, but I can't.

I should just go back to the suite. In fact, the elevators are right near the restrooms. Of course Mom and Dad will think that I was kidnapped and notify the captain. I take my phone out to text Graham, but realize that I'm completely out of battery. Reluctantly, I head back into the club and stop at the bar to order myself another drink. If I can't leave, I may as well finish getting drunk.

"Nice moves out there," says a voice behind me.

I turn around to find the cute guy I noticed earlier in the restaurant. He has this great dark, wavy hair and chocolaty brown eyes. And up close I notice a few dimples when he smiles. *Good find, Douchewell.*

"Oh, hey!" I say. Then I realize what moves he was referring to and a wave of humiliation comes over me. "Those moves weren't my idea, just so you know."

"No, you looked good. Your boyfriend is a very enthusiastic dancer."

"Oh please, that's not my boyfriend. Just a family friend hell-bent on ruining my vacation."

Okay fine, that's not completely true, but I'm in a *mood* right now.

"That's too bad. Well, not the part about him not being your boyfriend; the part about him ruining your vacation. So you're here with your family?"

"Unfortunately. Were those your parents I saw you with in the restaurant?"

"Yep. Were those yours?"

I nod. "Sucks for us, huh?"

"Royally."

"I'm Summer," I say. "From Salem, Mass."

"Hi Summer, I'm Jackson. From Windsor, Connecticut."

"Cool," I say, as if I know anything about Windsor, Connecticut. We step up to the bar and Jackson orders us two Red Bull and Vodkas. The bartender studies Jackson's ID for a long time.

"You look young," I say.

"I know," says Jackson. "But I'm twenty-one."

So he's a younger man. That's okay. What difference is a couple of years? I like to think that I look young myself. The bartender hands me my own ID back in about four seconds. *Jerk.*

"Salem, huh?" asks Jackson, while we wait for our drinks. "Are you a witch?"

"That's funny." I roll my eyes. "I've never heard that one before."

Jackson laughs. "Okay then, next question. You want to dance?"

The last thing I ever want to do again is dance. But then I remember The Prophecy and the lifetime of living in my parents' basement laid out in front of me, and I smile up at Jackson and nod in agreement. Perhaps this night can be salvaged after all. As we make our way onto the dance floor, I catch a glimpse of my parents through the crowd. They're back on the dance floor—minus Angel Cake O'Brien—and Graham is standing by watching them attempt to swing dance. *Triple step-triple step-right left right.* Honestly, how they're managing to dance like that to a Rihanna song is impressive and horrifying all at the same time.

I push Jackson to a location as far away from my family as I can get. I do feel a bit bad about leaving Graham alone with my parents, but another glance in their direction finds him suddenly dancing with a deeply-tanned blonde in a slinky red dress.

My stomach drops. However intimately I thought Graham was dancing with me earlier in the night, it was nothing compared to how he's dancing with this woman. And I say *woman* rather than *girl* because she is easily in her forties.

Well. Never mind them. Graham's a cougar magnet. I knew that. I've known that ever since he started dating a cocktail waitress nearly a decade his senior. And it's not like he was going to just stand there with my parents all night. He had to do *something*, didn't he? Still, can't Cougar Barbie at least try to show a little restraint? Not that Graham looks particularly offended by any of it. On the bright side, at least I now have confirmation of Graham's type.

Leather skin. Fake boobs. No shame.

Duly noted.

Secure in my freckled, strawberry-blondeness, I turn back to Jackson and push him further into the crowd. Maybe it's fate that my parents showed up here tonight and ruined whatever was happening between Graham and me. Otherwise I wouldn't be dancing with Jackson. Maybe Jackson is The One. Maybe in a month's time I'll be packing a U-Haul for Windsor, Connecticut and we'll be toasting champagne and laughing about how we met on a cruise ship and he asked me if I was a witch.

Time to turn on the charm.

"I love this song!"

Yikes. My voice came out quite shrill. To be honest, I don't even know this song. Jackson doesn't seem to mind though. He pulls me tightly into his chest and I push everybody and everything else from my thoughts.

Jackson nuzzles my neck and the room kind of starts to spin. I try to focus all of my attention on where I am at this very moment. Jackson is where it's at right now. Jackson is the reason I came on this trip.

This is good. I'm living life on my own terms. Sure Mom and Dad are about twenty yards away, but I don't even care anymore. Maybe Graham was right about ripping off the bandage. I hold my drink up in the air with one hand, keeping the other firmly around Jackson's neck.

This is how life should be. This is the new me.

***

Well that was a dumb idea.

Let it be known that a hangover, on a cruise ship, is not a good thing. Not a good thing at all. I'm lying in a bed that won't stop moving.

Back and forth, back and forth, rock rock rock. It's like my parents are swing dancing all over my stomach. Speaking of which, I see now that I wasn't dancing with Jackson because I no longer cared about what my parents thought. No, I was dancing with Jackson because I was piss drunk.

It's only seven-thirty when I wake up, but staying in bed is not doing me any favors. I drag myself into the shower, willing the warm water to bring me back to life. It doesn't. I pull on a pair of shorts and a t-shirt and knot my wet hair into a messy bun. I grab my sunglasses and purse and walk silently to the door of the suite. Graham is probably dead to the world at this hour, but still, I open the door as quietly as I can. I have no interest in finding out if Cougar Barbie spent the night. I also have no interest in hearing a lecture from Graham about my behavior.

You see, I sort of remember kissing Jackson in various parts of the ship. It started at the club while we were dancing…then we moved outside to the deck, looking up at the stars and stuff…then we were aimlessly riding up and down in an elevator, coming up for air only when other passengers got on…then, the fitness center? That was odd. I vaguely remember sitting on some sort of workout apparatus. Anyway, I was having a good time with a potential future husband. Progress was being made.

That is, until Graham materialized swami-like from the corner of the pool deck. Jackson and I were lying on a lounge chair, fingers intertwined, when Graham was just suddenly *there,* chastising me for leaving the club alone with a strange man. Jackson stood up and said a bunch of drunk, tough guy stuff like *She can be with whoever she wants, man*! until Graham basically shoved him back into the lounge chair and told him to shut it.

Then he grabbed me by the hand and dragged me back through the buffet to the elevators. I remember giving him a hard time as he silently escorted me all the way back to the suite. I said really smart drunk things like *You can't control me!* and *But he was a really nice guy!* Graham didn't bother responding and instead simply deposited me fully clothed into bed.

What right did he have to do that? I am perfectly capable of taking care of myself. You didn't see me rushing over and telling that woman in the slinky red dress to take her paws off of Graham, did you? No, because that would have come off as catty.

But when a man does it to a woman, under the pretense of *looking out for her*, it's totally okay. How am I ever supposed to meet anybody under these conditions? Trying to date with Graham around is turning out even worse than trying to date while living in my parents' basement.

I close the door quietly behind me and start out on the ten-minute journey to the buffet for some toast and ginger ale. I smile weakly as the woman at the entrance squirts my hands with anti-bacterial spray.

"Happy Happy! Washy Washy!"

Barfy Barfy! Pukey Pukey!

The ship is moving along at a fairly good clip. One glance at the moving water while walking in the opposite direction sets my head spinning. I steady myself against a handrail, praying that I don't throw up in the middle of the buffet. I can't even imagine the sanitation process that would occur if that ever happened. An army of happy happy washy washy ladies would probably converge on the mess, spraying it into oblivion. I put a couple of pieces of toast on my plate—looking wistfully at the piles of chocolate croissants and cinnamon buns that will have to wait for another day—and find myself a shady lounge chair by the pool. I stretch out with my plate on my lap and take a long sip of soda.

"Summer? Is that you?"

I look up to find Jackson standing there smiling down at me. With my huge sunglasses and my total lack of make-up, I can see why he might be unsure of my identity.

"Hey!" I say, sitting up a bit in my chair. "How you feeling today?" He sits down sideways on the lounge chair next to me. I notice, with a bit of superficial satisfaction, that he really is quite good looking. At least I didn't have my beer goggles on last night.

"I've got a little bit of a headache. But otherwise, not too bad."

"Lucky."

"Sorry," he says, reaching over and patting my thigh. "We had a good time though. At least I thought we did."

"We did," I say, taking his hand and giving it a squeeze. "I'm just sorry about, my um, my friend…ruining everything."

"Friend huh? He seemed more like your brother, or a bodyguard."

"Close. He's my brother's friend. Don't ask why I'm on a cruise with my brother's friend and not my actual brother. Don't ask how or why he tracked us down last night either."

Jackson shrugs. "He was just looking out for you, I guess."

I roll my eyes. "He doesn't need to look out for me."

"So do you have any plans for later?" he asks. "Assuming your bodyguard lets you out?"

"Plans that involve drinking? No, thanks."

"How about plans that involve going to a movie?"

"I could do that," I say. Sitting in a cool, dark movie theater sounds like heaven actually. That might be the best place to avoid feeling the movement of the ship. Maybe I'll just head there straight after breakfast.

"Great," says Jackson. "I'll be right back, I'm going to grab myself a Bloody Mary. Hair of the dog and all that." I watch him walk off to the bar, looking adorable in his Hollister t-shirt and leather strap bracelet wrapped around his wrist.

I haven't shopped at Hollister since high school, is what I'm thinking when I notice a white plastic rectangle on the lounge chair that Jackson had been sitting in. Thinking it's his cabin key, I pick it up for safe keeping until he gets back. I flip it over.

Windsor High School Student ID

I stare at the words. I have an ID card too, from the middle school that I work at. Only, it doesn't say Student ID on it. It says Faculty ID, because I am a member of the faculty, whereas this one clearly says Student ID. To really drive the point home, there is a picture of Jackson smack dab in the middle of it wearing a Windsor High School t-shirt. And also, there is his name.

Jackson Mahoney. Class of—

Son of a bitch. I do some quick calculations in my head, figuring Jackson to be sixteen years old. I feel sick. I mean, sicker than I already felt. How much trouble could I be in for this? I could be on the news! *Middle school librarian seduces minor.* Is making out considered seduction? Is it considered rape? Will I need to register as a sex offender? They went over these types of things during my job training, but I wasn't exactly taking notes since I didn't intend to put the moves on my pre-pubescent students. This has got to be considered extenuating circumstances. He looks much more mature than sixteen—how was I to know?

Oh God. As I watch him walking back to the pool with a Bloody Mary in his hand, I can totally see it. Of course he's sixteen. He's tall and muscular and everything, but his face is young. And those dimples. He's practically a toddler. Never mind that he was eating dinner with his *parents* for Pete's sake. The only grown adult in this world who goes on a cruise alone with her parents is *me*. A jury would have me convicted in about thirty seconds. Did Graham figure this out last night? Is that why he was so interested in breaking us up? I quickly hide the ID card as Jackson approaches.

"So what are you doing on a cruise with your parents anyway?" I ask as he sits down in the chair beside me.

"Just spending some quality time with them before I go back to school in September."

"Where do you go to school?"

"UConn."

"What are you majoring in?"

"Computer Science. I'm applying to Google when I graduate."

Google. Good one.

This kid's thought of everything, but I've heard enough.

"I didn't know that Google was looking to hire *high school students*!" I whip the ID card at his chest. Jackson catches it clumsily, his face turning red.

"Where'd you get this?" he asks.

"It fell out of your back pocket, dumbass." I stare at him and shake my head. "You realize I could go to jail for this?"

"You can't go to jail for making out." Apparently he's done some research.

"Yeah, well thankfully that's all we did," I say in a whisper. I don't even want to be seen with him right now. And to think, I gave Graham a hard time about not bringing this child back to my room with me.

"Sorry," he says, unconvincingly. "But you were flirting with me. What was I supposed to do?"

"Gee, I don't know. Maybe not pretend to be a grown adult

when you haven't even taken your SAT's yet?"

"I've taken the PSAT's."

"I'm a school librarian! You're two years older than some of my students!"

"And I'm sure they would all be jealous of me," says Jackson, giving me a wink.

"How'd you even get served last night?"

"Fake ID."

Fake ID. Great. How is a girl supposed to fulfill a prophecy when there are teenagers with fake ID's running rampant all over this boat?

"And those people at the restaurant?" I ask. "They can't possibly be your parents."

"Grandparents."

"Of course," I sigh. "May I ask how old your actual parents are?"

"Thirty-five."

I nod slowly. His parents are nine years my senior. Nine years. I do believe it's time to go.

"Well, kiddo, I'll see you around." I stand up and gather my things. "Try to find yourself a nice girl your own age, okay?"

Jackson leans back in the lounge chair and takes a sip of his Bloody Mary.

"I don't have any regrets," he says, squinting up at me. "And I don't think you should either."

"Of course *you* don't have any regrets." I grab the Bloody Mary out of his hand and throw it, glass and all, into the trash. "Guys get high fives for hooking up with their teachers. You know what the teachers get? Added to the sex offender registry."

I storm off through the sliding glass doors, humiliated.

10

Water. Water. Flying fish. Water.

Graham finds me on the top deck, staring into the sea and contemplating the weirdness of what just happened. I'd say that he's the last person I want to see right now, but that's not true. The order of people that I don't wish to see right now actually goes: Jackson, Mom, Dad, Eric, Angel Cake O'Brien, Graham. So he's not actually doing too badly.

"Don't jump," he says, joining me at the railing. He's wearing a neon pink and white striped polo shirt. "It's only our second day."

I give him a strained smile. "How do you keep managing to track me down?"

"I tried your phone first, but I heard it ringing from your bedroom. Catch." He tosses the phone at me.

"Graham!" I catch it tightly between my hands and clutch it to my chest. "That's not the smartest thing to do near the railing!"

"You're welcome. Anyway, I thought the next best idea was to wander around a cruise ship the size of New York City until I randomly found you."

"Good plan. Is that how you found me last night?"

"Maybe."

I shove the phone into my bag and we stand there in awkward silence for a few moments, staring out at the water.

"Look, I'm sorry if I was obnoxious last night," I say. "But you embarrassed me, and then my father started dancing with a drag queen, and then I saw my parents swing dancing to hip hop music, and then you were…well, never mind. It was all just a bit too much."

"Oh, come on," says Graham. "You're still going to insist that I embarrassed you?"

"Of course you embarrassed me."

"But it was still kind of funny, wasn't it? *They're doing chest bumping.* Remember that?"

I try not to laugh, but find it difficult.

"Okay fine, that part was funny. But the actual chest bumping? Not cool. And the whole rest of it was something out of a Stephen King novel. I mean my dad was *twerking.*"

"That part wasn't funny, it was hilarious."

I just shake my head. "What happened to that woman anyway? Angel Cake?"

"A little birdie may have whispered in her ear that your father is a happily married man. Then she left to get a drink and never came back."

"A little birdie, huh?"

Graham shrugs.

"Well, thanks. I was starting to feel sorry for my mother."

"We're all entitled to get carried away once in a while," he says. "Even your dad. Even *you.* I just feel like I need to watch out for you, since Eric's not here. You know I wasn't trying to ruin your good time, or your *plans.*"

I glance over at him. Plans? How could he possibly know my plans?

"I don't have any plans."

"No, of course not. I'm just teasing you." Graham gives me a wink.

A wink? What was the wink for? Was that an *I'm just teasing you* wink? Or was it an *I'm going to claim that I'm just teasing you but I actually know all about your pathetic plans to meet a man because I am some sort of mystic who can materialize out of thin air on pool decks?* Hmmph.

"Well, that's thoughtful of you," I say, "but you really don't need to look out for me."

"You needed me last night when you wandered off with that guy."

"No, I didn't. Everything was under control."

"Oh really? Didn't you think your parents might wonder what happened to you? I had to tell them that you texted me saying you felt sick and were going to bed. Then I told them I was going back to the room to check on you."

"Oh," I say, suddenly feeling a bit guilty. I hadn't even thought of that. "Well, thanks. I didn't mean for you to have to make up a bunch of lies. I'm sorry."

"It's okay, I was happy to help. You didn't need them freaking out on your first night here."

I smile. "So, um, just out of curiosity, what was it that you didn't like about Jackson?"

Graham shrugs. "Nothing in particular. It wouldn't have mattered if you had disappeared with the Pope. I still would have gone looking for you. You have to be careful with strange men. I should know."

I nod. "You are indeed a strange man. Hey, do you want to know a secret about Jackson?" I know I'm going to regret this, but I feel like he should know that he didn't actually ruin anything.

"Sure." Graham's eyes light up. "Was he heir to the Oscar Meyer fortune and I ruined a lifetime of free bologna for you?"

I laugh. "Well that is every girl's dream. But no, nothing like that."

I put my elbows on the railing and rub my forehead with my palms. "I, um, I ran into him this morning, and he dropped his Student ID card." A strong gust of wind mercifully carries away the words *Student ID card*.

"What did you say?"

I lift my head and look him in the face. "He dropped his Student ID card. Jackson wasn't a strange man, Graham, he was a strange *boy*. He's sixteen years old."

Graham just stares at me for a few seconds before he bursts out laughing. I stand by quietly, waiting until he's finished.

"Are you finished?" A small smile breaks through my façade.

"Yes, I'm sorry," he says, somewhat, though not totally, composing himself. Maybe I jumped the gun by deciding to confide in him. He's easy to talk to and all, but I can totally see why he and my brother get along so well.

He wipes his eyes and lets out a long whistle. "Now that I think of it, I might have seen him in the arcade racking up Skeeball tickets this morning."

"I don't know why I even told you," I say. "It's humiliating."

"Oh, it's not that bad." Graham slides a few steps over and pulls me into a hug. Then I feel him shaking with silent laughter. I pull myself free and shove him hard in the chest. Of course he doesn't budge, but it still felt good to shove somebody.

"I'm glad you find this so amusing," I say. "It's your fault, you know. If I hadn't been so mad at you I never would have danced with him."

"My fault!"

"Yes, your fault! You humiliated me in front of my parents, tossing me around like we were in some club in Havana."

"Are we back to that again? Look, you could have just gone back to the suite. I didn't tell you to run off and revenge dance with random guys."

True. But going back to the suite alone wasn't going to fulfill any prophecies. Of course I can't tell that to Graham.

"It wasn't *revenge*. Revenge would imply that I was trying to make you jealous, when in reality I was just trying to get as far away from you as possible. What was your excuse for dancing with that bimbo?"

Graham looks at me with raised eyebrows.

"You saw that, eh?"

"She was hard to miss."

"Not jealous, you say?"

"Nope."

"I didn't know I needed an excuse."

"She was like, forty."

"Remind me again how old your guy was?"

"Touché," I laugh. "Okay, fine. Maybe we should just stay out of each other's love lives."

Graham looks at me in silence for a few seconds. I'm unable to read his expression and it's making me inexplicably uncomfortable. Did I say something wrong?

"Deal," he says at last. "So, do you want to get a couple's massage?"

"Are you insane?"

"Sort of. See, there was actually a reason I came looking for you in the first place. Apparently Eric's girlfriend booked appointments at the spa for this morning." Graham glances at his watch. "Fifteen minutes from now, actually. It'd be a shame for them to go to waste."

"I'm *not* getting a couple's massage with you."

"No worries. She booked pedicure appointments for the two of you."

"So you're going to get a pedicure?"

"Sure. I'm overdue."

"This vacation just keeps getting stranger," I say. "Alright, fine. Let's go get our toenails painted."

The spa is on Deck Eleven, but after we get on the elevator Graham pushes the button for Deck Nine.

"Where are we going?" I ask.

"We just have to make a quick stop," he replies, looking a bit guilty.

Deck Nine…Deck Nine…oh no. All those months of double-checking our room numbers, now I remember. Mom and Dad are on Deck Nine.

"Come on!" I cry. "The spa is supposed to be *relaxing!*"

"Sorry," says Graham. "You and I may not be getting a couple's massage, but Tanya ordered one for your mom and dad. I think she was trying to suck up to her future in-laws."

"You know what would have really won them over? Showing up for this vacation."

Graham laughs. "Look on the bright side, maybe she ordered

them some kind of weird seaweed wrap."

We get off the elevator and head down the long corridor to Mom and Dad's suite. This is going to be bad. I mean, my parents have never done anything as crazy as going to a spa. It's one of the items on their list of things that only rich people do, right below owning a swimming pool and going to Disney World. Besides, my mother claims to hate massages, although I think the real reason is that the towels, sheets, and masseur's hands could never be sterilized to her excessively paranoid standards. Never mind the fact that this is the first time I'll be seeing them since the fiasco at the club last night. Who knows what kind of scolding my mother has in store for me. Suddenly I want nothing more than for Graham not to witness this.

"You don't have to come with us," I say, throwing myself in front of Mom and Dad's door. "Why don't you go climb the rock wall, or something similarly masculine?"

"Scared of heights," he replies, with a shrug. "And rocks. And walls. But mostly it's the height thing."

"Wuss."

Reluctantly, I step aside and Graham knocks on the door. We file into Mom and Dad's suite, which is just as lovely as ours except that it's a completely cluttered mess. There are underwear and shoes and travel-sized bottles everywhere, literally everywhere. It looks like The Duffle exploded. There is a bag of cotton balls in the kitchen sink.

The two of us wait while Mom and Dad rush around finishing up their last minute preparations. If I asked a stranger where they thought my parents were headed, they would probably say colonoscopy appointments. Nobody would ever guess luxury spa. I sit down on the couch, anxiously anticipating Mom bringing up the subject of last night. When she finally says my name—in between filling a fanny pack with antibacterial wipes and putting two changes of underwear into a plastic supermarket bag—I nearly jump off the couch.

"Are you feeling better today?" she asks. "Graham said you left last night because you weren't feeling well."

"Oh, yes. Much better, thanks."

She must be easing into it. Any second now she's going to tell me that I looked like I was *hot to trot*, and remind me that men are only interested in one thing.

"It's too bad, because I was really enjoying watching you dance!" she says. "Weren't you enjoying watching her dance, Richard?"

"Oh, yes," agrees Dad. "She looked, um, quite lovely."

"She has such rhythm!" says Mom. "I never knew she had such rhythm!"

Wait, what? I've got *rhythm*? Mom *liked* watching me dance that way?

"Um, thanks," I say. "But it was mostly Graham. He's the one with all the rhythm. He just kind of…tossed me about."

"I should have known," says Mom, nodding enthusiastically. "He was always such a fabulous piano player. What fun you two were having!"

I just stare back at Mom, speechless.

Graham gives me a smug smile.

11

Mom and Dad come out of the changing rooms wearing fluffy white bathrobes and water shoes.

"I don't think there's a pool here, guys," I say, gesturing to their feet.

"I'm not walking around barefoot on this filthy carpet!"

The spa receptionist glances up at the words *filthy carpet*. In reality, the carpet is plush, white, and immaculately clean. The entire place smells like coconut oil and green tea. I'd hate to hear Mom's thoughts on the YMCA.

"Warts," chimes in Dad.

Mom and Dad have a debilitating fear of being barefoot, as if the soles of their feet are two petri dishes just waiting to be cultured.

"You're not going to get warts here, Dad." I roll my eyes at the receptionist. Her name is Sophia and she's been trying unsuccessfully to make my parents comfortable. Just getting them into the fluffy white bathrobes involved a ten-minute discussion of onboard laundering procedures.

"Maybe you would like some champagne?" she asks.

"Oy, please," says Mom.

Sophia looks a bit uncertain as she picks up a bottle of champagne and starts to pour a glass. She glances over at me.

I shake my head. "That means no."

She puts the bottle down. "Chocolate covered strawberry?" She holds the bowl out for them. Dad is about to take one, but Mom looks at them through her bifocals and crinkles up her nose.

"Were they washed?"

"Mom!" This is so embarrassing. Would they ask the workers in the dining room if the zucchini had been washed?

Yes. Yes they would.

Before Mom can request that Sophia rinse the chocolate covered strawberries under hot water, they are called away to another room for their massage. Sophia looks relieved and quickly directs me and Graham to the row of pedicure tubs. I step out of my flip-flops and plunge my feet into the warm, bubbly water. Sophia brings us champagne and the bowl of chocolate covered strawberries, which we gladly accept.

"You think they give happy endings here?" Graham asks.

"Stop it!" I say, laughing. "You're going to get us kicked out of here." I sink back into my chair, trying to disappear. I don't think that Sophia heard him, but she does glance back at us with a look in her eye that seems to say *Not while I'm on the clock, honey. But maybe later.* I don't know why I'm surprised.

Whistling, Graham picks up an issue of *Us Weekly* and opens it to the middle.

"You seem disturbingly comfortable here."

Graham grins. "When I got my first big paycheck, I took my

girlfriend to Vegas for the weekend. We spent a lot of time at the Bellagio spa."

"That's kind of weird."

"Why's it weird?"

"I don't know. It just seems like a girlish thing to do."

"I pay no heed to societal norms."

"You can say that again."

Okay, so I don't really think it's that weird. I just have this odd, squirmy sort of feeling in my stomach when I think about Graham being at a hotel in Vegas with a girlfriend.

"So, which girlfriend was that?" I ask, trying to sound casual.

"Sarah."

I nod, trying to remember her face. A redhead, I believe, or maybe a brunette. I'm not even sure why I'm asking for details.

"What happened to her?"

"She took a chunk of my money and moved to New Hampshire with our landlord."

Ouch. I'd always assumed that Graham enjoyed moving on to the next flavor of the week. I never considered that he might occasionally have been the one who got hurt. I sneak a glance at him from the side as he continues to read his magazine. His brow is furrowed as he scans through an article about the Kardashians. It suddenly strikes me what a fool this Sarah must have been. I wonder if the landlord was worth it.

"I'm sorry," I say. "Eric never mentioned that to me." I say it as if Eric and I talk all the time.

"That's because I didn't tell Eric." Graham puts down the magazine and turns to look at me. "He's my best friend, but he's not the most sensitive guy in the world. I was embarrassed, so I told him that it was a mutual split." He picks the magazine up again and starts flipping through the pages.

"Why are you telling me this?"

"Perspective. Getting duped by a sixteen-year-old you met yesterday doesn't seem like the worst thing in the world now, does it? It's just a blip on the radar. Hey, look. Oprah gained thirty pounds." He holds the magazine up so I can see.

As I take it from him, our fingers briefly touch. My cheeks feel a bit warm as I examine Oprah in more detail.

"So what are you up to tonight?" I ask, not taking my eyes off the magazine. "Jackson asked me to go to a movie, but obviously that's not happening."

"Especially if it's rated R."

"Very funny."

"You still want to go?" asks Graham. "I'll take you."

The minor warmth in my cheeks increases to a small inferno that I hope is not noticeable. I can always blame it on my feet being plunged into a tub of hot water, although that doesn't explain the butterflies in my stomach. But nobody needs to know about those.

I should probably say no to Graham's offer, since sitting in a movie theater with a man is a surefire way not to meet another man. But I still have plenty of nights left for that, and I still feel pretty sick. I can't even imagine going out to a bar or anything. Maybe by the time the movie lets out I'll feel ready to go back on the prowl.

"Um, yeah. Sure," I say. "Thanks. An early one though, okay?"

"Sure," says Graham. "I know you've got places to go and under-aged men to see."

"Funny. You're not planning to talk through the entire movie are you?"

"Nope. We'll be sloppily making out for most of it."

"Gross." I throw the magazine onto his lap. Now my palms are starting to sweat. And the butterflies are back. But they're tiny. Barely out of their cocoons, really.

The butterflies are interrupted by a shriek from one of the massage rooms.

"Oy! Get it off! Richard! Make them take it off!"

My eyes widen and I clamp a hand over my mouth.

"Is that your mom?" asks Graham.

"Of *course* that's my mom! What the heck is going on in there?"

The sound of my mother's voice is followed by a loud thud, and then several smaller thuds. Sophia jumps up from behind the reception desk and rushes into the massage room.

"Somebody call the infirmary!" she shouts.

"*You're* the receptionist!" shouts somebody else.

Sophia runs back out and punches some numbers into her phone.

"Can we please have a medic up here?" she asks. "There's been an accident. Yes. Thank you."

"An accident?" I mouth the words to Graham. I jump out of the pedicure tub, quickly dry my feet off with a towel, and rush into the massage room. Mom is lying face down on the floor surrounded by hot stones. A technician has draped a sheet over her body, making it look a bit like a murder scene.

The masseur is sitting on a stool looking quite pale. Dad is sitting up on the massage table with a sheet over his lap. Scented candles burn peacefully behind him. It's an image that I'll never get out of my head.

"Mom! What happened?" I say, crouching down next to her. "Are you okay?"

"I'm having a nervous breakdown," she mumbles into the carpet.

"Besides that, what happened?"

Mom seems unable to form any further words, so the masseur takes over.

"I am so sorry, Miss. I swear I did nothing! I began to place the hot stones on her back, just as I always do, when she started to scream *Get it off! Get it off!*" He makes sweeping *get it off* motions with his arms. "Before I had a chance to remove the stones…BOOM!"—he claps his hands together—"she had thrown herself off the table and onto the floor! I did nothing! I swear to you! I *only* placed the stones!"

He is clearly terrified of being accused of attacking an old woman and losing his job. He has my full sympathy.

"It's okay," I reassure him. "It's not your fault."

"Not his fault?" says Mom, turning her head to the side in order to fix one eye on me. "He burned me with hot coals!"

"They're hot *stones*, Mom. This is a hot stone massage. Nobody burned you with coals."

"It felt like hot coals."

"Okay fine, they felt like hot coals to you. But did that make it necessary to *throw yourself* onto the floor?"

"I had a panic attack when he refused to take them off!"

"I was trying to take them off!" argues the masseur. "I took off one, and then the next, but before I could reach for the third she had thrown herself off the table! She flopped right off of it like…like a fish!"

I fight back a giggle at the image of Mom flopping around on the deck of a fishing vessel. She would never forgive me if I laughed right now.

"Mom, why would you think it was a good idea to throw yourself off a four-foot high table?"

"Because I couldn't breathe! The stones were crushing me!"

"I thought they were burning you?"

"They were burning and crushing me!"

A regular Giles Corey she's turning out to be. I pick a lukewarm stone up off the floor that's about the size of a credit card, and wave it in her face. "This? This was burning and crushing you?"

"Summer," says Dad. "Your mother is very sensitive."

"I think I broke my back!"

"Maybe you shouldn't have *thrown yourself off of a table*!"

Just to make the situation into more of a British comedy, Graham enters the room wearing a pair of bright pink flip-flops about four sizes too small. He joins us down on the floor.

"It's alright, Joan. Someone from the infirmary is on their way up to check you out and get you back on your feet."

"Thank God you're here!" says Mom, reaching over and squeezing Graham's arm. She would never say those words to me.

"She threw herself off the table," I say, very matter-of-factly. Graham just looks at me and shrugs.

"Not everyone is cut out for these new age shenanigans, that's all. Hot stones and seaweed wraps, that's no way to relax. Just give me a glass of wine, a hot bath, and a little Michael Bolton, am I right Mrs. H?"

Mom smiles admiringly up at him, nodding in agreement.

What the hell is he talking about? Michael Bolton in a bathtub?

Before I can say anything, the medic shows up and checks Mom for broken bones. Luckily, everything appears to be in working order. When she tells him that she's having a nervous breakdown, he gives her a brown paper bag to breathe into. She takes a couple of deep breaths, declares that she's going to suffocate, and thrusts the bag at the medic.

That's the final straw for me. I wait until Mom is back on her feet, before I head back out to the waiting area. Graham follows shortly behind. A few minutes later the medic walks Mom out and sits her down in a chair with a cup of water.

"Should we sue?" she asks me.

"You threw yourself off the table. How is that the spa's fault?"

"They shouldn't have put those stones on me."

"It was a hot…stone…massage." I annunciate each word. "I don't think you have a case."

Graham nudges me in the elbow. "Mrs. Hartwell, they most certainly should have asked your permission before placing those hot stones on your back. I agree with you one hundred percent. But you don't want to put a damper on the rest of this lovely trip, do you? Maybe we should just let this one go."

"I probably won't even be able to walk tomorrow."

"If that's the case, then I know just the attorney to call. But why don't we wait until tomorrow before making any drastic decisions?"

Mom nods reluctantly, and glances in the direction of the massage room. "Tell your father that I'm going back to the cabin to lie down."

"Okay," I say. "Feel better."

A few seconds after the door shuts, Dad emerges from the massage room looking like he's just been through the Spanish Inquisition—not exactly the poster child for rest and relaxation. Sophia rushes over and hands him a complimentary gift bag.

"Just a few things to show our appreciation," she says. "Body oils, lotions, and a coupon for the spa gift shop."

So basically a bag full of totally useless items. Dad just stands there with the bag in his hand, looking a bit dazed.

"Come back anytime!" she says, practically pushing him out the door.

"Mom went back to the room!" I call after him, as the door swings shut. I have no idea if he heard me.

Oh well.

Graham and I stand there for a few seconds, enjoying the silence. Then he takes my hand and leads me back over to the pedicure tubs.

"That went about as well as I expected," I say, settling back into the chair. "What do you think?"

"I think that I know why you're stressed out all the time."

"Yes, thank you! People always think I'm exaggerating when I talk about my parents. But I'm not. It's rough." I swish my feet around in the tub. "What was all that talk about listening to Michael Bolton in the bathtub? Is that what you do when you get home from a long day of building fart apps?"

Graham laughs."I just know how to speak her language, Sum. You go in there like gangbusters, telling her that she's wrong, and she's only going to fight you. You're not wrong that they're stressful people to deal with. But you are wrong in the way you deal with them."

"How is it that you know exactly how to deal with my parents, and I, after all these years, still have no idea?"

"It's a gift." Graham shrugs.

"That's an odd gift to have received."

"We don't get to pick and choose," he replies. "So, are we still on for that movie?"

12

It appears that going to see *Back to the Future Part III* on a cruise ship is not high on many people's agenda. I don't know if it's throwback movie night, or if all of the modern day movies accidentally got dropped overboard, but this is what they've decided to show.

Aside from a giggling group of teenagers that I quickly scan for Jackson, Graham and I are pretty much alone in the small theater. I feel very uncomfortable sitting so close to him. I know it's stupid since last night we were slow dancing with our bodies mashed together, and right now all that's happening is a slight contact between our elbows, but *still*. I'm so tense. I have this fear that if I so much as breathe too deeply, he's going to think that I'm turned on and lusting after him. And then he'll turn to me and say, *I'm sorry, I'm dating that blonde in the red dress from the other night, didn't you know?*

No way am I putting myself through that again.

I know what you're thinking. You're thinking that I'm out of my mind and letting irrational fear control my life. Well, yes. Yes I am. Irrational fear is in my DNA. Ask my parents what will happen if they walk in the rain without an umbrella. At some level they know that it's not going to kill them, but they still like to spare themselves the discomfort of getting wet.

Anyway, I shouldn't even be here. All of the single men on this ship are out there, right this second, being snatched up by all of the single women. And where am I? Sitting here watching Christopher Lloyd prance around in a pair of leather chaps. After tonight I am ditching Graham and getting down to business. I mean it.

Aside from the occasional sarcastic observation about the mechanics of time traveling into the Old West, Graham surprises me by keeping his mouth shut throughout most of the movie. The occasional bumping of our elbows never makes as much of a scandal as I thought it would, and I consume a bag and a half of gummy bears. All in all, it's kind of the perfect evening. About halfway through the movie I even resume a normal breathing pattern.

The theater lets us out near the piano bar, where it appears to be Elton John night. I can hear a decent rendition of *Rocket Man* coming from inside.

"So, where are you off to?" asks Graham. We've come to a stop outside the bar where twinkling white Christmas lights catch my eye. It looks so inviting, but I shouldn't go in there with Graham. There's no point.

"I don't know, maybe just to the coffee shop or something. I brought a book." I pat my handbag to illustrate just how cool I am.

"Okay," says Graham. "I was thinking about maybe going in the piano bar, if you wanted to come with." He points to the

Christmas light encrusted piece of heaven behind us. Maybe just a few minutes wouldn't hurt.

Christmas light encrusted piece of heaven behind us. Maybe just a few minutes wouldn't hurt.

"Um, okay," I say. "Just briefly though. I don't even know if I'll get a drink."

"Of course. Places to go, people to see. Coffee shops to sit in."

Graham leads the way and we settle into two large leather chairs by the windows. Graham orders a Manhattan and I order a white wine.

Just one drink, that's it.

Our seats overlook the pool on the top deck, giving us a nice view of the late night swimmers. And when I say "swimmers," I mean "teenagers making out in the hot tub." A couple of older women, who were flirting with the bartender when we walked in, have now turned their attention to Graham. They whisper something to each other and start smiling in his direction.

"Cougar alert," I mutter.

"Duly noted," he mutters back, taking a sip of his Manhattan.

"What is it with you?" I ask.

"What do you mean?"

"I mean you're like a magnet for women of a certain age."

"Am I?" Graham raises an eyebrow, plucks the maraschino cherry out of his drink, and pops it into his mouth.

"Yes, you are. Remember last night when you were dancing with what's-her-name?"

"Lana?"

"I guess so, unless there were others."

Graham smirks and takes a sip of his drink. "Jealous?"

"I already told you this morning that I wasn't jealous. I'm just a little curious if I need to disinfect the hot tub."

"In case you forgot," says Graham, "it was me who brought you back to the suite in your less-than-admirable state last night."

"And I thank you for that." I tip my wine glass towards him. "But I was passed out cold and have no idea if you left again to go fetch what's-her-name."

"Lana."

"Right, Lana. How old is Lana? Fifty-five? Sixty?"

"Thirty-eight. Thirty-nine at the most."

I raise an eyebrow.

"Forty. But not a day over." Graham gives me a crooked smile.

"That's more like it." I take a sip of wine.

"Let me ask you a question," says Graham.

"After you refused to answer mine?"

"I'm being serious now."

"Okay, fine."

"On any given day, exactly how many bottles of sunscreen do you need to apply?"

"Very funny." I roll my eyes. "I thought you were being serious?"

"Sorry. I do have an actual question for you."

"One more chance. Spit it out."

"Why did you hook up with that teenager last night?"

The question catches me a bit off guard.

"I didn't *know* he was a teenager at the time," I say. "I thought we went over this?"

"That's not what I meant. I meant in general, why did you

decide to hook up with some random guy? That doesn't seem like you."

"If I'm not mistaken, it was *you* that convinced me to go out dancing," I say.

"I just wanted you to have a few drinks and loosen up," says Graham, looking at me over the top of his glass. "Maybe dance with me a bit."

"I *did* dance with you. And after that you were dancing with Lana." I try to ignore the feeling that Graham is flirting with me.

"Not until after you disappeared the first time."

"I only disappeared because Mom and Dad showed up and you embarrassed me."

"You still haven't answered the question."

I sigh. "Look, I don't get out very much when I'm at home. So I saw a cute guy and I thought I should try to increase my odds."

"Increase what odds?" asks Graham.

"My odds of meeting somebody, duh." I wish those two ladies would hurry up and hit on Graham so he'll stop asking me uncomfortable questions.

Graham nods slowly. "So that's your plan, isn't it?"

"What plan? Why do you keep implying that I have some sort of *plan*?"

"Your plan to meet Mr. Right. I knew you were up to something."

"It's not a *plan*," I say, trying to hide my embarrassment. "It's just an idea that I had about something that maybe I would try to do while I was going to be here anyway…"

"So… a plan?"

"Maybe."

"That's a tall order."

"Look, you know how overprotective my parents are. This trip, these eight days of quasi-freedom, this is the only chance I've got. If I ever want to get out of that house, I've got to take some initiative. So yes, I needed to have *a plan*."

There, I said it. Maybe if I tell him the truth, he'll realize that hanging around with me all week isn't going to help fulfill The Prophecy.

"And taking initiative means finding a man to whisk you away?"

"You don't have to make it sound so Disney princess. But yeah, the easiest way for me to get out of that house is if I get married."

"I'll buy that. But why take the easy way out?"

"What do you mean?"

"I mean, you're twenty-six years old. You could just pack your stuff and hit the road. Who cares if your parents don't like it? They'll get over it."

"I know how old I am. I know that I could hop a flight to Paris or get a tattoo. I understand that they have no legal hold over me anymore." I stare out the window trying to put into words what it is that stops me from living my life. "It's just that they seem so fragile, you know? I think that if I were to do any of those things, they would both end up in the mental institution. Imagine if I told my mother that I was going backpacking across Europe?"

"I'm not telling you to go backpacking across Europe. I'm telling you to rent an apartment a few blocks away from them."

"It doesn't matter how close it is," I say. "They don't want me living by myself. And they don't want me living with a roommate either, because every once in a while they see on the news that someone was murdered by their roommate. Mom would have a legit nervous breakdown."

"You realize that she's never had a legit nervous breakdown, right?"

"What's your point?"

"Maybe you're not giving them enough credit," says Graham. "Maybe you should do something crazy and freak them out a little bit. Maybe it would put some hair on their chests. *Maybe* they'd get over it."

"Maybe," I shrug. "Or maybe they'd both drop dead and it would all be my fault."

"So you're not living your life because you're afraid of hurting your parents?"

I chew my lip and keep my eyes firmly on the teenaged girl being felt up in the hot tub. "My parents drive me insane, Graham. But what kind of person would I be if I intentionally tried to hurt them?"

Graham leans forward and rests his hand on my knee. I glance down at it nervously. "I would never in a million years suggest that you intentionally hurt anybody. But sticking up for yourself does not make you a bad person. Do you really think this is the kind of life your parents want you to live?"

I look at him, wide-eyed and incredulous. "*Of course* this is the kind of life they want me to live! They're the ones that give me such a hard time when I try to have a life that I've given up completely! It's their fault that I'm looking for my future husband on an eight-day cruise! They've turned me into some kind of desperate middle-aged divorcee, and I'm not even thirty yet."

"It's not their fault," disagrees Graham. "Not completely."

"So you're blaming me?"

"Yep."

"Okay, Dr. Phil, what is it that I'm supposed to do then?"

"How do you think Eric managed to escape all of this?"

"They were never this suffocating with him. Probably because he's a boy."

"That's not what Eric tells me," says Graham. "I've heard similar childhood stories from him. But you know what he told me?"

"What?" I'm curious to hear this.

"For the most part, he went along with them, just like you. But every once in a while, he would refuse. Maybe he wouldn't wear a winter hat if it were above forty degrees outside. He stood up for himself a little bit at a time, and eventually he built up your parents' immunity. Now he goes hang-gliding in Costa Rica and they don't even flinch."

"So what you're saying is, he's been giving them a drop of poison every day for the past twenty-eight years?" I can't help but smile at Graham's theory.

"Exactly."

"But how does this help *me*? I'm twenty-six years behind the game." I take a long sip of wine. It's not easy to hear a real live person—not just the little voice in the back of my head—tell me that it's my own fault my parents walk all over me.

"It's never too late," says Graham, placing his empty glass on the table, and leaning in conspiratorially. He places a hand on my knee and looks into my eyes. "If you'd like, we can start tomorrow."

"Start what, exactly?" This does not sound good, but I can't find the words to argue. Not with Graham's hand on my knee and his eyes boring into mine.

"Poisoning your parents."

A couple at a nearby table gives us a funny look. I snap out of my trance long enough to kick Graham in the shin.

"Sshh! What are you even talking about? You think I'm going to get a tattoo or something?"

"You have a problem with tattoos?"

"Yes," I admit. "I am slightly averse to having a needle jabbed repeatedly into my flesh."

"We'll save that one for the end of the week then," says Graham. "I'm talking about doing some simple things that your parents would never approve of, and realizing that it's not the end of the world."

"You realize we're sailing to Bermuda, right? I don't think there are many opportunities for wild and crazy activities. There's mostly just, like, golf."

"I'll come up with something," says Graham. "We're going to change your life."

Change my life? I was supposed to be doing that on my own, and it certainly wasn't supposed to involve Graham. I can't help but smile though as he waits for my response. He looks so excited about the idea. Like he thinks we're actually going to succeed in defeating Mom and Dad's sixty-five years worth of fear and paranoia.

"The last time I tried to do something my parents wouldn't

approve of, I hooked up with a sixteen year old," I point out.

"That's why you need me. I mean, if you still insist on searching for Mr. Right, you're on your own. I'm not going to spend my week trying to find you a husband. I'm going to spend my week teaching you that you don't need one."

"So my nights will still be my own?"

"You can nail every guy on this ship if you want to."

"Gross."

"Right, don't do that. You can get a *cup of coffee* with every guy on this ship if you want to. But I'm pretty confident that you'll find our daytime activities slightly more fulfilling."

"Okay, fine," I say. "But I have one rule. I refuse to play volleyball."

"That's your one rule? Volleyball? So I could make you get one of those tattoos on your eyelids where it looks like your eyes are open even when they're closed?"

"I know you, Graham. You're not crazy enough to make me get eyelid tattoos, but you are annoying enough to make me play a game of pool volleyball."

"Maybe you don't know me as well as you think you do. What's the big deal about volleyball, anyway?"

"I used to get yelled at in gym class when I was a kid, for missing the ball. *Douchewell sucks!* That's what they would say." I take a long sip of wine. Sometimes I think I've got gym-class-induced post-traumatic stress disorder. GCIPTSD.

"I'm sorry that you had to put up with that nickname," says Graham, quietly. "I really am. If I ever hurt your feelings when we were younger, I'm sorry about that too."

"I appreciate that," I say, giving him a smile. "But it was never you. It was always Eric, or some idiots from school, or basically everybody else on Earth. But I specifically remember that it wasn't you. You were always nice to me."

"I'm glad," says Graham. "Nobody deserves that."

We sit in silence for a few seconds.

"So, it looks like you've got your work cut out for you," I say.

"Looks like I do," says Graham. "Do you want to shake on it?" He holds out his hand and I shake it, holding on a bit longer than I should have. Or perhaps he held on a bit longer than *he* should have. A mischievous grin works its way across Graham's face—a grin that I do not like one bit.

Well, maybe I like it just a little.

13

I swear they have a tracking device on me. Mom and Dad are here, in this bar, heading right towards us.

"You've got to be kidding me," I mumble. Graham's face lights up.

"Good for them," he says. He jumps up and walks over to meet them halfway, shaking Dad's hand and bending down to whisper something into my mother's ear.

He goes over to the bar while Mom and Dad make their way to where I'm sitting. They drag a couple of heavy leather chairs over, and Mom shoves her forearm in my face.

"Look at this," she says. "I think I picked up something at the spa."

"What? Where?" I can't see a thing.

"Right there." Mom points to a tiny red bump. A speck, really.

"It's nothing," I say, staring at the miniscule thing. "It's probably just a bug bite."

"Oy!"

"What? A bug bite's not a big deal."

"What if it's from a flesh-eating bug?"

"Like a flesh-eating bacteria? Did you go swimming in the Amazon?"

"Who knows how clean those bathrobes were?" She makes the same face that you would make had you just stepped into a steaming pile of fecal matter. She settles into one of the chairs and puts her pocketbook on her lap, looking extremely uncomfortable. Dad is staring out the window at the teenagers in the hot tub.

"You guys shouldn't have gone to the spa if you were going to make such a big deal out of everything," I say. "Was there anything that you did enjoy?"

"I fell off the table and almost died, in case you forgot," says Mom.

"You did not almost die. And you *threw yourself* off the table, so you've got nobody to blame but yourself."

"I still think I might sue the cruise line."

I roll my eyes. "Did you like any part of the massage? Before they put the hot stones of death on you, I mean?"

"All of the rubbing and squeezing made me queasy. And that man barely spoke any English."

"What does the masseur not speaking English have to do with whether or not you enjoyed your massage?"

Mom is unable to come up with a logical response, so we sit in silence until I think of a new subject to discuss. I wish Graham would hurry up and come back already. I glance in the direction of the bar and see that the two cougars have started chatting him up. Great.

"So Dad, what do you want to do when we dock tomorrow?"

"I'd like to see the Perfumery," says Dad, a bit morosely. Also, he's repeating exactly what I heard Mom say she wanted to do.

"Really?" I ask. "What about Fort Hamilton? You know, something a bit more masculine?"

"I did see that in one of the brochures," says Dad, brightening up a bit. "I might like to see that."

"If there's time," says Mom. "You also wanted to do some shopping in town."

Right. I bet Dad's been dying to visit the Vera Bradley boutique. Well, whatever. I shouldn't push the issue as I suspect that I will be accompanying my parents around the island, and I would much rather go shopping than take a bunch of pictures next to a cannon. I figure my parents will only need one day of sightseeing before they decide that they've had enough sun; and since we're docked in Bermuda for three days, that still leaves me plenty of time to myself.

"A Manhattan for the gentleman," says Graham, finally returning with some drinks. He hands a glass to Dad. "And a Jager Bomb for the lady." He hands Mom a beer and a shot glass.

"A *what*?" Mom looks horrified. I choke back a laugh.

"A Jager Bomb. It's a beer, with a shot of Jager. You drop the shot glass into the beer, and then you down it."

"But I asked you for a Chablis!"

"Oh, did you? I must have misheard you with all the music." Graham winks at me. The piano player has been on a break for the past twenty minutes. "If you don't want it, I'm sure Summer will drink it."

"You drink these things?" asks Mom, as if I regularly do shots while watching *Doctor Who* episodes in my bedroom.

"Um, yeah," I say. Graham is smiling at me. I know what he's thinking. This is his idea of a kick-off party for freaking out my parents. Okay, fine. I take the two glasses out of Mom's hands. I drop the shot glass into the beer and I chug it. God, that's disgusting. Graham claps.

"Could I try one?" asks Dad.

"You've already got a drink!" says Mom. "You'll be sick!"

"So what?" I say. "We're on vacation. If Dad wants to do a shot, he can do a shot."

Graham is already halfway to the bar. This is so strange. A few minutes later the waitress follows him back to the table carrying a tray with three more beers and three more shot glasses.

"Cheers, everybody! And Joan, you're not getting out of it this time." He places the drinks in front of himself, Mom, and Dad, and starts to count. "On three. One, two…three!"

Graham's already downed his drink while Mom is still studying the outside of her shot glass.

"I'm not putting this filthy thing into my beer!" she says.

"Oh, just shut up and drink it," says Dad. He drops his shot glass into the beer and chugs it. I watch wide-eyed with my mouth hanging open. Graham grabs Mom's shot glass out of her hand, pours it into her beer for her, and holds the glass right up to her face.

"Drink," he commands.

Mom, still in shock from Dad's rebuke, yet unable to say no to Graham, reaches for the glass and takes a cautious sip. She crinkles her nose.

"This is going to give me indigestion."

"Just shut up and drink it!" the three of us yell in unison. She drinks.

***

Okay, so night two went down the toilet.

Rather than doing what I was supposed to do in order to find myself a life partner, I spent the rest of the evening watching Mom and Dad get giggly over Jager Bombs.

Okay fine, it wasn't a total waste. After a beer, a shot, and a Manhattan, Dad was in hilariously rare form. And after Mom drank her beer, she drained an entire glass of Chablis. She kept mumbling something about deserving it after the trauma of falling off the massage table. Hey, whatever it takes to loosen her up.

Had it been just the three of us—Mom, Dad, and me—I would have been seriously depressed about spending an entire night drinking with my parents. But with Graham there, it was different. I was able to laugh at things that would have normally stressed me out—like when Dad took out his cell phone and started trying to figure out how to send text messages. Then Mom started peering at his phone through her bifocals and saying things like "Maybe you need to crash into the network?" and Dad kept saying "Can you hear me now?" like the guy from that old cell phone commercial. God, it was awful. But one wide-eyed glance at Graham and the stress just melted away. I could see the humor in the situation. I've always had a suspicion that there was humor to be found in my parents, but it's always been just out of my grasp.

During the course of the evening, Graham came up with a plan for the four of us to go to a place called Snorkel Park today. From what I read in the tourist brochures, it's a beach full of watersports. The upside is that it's very close to where we're docked, so Mom and Dad won't have to utilize any public transportation to get there. The downside is that it's a beach full of watersports. I mean, I was very grateful to him for the idea. As much as I like to imagine myself roaming the island alone, chances are I was going to end up hanging around with my parents. And if that's the case, I'd much rather do it with Graham by my side. But, still. It's a *beach full of watersports.* What exactly does he think Mom and Dad are going to do there? I also think it's a bit unfair that he talked them into it while they were both drunk.

Graham and I didn't stay long at the piano bar after Mom and Dad retired to their suite. It was almost two o'clock in the morning by that point. As I climbed into bed I realized that the thought of scouring the bars and clubs for a man hadn't even occurred to me, let alone appealed to me. I'd been having too much fun. I'd been having actual *fun* with my parents. The world that we live in is completely mad and unpredictable. Completely.

Anyway, today it's back to reality.

Getting Mom and Dad off of a cruise ship and onto foreign soil is no small task. It would have been bad enough if they were simply going to the perfume factory, but to the beach? Mom and Dad haven't set foot on a beach in years. Decades maybe. Okay fine, *technically* they've been to the beach. When I was in high school they used to drive up to Ogunquit, Maine in the middle of February to view the ocean, all bundled up in winter coats and scarves, and I would have to go with them. Not because I wanted to, but because they didn't think a sixteen-year-old girl was capable of staying home alone for the weekend. Of course if I had been Eric, they'd have had no problem with it. He would have stayed home and thrown one of those parties that you only see in the movies, and when Mom and Dad returned they would have said *We're so proud of you for taking such wonderful care of the house!* while half the population of the school snuck out the back door carrying shards of broken furniture. Yet I, who would never have even thought of doing such a thing, was the one who got stuck traipsing along the beach fifty feet behind them, freezing my tuchas off.

But I digress.

Mom's bringing The Duffle, packed with water shoes, water bottles, a variety of sunscreens, extra sneakers, socks, underwear, and towels. In addition to The Duffle, they're each wearing a fanny pack that says Foxwoods across the front. Dad's also wearing a backpack, which Mom keeps making him unzip so she can fool around inside looking for things. The last time she opened it I caught a glimpse of a pack of D batteries.

Graham and I thought it would be wise to meet them at their suite in order to help them mobilize more quickly. All I'm doing, however, is sitting on the bed trying not to say anything rude. Graham is buzzing around the room helping them locate additional items, and cramming them into bags. He picks a travel-sized flashlight up off the bed.

"Put that in the backpack," says Mom, motioning to Dad. Graham raises an eyebrow at me. I shrug and motion encouragingly towards Dad. Bringing them to a watersports park was his idea; he should have to suffer the consequences. Graham walks up behind Dad and slowly unzips the backpack. A wad of tissues pops out and flutters to the floor.

I fight back a giggle.

Graham picks up the tissues and stuffs them, along with the flashlight, back into the backpack. As he pulls the zipper back the other way, it gets caught on the fabric of his cuff. He yanks it firmly a couple of times.

I choke back a laugh.

Dad has been fiddling with the cap of his anxiety pill bottle the whole time and doesn't even realize what's going on. Graham continues to tug on the zipper, probably wishing that Dad would say something along the lines of *No worries, old boy, I'll take this backpack off immediately and spare both of us a lot of embarrassment.* But no such thing happens. What does happen is that Dad gets the pill bottle open, pops a few tablets into his mouth, and turns to head into the bathroom, dragging Graham along with him. Graham gives the zipper one last frantic tug and comes free—leaving a hole in the cuff of his sweatshirt. Dad steps into the bathroom and shuts the door, none the wiser.

"I hope that wasn't expensive," I say, as he joins me in sitting on the bed.

"Nope," says Graham. He smiles, but I sense a slight strain. They might be getting to him. *Finally.*

"So, what are we doing at this, what is it called?" asks Mom. "*Snorkel* Park?" She says the word snorkel as if it's covered in a thick layer of Ebola virus.

"Oh, we'll see," says Graham, glancing at me and giving me a wink. "They've got a little of everything. Snorkeling, paddle boats, parasailing—"

"PARASAILING?" Mom's knees fail her and she sinks onto the bed.

"You like parasailing?" asks Graham.

"No, I do not like parasailing! What about the perfume factory?" she asks. "What about the Vera Bradley shop? For God's sake, what about the *glass blowing factory*? Why aren't we doing things like *that*?"

"There's plenty of time for that later. We're docked for three days. Of course, if you'd like to do those things today, you're more than welcome." Graham motions toward the window, indicating Mom and Dad's freedom to explore the island alone. "But Summer and I will be at Snorkel Park."

Mom dismisses the idea with a laugh, as if he just told her she should make a solo expedition to the Galapagos Islands, and returns to shoving things into bags.

14

Snorkel Park is a conglomeration of all things my parents hate: sun, water, and sports.

Sure, the sun provides life-giving energy and warmth for every being on the planet. Sure, without it we would all die. That may make the sun likeable enough for some people, but not Mom and Dad. They haven't been able to get past skin cancer. That one flaw in the character of our jolly yellow friend in the sky has rendered it, in my parents' minds, a totally evil being. They look into the sky and they see the Eye of Sauron. *One ring to rule them all. One ring to cause irregularly shaped melanomas.*

Water might also appear to be an agreeable element. We need it to drink and to water our plants, and much like the sun, we would all die without it. But Mom and Dad are no fools. Water can also cause 1) drowning, 2) cramps, and 3) your sunscreen to wash off.

And then we have sports. Anything that requires physical exertion, or the pushing of oneself to one's limits, can just get in line next to water and the sun as three of the greatest evils the world has ever known. No offense, cancer, AIDS, and Hitler.

So here we are, on a sunny day, at a watersports park.

Deep breaths, Douchewell.

To be honest, I'm feeling a bit exhilarated as we walk through the stone entrance tunnel and onto the beach. If Graham weren't here, I would be at the Vera Bradley shop right now sifting through racks of old lady handbags. Living with my parents for my entire life has obviously had some influence on my opinions of the world. As such, watersports have never quite made it to the top of my to-do list. But now that I'm here, I find myself rather eager to try something.

Normally, even if I'd really wanted to try something, I would never have attempted to come here knowing Mom and Dad's typical reaction. I wouldn't have wanted to cause them any grief. Don't get me wrong; I still don't want to cause them grief. But that's the beauty of today. Graham is fully responsible for whatever happens to me. If I fall and break my neck, well, it's not like any of this was my idea. Blame Graham. Or if I should get cut loose from the boat and start drifting across the Atlantic, dangling from a rogue parasail, Mom had better not give *me* the evil eye. Take it up with Graham. I'm just the innocent victim.

Graham's given me quite the gift of freedom, actually. If there were ever a time in my life to try something a little extreme, it's now.

I know I sound ridiculous. Watersports are tame to most normal human beings. It's not like I'm shooting off into outer space on Virgin Galactica—though Mom and Dad probably rank them on the same end of the risk scale. I know that normal people do these things every single day, and that it's safe to assume that whatever happens, Mom and Dad will get over it.

That's what Graham said last night, and I'm going to trust him. Mom and Dad will get over it, and maybe the next time I tell them that I didn't get an oil change at precisely three thousand miles, they'll realize that it's not the end of the world.

Maybe.

"Those look nice," says Mom, pointing in the direction of a paddleboat that's out in the water. An elderly couple, wearing matching floppy straw hats, is slowly paddling around. A bird lands on the back of the boat and pecks at the surface of the water.

"Jet Ski Safari," says Graham.

"Excuse me?"

"Jet Ski Safari," he repeats, a bit louder. "That's what we're doing. I've already booked it."

I raise my eyebrows. "You've already booked it?"

"Surprise!" He flashes me a please-don't-kill-me kind of smile.

I don't know what I was expecting. This is Graham I'm dealing with. It's not like he came all the way to Bermuda to pedal around in circles on a paddleboat with my parents. Still, I had some hope that he would take it easy on me, at least at first.

"Um, okay," I say, trying to squelch the visions of Jet Skis crashing into docks that are running through my mind. "Sure. Let's just get Mom and Dad set up with the paddleboats first."

"You misunderstood me," says Graham. "We're all doing it. I've booked Jet Skis for Joan and Richard too."

At the sound of their names, Mom and Dad look at Graham, their faces indistinguishable from those who have looked into the eyes of Medusa.

"Oy, God!" says Mom.

"But we can't!" says Dad.

"I'm having a nervous breakdown!" says Mom.

"But we can't!" repeats Dad.

This could go on all day.

"Jet Skis are for assholes!" says Mom.

"Joan," interrupts Graham, "you know that I love you, but that's a pretty broad generalization to make of people who are just having fun. You should know that your own son went jet skiing with me in Aruba last year, and even though some may beg to differ—" Graham shoots me a meaningful look, "I don't typically classify him among the assholes. Besides, paddleboats are lame."

"But, but, we can't!" says Dad.

"Are you over the age of sixteen?" asks Graham.

"Well, yes."

"Are you under three hundred seventy-five pounds?"

"I think so."

"Well then, Richard, you most certainly can do it."

"But where will I put my cell phone?"

"Minor detail. All will be well. Trust me."

Trust him? Graham can't be serious. When I said that Mom and Dad would get over this, I meant that they'd get over seeing *me* on a Jet Ski. Putting *them* on Jet Skis is a completely different story. They would never get over that, and do you know why? Because they would die.

I don't know if they would die of fear, or if they would die from falling into the ocean, but one way or another, they would not survive this. I don't care what the guidelines say—Mom's body is not capable of withstanding that kind of wind resistance. It would be like strapping her into a G-force simulator. I mean, sometimes when it's very windy outside she'll grab onto the side of a building and pretend like she can't walk.

Sure, Graham and I talked about poisoning my parents, but that was metaphorically speaking. Right now, Graham is about to literally kill my parents.

"You are not putting my parents on *Jet Skis!*" I shriek.

Graham ignores me and starts herding the three of us down the beach, marching us toward a wooden shack with the words Jet Ski Safari Tours painted across the front. He puts his elbows up on the counter and bounces up and down on his toes, waiting for the attendant. I whack him on the arm.

"Did you hear me?" I ask. "I said you are *not* putting my *parents* on Jet Skis!" I hope that rearranging the emphasis on my words will make him see the error of his ways. It does not.

"Oh, I heard you," says Graham. "But it's not up to you, it's up to them. Your parents are free to leave if they want. The funny thing is, they're not leaving."

I look over at Mom and Dad. They still look stunned, but now they're flipping through pamphlets and speaking to the man behind the counter. I hear Dad mutter something about his cell phone.

"Why do you think they're still here?" asks Graham.

I shake my head, bewildered. Why *are* they still here? I would have expected them to scurry back to the ship by now. I can't say that I would have blamed them.

"I think," says Graham, "that on some level, they actually want to do this. And much like you, I think that they know they would never decide to do it on their own. They're going to thank me later."

"Don't flatter yourself," I say. "There is no way they want to do this."

"They're stronger than you give them credit for, Sum. You've just never tested them properly. And vice-versa. Ah, here he is."

The man behind the counter has finally made his way over to us. He looks a lot like the dead guy from *Weekend at Bernie's*. His name is Don and he's wearing an open Hawaiian shirt and sunglasses and acts like it's the most normal thing in the world that we want to put two elderly nervous wrecks on Jet Skis.

"Are you sure you're okay with this?" I ask Mom and Dad, crinkling my nose. "Don't let Graham pressure you into anything."

"And don't let Summer discourage you from anything!" chimes in Graham.

"Not at all. I'm ready!" says Dad. He does a few knee bends and cracks his knuckles. "Let's cut some cheese!"

"I think you mean cut some—actually, I have no idea what you mean." I shake my head. "Are you *really* sure you want to do this?"

"Don says I can purchase one of these waterproof cell phone cases!" He happily hands over a twenty-dollar bill in exchange for a neon pink zippered case.

"You know you could just leave it here with the rest of our stuff?" I pat my beach bag.

"No, I like to have it with me. Just in case." Dad puts his cell phone into the pink zippered case, and then zippers the cell phone case inside his fanny pack. Apparently the safety of his cell phone was his only concern.

"What about you, Mom?" I ask. What could possibly convince Mom that riding a Jet Ski is a good idea?

"If Don and Graham say that it's safe, I'm going to trust them." She puts her hand on Graham's forearm and gives it a firm squeeze. Well, okay. I always knew that she would follow Graham through the gates of Hell, but I didn't realize she had so much trust in Don, whom she met about six minutes ago. Meanwhile, she didn't even trust her own daughter enough to drive her into Boston.

Anyway, it's settled. For some bizarre reason, possibly involving an alternate reality, Mom and Dad are gung-ho for jet skiing. There are eight people in our tour group, and Don hands out life jackets to all of us. It takes quite a few adjustments before Mom is able to wear hers without announcing that she's suffocating.

It takes equally long for Mom and Dad to get situated on their Jet Skis. First Dad sits down backwards, and then, upon trying to turn around, snags his fanny pack on who knows what, causing it to fall off of his waist and into the water. Don fishes it out. Dad unzips the fanny pack, removes the pink zippered cell phone case, unzips *that*, and holds the cell phone triumphantly in the air.

"I've got it!" he shouts. "And it's not even wet!" He shakes the phone in the air, and then, with a resounding plop, drops it straight into the ocean. In a moment that I shall relive over and over in my mind for all eternity, Dad leaps off the Jet Ski like he's in a Bond movie, and splashes around in the water as if he's saving a drowning child. Finally the splashing ceases as Dad concedes that the phone has sunk beyond his reach. Don fishes him out of the water and places him safely back onto the Jet Ski.

Poor Dad looks completely poleaxed. I don't even mean that figuratively. I mean he literally looks as if he were attacked with a poleaxe. Stunned, if you will. Don reassures him that if there is any sort of emergency, he has the ability to communicate with the mainland. Dad nods his understanding, and gazes forlornly into the sea.

Mom makes it onto her Jet Ski without too much trouble, but the gentle bobbing motion of the water sets off a stream of complaints about motion sickness. She immediately climbs off the Jet Ski, staggers backwards in dramatic fashion, and steps right off the edge of the dock.

Splash.

Don fishes her out—he's getting quite good at this—and places her back onto the Jet Ski. He promises her that once she's moving at full speed, motion sickness shouldn't be a problem. It's cute that he thinks she's going to move at full speed. At any rate, the shock of the water seems to have temporarily taken her mind off of the motion sickness. She sits hunched over the handlebars—dripping wet and seething, but quiet.

Graham and I stand side by side on the dock, patiently observing. The funny thing is that nothing that happened just now has stressed me out. Mom and Dad have both fallen into the ocean, and my heart rate hasn't increased in the slightest. I mean, I'm not a monster. Mom and Dad both have life jackets on, so I knew they were never in any real physical danger. And as far as their emotional well being goes, I have peace of mind knowing that none of this can be blamed on me. This was all Graham's idea, and I'm as innocent a victim in all of this as they are.

"This is a bit different for them, huh?" asks Graham.

"It's completely unreal," I laugh. "You've got some sort of weird power over them. Or maybe it's *Don*. Maybe he's a wizard."

"It's definitely me," says Graham. "And I don't just have magical powers over them." He gives me a wink.

"Yeah, right," I say. "Come on, Gandalf. It's our turn."

Once Graham and I are onboard, Don gives us a quick orientation session. Driving doesn't seem very difficult. Basically I have to squeeze the throttles if I want to go, and ease off of them if I want to slow down or stop. Still, I keep picturing myself getting stuck in a tailspin until Don comes to rescue me. Meanwhile, I imagine Graham zipping off into the sunset and not looking back.

Speaking of Graham, he looks pretty good. He's wearing this dark blue swimsuit with little red lobsters all over it. It's something you would expect a three year old to be wearing, but for Graham it's very subdued and kind of adorable. And also, he's shirtless. Well, except for the life vest. And yes, I know that I've seen him shirtless before and that men go shirtless all the time and it's no big deal to a normal mature woman. But, hello, he's all oiled up with sunscreen, and there is a huge difference between seeing your pasty white cousin shirtless on the Fourth of July, and seeing Graham Blenderman shirtless on a Jet Ski.

Crap. I'm on a Jet Ski!

15

Okay. This is *amazing*.

It isn't terrifying, or crazy, or something that only assholes do. No, it's just fun, and I can't believe I almost missed it.

As soon as we were instructed to head away from the dock, I squeezed the throttles, prayed that I not make a fool of myself, and off I went. And it was *fine*. I didn't crash into anything, or get stuck anywhere, or flip over and get crushed under seven hundred pounds of fiberglass. I simply drove along, at approximately thirty miles per hour, and enjoyed the spray of the ocean in my face.

Of course, I can't speak for Mom and Dad. They're puttering along like they're on scooters at Wal-Mart, and seem to be communicating through primal screams. Luckily, most of their screaming is carried off into time and space by the ocean breeze, so I never actually have to hear a word they're saying. They seem okay though, from afar. My parents are on Jet Skis and they seem okay. Maybe they're not *great*, but they're alive, which is more than I expected.

The tour we're on takes us all along the western end of

Bermuda, stopping at various shipwrecks, drawbridges, and coral reefs so that we can do some sightseeing. The water is crystal clear, allowing us an amazing view of everything below the surface—including the colorful tropical fish that swim up to us every time we stop.

Eventually we arrive at a small, private beach, and Don tells us that we have some extra time to swim, or just hang out and relax, before heading back to Snorkel Park. Mom looks very *Life of Pi* as she comes ashore, as if she's just spent several months at sea with an orangutan and a Bengal tiger, but Dad is actually smiling. His hair is standing on end, just as it was when he stepped out of Graham's Camaro the other day, but this time I don't think that anybody could accuse him of being a terrorist. He still looks completely out of his element, of course. But at the same time, he looks rather exhilarated.

The two of them quickly locate the only tree on the beach and huddle beneath it as Mom tries to salvage the wet contents of Dad's fanny pack. I watch as she pulls out a soggy roll of Tums and somberly shakes her head. *Time of death: 11:15.*

I'm not sure where Graham's wandered off to, so I walk alone to the edge of the water. I take off my tank top and shorts and sit down in just my swimsuit, letting the water lap around my feet. I tilt my head back, close my eyes, and let the warm sun wash over me. I want to remember this moment. I want to—

"Ahhh!" A bucket of water splashes over my head. "What the *hell?*"

Graham sits down next to me, laughing. "Sorry, I couldn't resist. You looked way too relaxed." He tosses a yellow plastic sand bucket over his shoulder and onto the beach.

"You're so rude," I say, laughing and pushing wet hair out of my eyes. At least the water was warm.

"Am not. It's just that if you're lounging in the sand with your head back and your eyes closed, you're asking for it."

"I wasn't asking for anything."

"Difference of opinion. So, are you having fun?"

"I *was* having fun."

"Oh, come on. Get me back if it makes you feel better. Go on." He leans back on his elbows and closes his eyes. God, he looks good without that damn life vest covering everything up.

"I'll get you back," I say, looking him over while his eyes are still shut. "Just not right now. It has to be when you're least expecting it."

"I guess I'll have to sleep with one eye open then," says Graham. He turns his head toward me and opens one eye. I quickly look away.

"Are my parents still under that tree?" I ask, changing the subject, and turning to look over my shoulder.

"Still there," says Graham, following my gaze. "How are they holding up? Ready to murder me?"

"They seem fine," I say, shaking my head. "I can't believe Mom's not yelling at me about using hand signals, or for not coming to a complete stop every time I turn. I mean, they were complete wackos when I was learning to drive a car."

"They're too busy worrying about themselves to be worried about you. Don't you see? Keeping them busy might be the key to your freedom."

I laugh. "So, what? When we get home I have to sign them up for all kinds of extreme activities? Maybe Tuesday nights can be sumo wrestling."

"It's a thought," says Graham. "Either way, we're making major progress."

I smile and turn my attention back to our beautiful surroundings, trying to take a mental picture. When it gets cold and miserable back home, I want to be able to remember this place exactly the way it is right now. I want to take it all in. I want to—

"Ahhh!" A sweatshirt lands on my head. "What the *hell*?"

"Put that on," says Mom. "Or you'll get a burn."

Graham snorts.

"Where did she even *get* this?" I whisper as I start to pull my arms through the sleeves. I freeze when I notice the look on Graham's face. "What?"

"What do you think you're doing?"

"What do you mean?"

"You can't put that thing on. You just made a ton of progress today. You went *Jet Skiing* with your parents. Now you're going to cave over a sweatshirt?"

"I'm not caving, I just don't want her to worry about me getting a burn."

"But you were okay with her worrying about you on a Jet Ski?"

"The Jet Ski was *your* doing, Blenderman, not mine. This is all me. If I don't put the sweatshirt on and I get a burn, I've got nobody to blame but myself."

"Who cares if you have to blame yourself? It's called living your life and making your own mistakes and choices. Honestly, Summer, you need to grow a pair."

My jaw drops open. "I don't need to grow a pair of anything. And I'm putting the sweatshirt *on*."

"No, you're not."

"Yes, I am!"

"Do you *want* to put the sweatshirt on?"

"Of course not!"

"Then don't!"

"I have to!"

"That doesn't make any sense!"

Graham reaches over to pull the sweatshirt away from me, while I struggle to shove my arms into the sleeves. We go back and forth for a while, practically wrestling in the water—laughing and screaming, and looking much like a scene out of some awful chick-lit novel. Graham finally grabs hold of a sleeve that happens to have my arm halfway through it, and pulls me over on top of him. His free hand grabs onto my waist, preventing me from rolling off the other side. I drop one hand into the sand above his shoulder in order to steady myself, and feel his wet, sandy, grip tighten against my bare skin. Swallowing hard, I suddenly wish that Don and the rest of the Jet Ski Safari tour would disappear.

Graham must be thinking along those same lines, because I am suddenly aware of a subtle shift in the terrain beneath my hips. A slight rising of the tide, if you will. Now, I realize that I put myself in a compromising position—wearing a swimsuit and rolling around on the beach with a man—but even so, my cheeks heat up with embarrassment. I bite my lip and look down at Graham, my eyebrows raised. I'm caught between wanting to stand up as fast as humanly possible, and not wanting to move an inch. With my guard momentarily down, Graham gives me a wink, yanks the sweatshirt the rest of the way off of me, and whips it onto the beach.

I look up to find Mom and Dad still standing under their tree, watching everything. I must say, if ever I envisioned a man tearing off my clothes on a beach, it certainly didn't involve Mom and Dad looking on. I look briefly down into Graham's eyes again before rolling off of him and onto the sand. I lay there staring up at the sky, slightly mortified, and willing my heart back to a normal pace.

"Thank you," I say, at last. "I wasn't strong enough to do that myself."

"Oh, you're plenty strong enough," says Graham, rubbing his shoulder. "I think you pulled my arm out of its socket."

"I don't think that's all I did," I say with a nervous giggle, attempting to clear the air.

"Um, yeah. Sorry about that." Graham clears his throat and adjusts his waistband, likely the closest I've ever seen him come to being embarrassed.

"No, it's my fault," I say. "I shouldn't have been wrestling with you. That was weird of me. The same thing happened the other night when my parents saw me dancing. I was ready to dropkick you to the ground if that's what it took to make you stop. I'm like a drug addict."

"You're addicted to not causing your parents stress? That's got to be the lamest thing I've ever heard."

I laugh. "I don't know why you expected anything different, Blenderman. You've known me for a long time. I take pictures of my cat doing handstands."

"Because we had a plan, remember?" Graham rolls onto his side and props himself up on his elbow. "The whole point of which was to stress out your parents."

"I know, I know. Blah, blah blah."

"Don't blah blah blah me," says Graham. "This is serious. In order for our plan to work, you need to be able to stick with it after we're back home—even when I'm not around to take the blame."

"I can still blame you, even if you're not there."

"Summer."

I roll my eyes. "Alright, I know. I've got to grow a pair. You're so eloquent."

"Damn straight. Grow a couple of pairs while you're at it. You've got to be willing to put in the effort."

"I am willing," I mumble. "It's just that this whole rebellion thing is a lot harder than I thought it would be."

"Of course it is. We're fighting a quarter century of learned behaviors over an eight-day cruise. It's borderline ludicrous. But we'll get there, Summer. One day at a time."

I sigh. "You do realize we've only got five more days?"

"Don't underestimate me," says Graham.

***

Mom was pretty mad about her sweatshirt.

She picked it up off the beach, all limp and sandy, and said— and I quote—*To hell with you!* That's what she said to her own daughter! Condemning me to eternal damnation just for getting her stupid sweatshirt wet. Well, I wasn't about to take that lying down. Oh no. I blamed the entire thing on Graham. It worked too, since she'd witnessed the whole thing—me struggling to get into it, Graham flinging it cruelly onto the beach. She even gave him a lecture on the dangers of ultraviolet rays—pronouncing each word very slowly, and making *ultraviolet ray* motions with her arms. Naturally, none of this made Graham very happy. But hey, you can't please all of the people all of the time. Besides, I've got five more days to grow a pair. No need to rush things.

I'm alone in the suite now, stretched out on the couch and completely exhausted from our day in the sun. Ideally, I would order room service and read a book in bed for the rest of the night. But instead, I need to work on finding myself a husband.

The whole idea sounds stupider every time I say it—and it sounded pretty stupid to begin with. But just because Graham doesn't think I should rely on a man to rescue me from the confines of my parents' basement, doesn't mean that I've completely renounced the idea. Sure, jet skiing was fun, and something I never would have done on my own, but I don't see how it's going to get me anywhere nearer to my goal of obtaining a life of my own. It's not like I'm going to jump on a Jet Ski and blast through the wall of my parents' basement yelling, *Yippee Ki-Yay Mother Fuckers!* As awesome as that is in my mind, it's just not realistic.

The Prophecy, on the other hand, has some merit. Women have been living at home until they're married for hundreds of years; just because my mother suggested it doesn't necessarily make it wrong. Why should I have to be the one to make history? So no, I'm not giving up on it yet. Besides, I've got to make at least one attempt with a man who's old enough to vote.

I shake my head at the memory of Jackson, heaving myself off the couch and into the bedroom to get changed. Mom and Dad have gone back to their suite to take a nap, and Graham is supposedly doing the same in his room. We haven't really talked about our plans for the rest of the evening. I don't want to guilt him into hanging out with me again, even if he does claim that he's doing it out of his own free will. He deserves some time on his own to do whatever he wants—perform in a variety show, make tie-dye t-shirts, meet women. An odd feeling creeps into my stomach as I remember him dancing with Lana the other night. Maybe he'd like to see her again. He certainly can't do that if he's got me and my parents chained to his ankle all night.

I make up my mind to take the choice out of his hands. I'll head out on my own for the evening before he wakes up from his nap. I can start with an early dinner at the buffet, and then, well, what do single people actually do on this boat? I pick the *Cruise Notes* daily activities sheet up off my bed and scan through it.

6:00 p.m. – Hawaiian Shirt Bingo
7:00 p.m. – Women's Open Mic Comedy Hour
8:00 p.m. – Senior Speed Dating with Stan

Okay, no. I throw the sheet back down on the bed. I'll just have to make my own fun. I put on a short black dress, and then realize how odd I'm going to look at the buffet while other people are still wearing swimsuits. It is only five o'clock. But maybe attention is a good thing. Maybe that's what my problem is. I put on a pair of red heels, and then take them off again. I don't want to attract *too* much attention. Or do I? I put them back on. No, I look ridiculous. I take them off.

I remove the black dress completely, and pull on a pair of black capri pants and a black t-shirt. Then I put the red heels back on. There. It's enough of a mix of daytime casual and nighttime chic that I may have just canceled myself out completely. It doesn't matter. The only plan I have right now is to sit at a bar and load up on Chardonnay until I'm able to make small talk with strangers. That doesn't sound weird or creepy or likely to end in my grisly murder, does it?

I didn't think so.

16

I've eaten way too many nuts.

And olives.

The olives are good, don't get me wrong, but there's a limit. Still, I just keep shoveling them in because that's what one does when one is sitting by oneself at a bar trying not to be self-conscious. Once in a while I get one with a pit, which makes things even worse because then not only am I sitting alone at a bar, but I'm sitting alone at a bar and spitting into a napkin. I shove the bowl of olives away and order another wine. Maybe I'll take the glass and go for a walk.

Dinner was kind of a disaster. I was sitting at a table by the pool, eating my dinner and reading a book, when a man stopped by and asked if he could borrow the salt. At least I think it was a man, since I handed him the salt without even looking up. A few minutes later, the same voice asked if he could borrow the pepper. Again, I handed it to him without looking up. It wasn't until I got to the end of the chapter that I realized he might have been attempting to start a conversation with me; or maybe he really just needed the salt and pepper. The point is that I'll never know because I was too absorbed in my stupid book. And do you want to know what I was reading? *Fifty Shades of Grey*. I just wanted to see what all the hoopla was about. The female teachers at my school are all crazy for it. It was in the middle of the millionth repetitive sex scene that a potential man of my dreams came over and asked me to borrow the salt, and I couldn't even be bothered to look up.

I stink at this.

Of course, now that I've been sitting at the atrium bar with my radar cranked all the way up, not a single person has tried to hit on me. It's a bit insulting. Maybe I just picked a lame place to hang out. I mean, about twenty minutes ago some parents came in with a couple of kids and ordered two chocolate milks. I look at my watch. Seven o'clock. Right. No way am I going to make it to a time when actual men are out.

I'm just about to slide off my stool when I feel somebody sit down beside me.

"Oh, hey Dad," I sigh. "What's up?"

That's who finally decided to come over and talk to me. My father.

"Your mother didn't feel like coming out after dinner. She's pretty tired after riding on the Jet Ski."

"And you're not?" I ask. I'm surprised. I figured if Mom were in for the night, Dad would automatically be in for the night too.

"I am," he says. "But I still thought I'd come out for a bit. I didn't want to miss anything." He looks eagerly around the bar, like he's expecting to see Marilyn Monroe. He orders a Manhattan from the bartender.

"Well, you weren't missing much here. Unless you count the

guy that sat down at the piano and played a bunch of Taylor Swift songs. 'Shake It Off' wasn't half bad."

"And now you've got your father to keep you company. Things keep getting better."

I laugh. "No, it's fine. I was getting lonely, to tell you the truth."

"Where's Graham?"

I shrug. "Taking a nap, last I knew. I wanted to give him a little space. He's been hanging out with us a lot."

"I like Graham," says Dad. "Always have. It was nice of him to come with us. Without Eric, I mean."

"I still can't believe Eric didn't show up. Are you going to yell at him when we get home?"

I wait while the bartender hands Dad his Manhattan, and he takes a sip. The same look of giddiness that he gets every time he has a drink crosses his face—like he's doing something that he shouldn't be doing. Like he's somewhat pumped that Mom decided to go to bed early.

"There's no use in yelling at him," he says, at last. "Eric's an adult."

"But he ditched us without even bothering to tell us ahead of time. That sucks. He should feel bad about it."

"Eric's never cared too much about other people's feelings," says Dad, taking another sip. "Even if I yelled at him, what would it matter? He does what he wants."

Eric does what he wants, that's for sure. The conversation I had with Graham the other night comes to mind. Eric's been doing whatever he wants ever since he was a kid, and that's why Mom and Dad have stopped trying to control his life. It's what

I've always been so jealous of. But now, I'm seeing proof of what I've always been afraid of—Dad looking so hurt and defeated. I don't want him to look like that when he talks about me. On the other hand, Eric did always take it to an extreme. All I want is to be able to decide for myself whether or not I need a sweater. Dad can't possibly be depressed about that kind of thing. Mom, on the other hand…

"He is kind of a self-centered jerk," I say.

"Nah, he's a good kid," says Dad. "He's just strong-willed. He's not like you. You're a good girl, Summer."

Dad smiles and pats me lightly on the head. I know he means well, but did Dad just call me weak? Are those really my choices—cause my parents grief, or be a weak-willed little mouse? Why is there no happy medium?

Sticking up for yourself does not make you a bad person. Graham's words from the other night come back to me. *I'm talking about doing some simple things that your parents would never approve of, and realizing that it's not the end of the world.*

Maybe that's my happy medium. Maybe stupid Blenderman actually has a point.

"So, Dad," I say. "How did you really feel about jet skiing today? Was it, um, was it okay?" He's a bit liquored up at the moment, so I'm either going to get a very honest answer, or the answer of a drunk person who thinks that just about everything is fantastic.

"I lost my cell phone."

"I know, Dad. I'm sorry. Besides that, though. What did you think?"

"Your mother said that it jostled her around too much. She

said she felt as if all of her bones were breaking into a thousand pieces."

I roll my eyes. "I'm sure she did. But what about *you*, Dad? What did *you* think?"

He pauses for a few moments, as if his own thoughts and opinions are too difficult to locate. I give him some time to dig.

"I think that I had fun," he says, slowly. "I always wanted to ride a motorcycle when I was a boy, and this was the closest I've ever come."

"You wanted to ride a motorcycle?"

"All the kids did when I was growing up. We wanted to be like James Dean."

"How come you never did?"

"Oh, you know. Grandma would have had a stroke if I ever went near one. And then I got married, and your mother always found them to be too dangerous. I mean, they *are* dangerous." He gives me a nervous glance, afraid that he inadvertently gave me the go-ahead to ride a motorcycle.

"So you really had fun? I'm glad. I kind of thought you'd be freaking out about the whole thing."

"Me? Freak out? Never. We'll leave that kind of thing to your mother."

I laugh. Three sips of a Manhattan are apparently all it takes for Dad to start talking nonsense.

"So, when we get back home, and I tell you that I'm going to an aerobics class at the indoor trampoline park, are you still going to worry about me breaking my neck?"

"Of course. Trampolines are one of the most dangerous inventions in the world. Where is there an indoor trampoline park, anyway?" He looks as if he's about to form the Committee to Shut Down the Indoor Trampoline Park.

"Near my work," I say. "It just opened. Some of the teachers have asked me to join them, but I've never gone. I didn't want to worry you and Mom."

Every so often, over the course of my life, I throw out the name of something that I would like to try, and I tack onto the end of it—*But I didn't want to worry you and Mom.* I've done this in regards to rollerblading, wine tasting, field hockey, Indian food, concerts, online shopping, haircuts, job interviews, and world travel, to name just a few. Part of me hopes that if I keep saying it, they will one day respond with—*Of course you should try it! Don't worry about us!*

"Good," says Dad. "The last thing we need is for you to wind up paralyzed."

Today is not that day.

"How many people do you know that have been paralyzed from a trampoline?"

"My cousin Morty's daughter, Deirdre."

"Deirdre is in Cirque Du Soleil, Dad. She broke her leg because she fell from a human chandelier."

True story. Deirdre was in physical therapy for a while, but she's definitely not paralyzed. And according to Facebook, she's already back with Cirque Du Soleil and touring Europe. I take a sip of wine and ponder the injustice of it all. My cousin, my own flesh and blood, is literally swinging from chandeliers—human or otherwise—all over Europe, while I'm here on a cruise ship with my Mom and Dad.

"Well, she has something. Scia…sciat…"

"Sciatica?"

"That's it."

I bury my face in my hands. Thanks to Cousin Deirdre's sciatica, I may never experience the joy of jumping on a trampoline.

"Don't you regret never having ridden a motorcycle?" I ask, lifting my head and raking my fingers down my cheeks. I catch sight of myself in the mirror behind the bar, looking a bit too much like Munch's *The Scream*. I readjust.

"Not really," says Dad. "It was my choice."

"But it wasn't your choice," I argue. "You never tried it because you were afraid of hurting Grandma or Mom. Their fear made the choice for you. Maybe I don't want to grow old having never jumped on a trampoline."

"If you do jump on a trampoline, you may never grow old at all." Dad nods slowly in agreement with himself.

I bite my lip and stare at the television behind the bar—almost laughing, but not quite able. How can one argue with such logic?

One cannot.

I sigh and grab more olives.

***

I walk Dad back to his suite, fully intending to stay out a bit longer on my manhunt. But by the time we get there, I realize how truly exhausted I am. It's much easier to just take the elevator up to my room than it is to make the ten-minute walk back to where all the action is. Sure, it's another night down the tubes, but at least I made an effort.

I push open the door to my suite—expecting peace and quiet—only to find Lana standing in the middle of the room wearing nothing but a beach cover-up and a pair of giant hoop earrings. And she's *squawking.*

"This suite is amaaaaazing!"

Before I can make my presence known, she's whipped her dress up over her head and tossed it onto the couch. Thankfully, and I am only thankful for this for about three seconds, she's wearing a bikini underneath. After those three seconds pass, I'm left with a double-D-chested, bikini-clad woman in my suite—and Graham, standing by the bar holding two empty martini glasses.

"I'm sorry," I mumble. "I didn't know you guys were in the middle of something. I'm just…I'm going to go to bed. It's late." I make a beeline for my bedroom, and quickly shut the door behind me. I hear the slider going out to our balcony open and close. A few seconds later, there's a knock.

"Summer?" says Graham, in a half whisper. I pull the door open a few inches.

"What?"

He has his forehead pressed up against the doorframe and is looking down at me. "Don't go to bed. Come out on the balcony with us."

"Are you crazy?"

"Look, I know what you think is going on here. But it's not like that. She invited herself over. To be honest, she kind of scares me."

"So, what do you want *me* to do about it?"

"Just hang out with us so she doesn't try to eat me alive."

I shut the door in his face and count to ten.

"I'll be out in a minute."

As much as I want to go to sleep, I also don't want to leave Graham and Lana out there alone. I kind of feel like I owe him something for getting me on a Jet Ski today—even if it is just saving him from a highly attractive older woman who wants to sleep with him. Does he really think I'm going to buy his story that he's not interested? Of *course* he's interested. I can't for the life of me figure out why he wants me out there. Maybe he's hoping for a three-way. Against my better judgment, I throw on my swimsuit and a cover-up and step out of my room. Graham is standing there holding a bright green martini.

"Appletini?"

"Thanks," I say, taking the glass. "You know, you could have warned me she'd be here."

"I didn't exactly plan on it. I told you, she invited herself. I was trying to get her back to her own cabin."

"I'm not buying your story, Blenderman."

"How come you disappeared before dinner tonight?" he asks, stopping me before I walk out the sliding door.

"I wanted to give you some time to yourself, to do whatever you wanted. Obviously I made the right move." I motion toward Lana, who is outside, leaning far out over the railing and sticking her butt directly into Graham's line of vision. I should probably warn her not to fall overboard, but I don't. Live and learn— that's what I always say.

"Yeah, thanks," says Graham. "It's just that I was just going to see if you wanted to go to the comedy show with me tonight. But when I came out of my room, you were gone. I had to eat dinner by myself at the buffet. That's where this one found me—" he jerks his head toward Lana, "and invited herself to be my date for the evening. Did you know that she laughs really, *really*, loudly?"

I giggle at the look of horror on Graham's face and then yank open the slider. "Come on, we'd better get out there before she injures herself."

At the sound of somebody stepping onto the balcony, Lana twirls around with a big smile on her face—most likely expecting to find a Speedo-clad Graham—but instead she finds me. Her smile fades.

"Oh," she says. "I thought you went to bed."

"Graham invited me out."

She looks me up and down, dismissing me with a shrug. I guess I don't pose much of a threat. I sit down on a lounge chair as she steps into the hot tub. Reggae music tinkles out from within the suite, and Graham steps through the door carrying two more martinis. He isn't wearing a Speedo, just a regular swimsuit in hot pink and navy blue stripes—and he's shirtless, yet again. I look away.

"Get over here, you," says Lana, her boobs floating atop the water.

"After you, Sum," says Graham. Lana shoots him a dirty look.

I reluctantly put my drink down, take off my cover-up, and step into the hot tub. Lana's boobs account for one person each, so there's already four of us in the two-person tub before Graham even attempts to get in. He looks from Lana, to me, to each of Lana's boobs, and then back to me, with a bemused expression on his face.

"Alright ladies, make way." He puts his drink down next to the tub and rubs his hands together. Then he sits in my lap.

"Graham! You're kind of heavy!" I try to push him off without actually touching him with my hands, the end result being a bit more intimate than I had intended.

"Whoa, hey there, Sum," he laughs, sliding onto the seat next to me.

I roll my eyes and wrap my arms around my chest, sinking down further under the water. Just kill me.

"Over here," says Lana, patting the two inches of bench next to her.

Graham slides over and now it's just a jumbled mess of legs and feet. Lana's holding her martini glass up in the air like we're on Spring Break in Miami.

"Love it!" she squeals.

Oy, please.

"So, um, Lana, who are you traveling with?" I ask, attempting to tone things down a bit.

"A couple of my girlfriends. Oh! That reminds me! Jessica and LuLu would *love* this place! Hand me my phone, will you?"

This place? Like our suite? I watch as Graham reaches over the side of the tub and picks up Lana's purse.

"Jess? It's me. You've got to come down to this suite, it's unbelievable. Yeah. That guy. I know, right? 6410. Yup. Of *course* bring LuLu! Okay. Okay, bye."

"They're on their way," she says. "They're an absolute *blast*. We used to all work together at Hooters."

And that's my cue.

I remain in the hot tub for about two more minutes before

excusing myself to use the bathroom. I don't bother coming back. Instead, I lock my bedroom door, put my pajamas on, and get into bed.

About ten minutes later I hear a giggling gaggle of Hooters waitresses traipse through the suite and out onto the balcony. I pull the blankets up over my head and pray that we hit an iceberg. Just one little iceberg, is that too much to ask? Women and children will load the lifeboats first, naturally.

Graham can go down with the ship.

17

Okay, okay. I don't actually want him to go down with the ship. Although, if he had been on the Titanic, some cougar from the Carpathia would have leaned over the railing and pulled him to safety before he even caught a chill. I just meant that I don't need all of this drama. I don't need all of these back and forth emotions. Especially when they all still seem to be one-sided, just like they were ten years ago.

All of my attempts at finding out what happened in the hot tub last night have failed miserably. Graham is so damn cryptic and full of innuendo that I can never tell when he's joking and when he's being serious. I mean, if he actually had engaged in hot tub fornication, would he really tell me about it? Or would he only make jokes if truly nothing had happened? Does it even matter? He doesn't owe me any explanations. We're just friends. Roommates. It must be nice being Graham, though. Every time I get close to a guy, he can rest easy knowing that it's likely going to end in disaster. Not that he cares.

I'm sitting alone on the pool deck the next morning with a chocolate croissant and my Kindle, killing some time before the four of us head to Horseshoe Bay Beach. It's early enough that I can sit in the sun without fear of immediate sunburn, and the sea breeze feels good on my face. The sound system is pumping out Calypso music, and I try to focus on, and appreciate, where I am right now. I am sailing across the open sea. I am staying in a luxury suite. I don't have a care in the world. I am lucky, *very* lucky. I close my eyes and take it all in.

"Reading anything good?"

I jump at the sound of a voice, and look up to find a scruffy young guy in a goatee and a Comic Con t-shirt staring down at my Kindle. Staring down at *Fifty Shades of Grey.*

"No!" I say, quickly hitting the power switch.

"You reading *Fifty Shades* or something?" he asks, narrowing his eyes.

My jaw drops. "How did you know?"

"That's the same reaction my mom had when I caught her reading it," he says, with a smile. He has a coffee in one hand, a Kindle in the other, and he takes a seat at the table next to mine. "Looks like we both had the same idea."

"*Fifty Shades*?"

"No," he laughs. "I mean the coffee and the reading. I needed a little quiet time this morning. Although, this stuff is barely tolerable."

"The coffee? What's wrong with it?" It tastes fine to me.

"I've been using my Chemex so much, that I can't stand the taste of anything else."

"What's a Chemex?"

"*What's a Chemex?* Just, the *only* way to make drinkable coffee. It was invented locally, in Massachusetts." He looks at me expectantly, as if his spouting of random facts should have cleared everything up, rather than make him sound like a pretentious tool.

"Never heard of it." I shrug.

"I guess I'm not surprised," he says, raising an eyebrow and taking a long sip. "Most people just flock to Starbucks. Like sheep."

"Excuse me?"

He shakes his head, as if just now realizing he was speaking aloud. "No offense. I just mean that most people accept Starbucks as real coffee, when it is *so* far from it."

I take a long, deliberate sip of my coffee while I study this guy in more detail. He's got a mop of unkempt curly hair, black, chunky framed glasses, and a few laugh lines around his eyes. He's not the most gorgeous looking creature I've ever seen—but he's definitely not in high school. I am definitely, fifty percent sure about that. He's also wearing a pair of skinny jeans with loafers. He's a total hipster; hence the Chemex and the coffee snobbery. But I never did put any restrictions on the type of guy I was going to pursue. Maybe we could be very happy together brewing our own coffee and kicking around a hacky-sack in Northampton. The powers that be have practically dumped this guy in my lap; I should think of The Prophecy and give him a chance.

"My name's Summer," I say, leaning over and reluctantly sticking out my hand. "And I'm going to pretend that you didn't just refer to me as a mindless sheep."

"Logan." He shakes my hand. "And really, it was nothing personal."

"Of course not," I say. "It was just an ignorant assumption about my ability to make my own decisions. So what are you reading, Logan? Something by David Foster Wallace?"

"Cat's Cradle. Heard of it? I know it's outside the realm of romance novels." He motions toward my Kindle.

I roll my eyes. "A, this book is far from romantic. B, I'm only reading it to see what the big deal is. And C, of course I've read Cat's Cradle. I'm a librarian. Books are my life."

"Really?" Logan looks at me in surprise. "What's your favorite book?"

"*The Lord of the Rings*." Not to flatter myself, but I can practically see the hearts forming in his eyes.

"That's not a book, it's a trilogy."

"Okay, fine. *The Fellowship of the Ring*. Happy?"

"Very," he says. "It's not every day you meet a girl who's into Hobbits."

It's not the most flattering compliment I've ever received, but this guy isn't exactly skilled at charming the ladies.

"It's not every day you meet a guy who can read," I say.

Logan laughs, even though I wasn't totally joking. Even if his t-shirt is adorned with a picture of a zombie shaking hands with Spiderman, it's refreshing to meet a man who reads. I can't imagine being able to discuss books with someone like Graham. I remember everything that he said about the books he was assigned in college. About *An American Tragedy* he said, and I quote, "It's longer than the goddamn Magna Carta." To which I asked if he'd actually read the goddamn Magna Carta, because it is actually quite interesting (to which he replied by flicking me in the head with a rubber band).

Logan and I return to reading our books, but I can't concentrate. What if I came off as rude? I don't want him to think I'm not interested. I mean, I'm *not* interested, but I should really push myself. Unfortunately, Logan could be the only man that talks to me today, and I'm on a tight schedule. It's not like people who are forced into arranged marriages love each other straight off the bat.

After a few minutes of nervously debating with myself, I look up. Logan is looking back at me with a pretentious smile on his face, like he's wondering if I ate quinoa this morning or just Cheerios. Whatever. Maybe that's what his smile looks like. I really shouldn't be so judgmental. I don't want to be like, well, like Logan.

"Can I help you?" I ask, feigning annoyance. Mostly feigning it.

"Do you want to maybe get a drink or something later?"

"You mean like an organic craft beer?"

Logan's eyes light up. "You know of a place?"

"No, but I'm sure we can track some down. It's a big boat."

"Sweet. It's a date then?"

"Sure, why not?" I say, thinking of about a million reasons but ignoring all of them.

***

It's about a half hour bus ride from King's Wharf to Horseshoe Bay Beach, and it is really quite a ride. Driving on the left side of the road is one thing, but the way the bus takes the corners on the narrow, highly vegetated road, is like something out of a movie. I would like to hold on for dear life, but the only thing next to me on the side-facing bench is Graham. I use every abdominal muscle I've got to hold myself in place.

Mom and Dad are seated directly across from us, and seem to have spiraled into a state of catatonic paralysis. They have been rendered incapable of speech—arms rigid, hands clinging white-knuckled onto the metal handrails, feet planted firmly on the floor. I should clarify that they are incapable of speech only until the bus goes around a corner and the tree branches snap against the windows. When that happens, Mom shrieks.

"Oy! Richard! How can they not have seatbelts?"

She goes limp, lets go of the handrails, and allows herself to be thrown against Dad in some sort of political statement about the hazards of the Bermuda transit system.

"This is insanity!" cries Dad. "Absolute insanity! I'm going to speak to the driver." As soon as he stands up, the bus takes a sharp turn, and Dad lurches forward with his right leg kicked back and his left arm stretched forward. His other arm grasps fruitlessly in the air behind him before he crashes head first into my lap.

"Dad!"

Graham, who jumped up one second too late in an attempt to catch him, is now on his knees on the floor. Strangers begin to get up from their seats to assist us. The bus continues along at the same speed.

"Stop the bus! Stop the bus!" Mom yells. The bus driver glances into the rear view mirror and continues driving.

Dad staggers back to his seat, visibly shaken, but uninjured.

"Do we need to call an ambulance?" asks Mom. "Should we call a lawyer?"

"Do you think we should?" asks Dad, looking around at the other passengers for advice. "Is that what people do?"

The bus driver glances into the rearview mirror again, this time slightly more interested.

"I think you're okay, sir," he says, slowing down the bus. "He's okay, everybody! Please, return to your seats!"

"What do you know?" asks Mom. "You're driving like a lunatic!"

"Mom," I hiss. "Don't make a scene!"

"What scene? He almost killed all of us!"

"It wasn't his fault. Dad shouldn't have stood up!"

"He wouldn't have stood up if this driver hadn't been driving like a lunatic!"

"That doesn't make any sense!"

The bus driver slows down and pulls over to the side of the road.

"Oh, thank God," says Mom. "Does anybody have their cell phone? We can have an ambulance meet us here."

I look out the window, noticing that there is no bus stop where we've stopped. The bus driver stands up and walks towards us.

"All of you, off the bus," he says.

"Excuse me?" says Mom.

"I want all of you off my bus." He points to the sign posted above the door. "Do you see that? *Wait until bus comes to a complete stop before leaving your seat.* It is clearly stated. You broke the rules, and now you want to call a lawyer? No. Get the hell off of my bus. All of you."

Mom looks out the window. There's nothing but vegetation.

"But where are we supposed to go?"

"You can walk. We're only a mile or so from the beach. Now get off."

The faces of the other passengers are quickly starting to change from concern to annoyance. I try not to look at them as we begin gathering up our things. Graham briefly tries to put up a fight, but there's not much to argue about when you know you're in the wrong. Dad broke the damn rules, standing up like he was Keanu Reeves on a mission to stop the bus from exploding. Why would he do that? He's usually so timid. I guess it doesn't really matter why anymore. We all file shamefully down the steps and stand there in a silent cloud of dust as the bus peels off down the road.

"Well, I guess we walk," says Graham, shrugging and smiling cheerfully.

He picks up my beach bag and heads off in the same direction as the bus. I follow after him, with my parents trailing about fifty feet behind. Every so often we slow down so that they can catch up—like a Slinky, but less fun.

18

We arrive at the entrance sign for Horseshoe Bay Beach, sweating and grouchy. Not only was the walk excruciatingly long, but hundreds of busses kept whizzing past us beeping and kicking up rocks—all of them filled with happy, relaxed tourists. Mom wanted to call for a taxi, but none of us could get any service on our cell phones. Besides, Graham was adamantly against the idea. I think that he actually enjoyed the walk, like he thought it was doing my parents some sort of good. Like it was toughening them up and increasing their mental fortitude. Perhaps. Or perhaps it was decreasing their life expectancy by fifteen years apiece.

Our moods deteriorate even further when we realize that the actual beach is at the bottom of yet another long dirt road. But we keep on trucking, trailing after Graham—our fearless and mentally unhinged leader—and eventually we step onto the beach.

I look out over the pastel pink sands and the turquoise water, and I realize that the arduous hike was worth every second. Well, maybe not every second. Maybe not the part when Dad stopped to shake out his shoes and show Mom his bunion, but most of it. The ocean is dotted with large rock formations that form small coves where they come close to the shore. Some adventurous souls are climbing and diving off the tops of them. I glance nervously at Graham. There is *no way* we're doing that. Then I glance over at Mom and Dad to see how they're enjoying the view.

"This is a nightmare!" shrieks Mom.

"What's the matter?"

"Where are we going to sit?"

I look out onto the beach, into a sea of chairs and striped umbrellas.

"Um, I don't know," I say. "How about right there? Or over there?"

"So close to the *people?*" She says it as if we've crash-landed on the Planet of the Apes.

"Just wait here," I say.

Graham and I walk over and rent four beach chairs and two umbrellas from the rental booth. Then we lead Mom and Dad down the beach, as far from *the people* as possible. The further we go, the less crowded it becomes, and when we finally put our stuff down in the sand, it's in a fairly empty area.

"See," I say, after we've gotten ourselves situated. "That wasn't the end of the world, was it?"

Mom refuses to acknowledge that I was right, and instead busies herself with picking miniscule bits of debris from the sand around her feet. I settle back into my chair, taking in the view. Gorgeous water. Sunshine. Graham disrobing directly in front of me.

Oh dear.

I'm thankful that I have my sunglasses on; otherwise he would have already noticed me staring. He flings his t-shirt—which is a color that I can only describe as American cheese—onto his beach towel, does a few completely unnecessary stretches, and heads off toward the water.

"Want to join me?" he calls over his shoulder.

Um, sort of. I mean, it looks really nice out there, but what are we going to do? Splash each other? Do that thing where the girl gets up on the guy's shoulders? What if we somehow end up wrestling again? I know it's unlikely, but with Graham you never know. My stomach gets a bit jittery at the thought of how yesterday's little wrestling match ended. At the feeling of, well…oh boy, now my cheeks are burning up. My cheeks are burning up and my stomach is in knots over the thought of a guy who wears American-cheese-colored clothing.

Get a grip, Douchewell.

I just have to go out there and bob around in the waves, making sure to keep a safe distance at all times. It shouldn't be too difficult with Mom and Dad looking on. Not that that made any difference yesterday.

"Sure, I'll be there in a few minutes," I call back.

"You should drape a towel over your legs," says Mom, gesturing to the six inches of leg that are sticking out from under the shade of my umbrella.

And that was long enough.

I take off my tank top and shorts and head down the beach. I shouldn't be surprised, but in the past couple of minutes a few women have joined Graham in the water. I'm tempted to turn around and go back to my parents, but decide to choose the lesser of two evils. I'll just hang out in the water by myself. It's better this way. I wade in slowly at first, until I realize how warm it is—then I plunge in up to my neck. The water is crystal clear straight down to the bottom, and I can see the sand swirling around where I've sunk in my feet. I bob gently up and down with the waves, occasionally glancing at Graham and his new friends.

My stomach drops when I realize that one of them is Lana. Great. Did she follow us here?

I turn around and face the ocean, pretending to soak up the scenery. Last night in the hot tub I learned that Lana and her friends are celebrating Lana's divorce. She's been having the time of her life and really enjoys meeting new people. Good for her. What do I care? I have a date with Logan tonight. Good old book-reading, hipster Logan. I tilt my head back into the warm water and try to just enjoy the moment. I am floating in the ocean. I am in paradise. I do not have a care in the world.

"I can't believe the *size* of that thing!" shrieks Lana.

And I'm getting out.

Lana is pointing at the water in the vicinity of Graham's shorts. I raise my eyebrows as I pass by.

"It's a fish," says Graham.

"A *huge* fish," adds Lana. "Oh my gosh! Here it comes again!" She lets out a cry and launches herself into Graham's arms.

I continue on my way and don't look back until I've reached the safety of my chair.

"You weren't out there very long," says Mom, looking up from her magazine.

"It was long enough." I gesture toward the water so Mom can

see what's going on. Now Graham's got Lana up on his shoulders.

"Oy, please. Who needs that?" says Mom. "They should go read a book."

I smile. Mom does drive me berserk, but once in a while she knows just what to say. I watch in disgusted silence for a few more minutes. Eventually, Lana climbs down from Graham's shoulders and floats on her back—her enormous flotation devices protruding from the water. Lovely. I shake away the image and take my Kindle out of my bag. *Fifty Shades of Grey* ought to take my mind off of things for a while. I am absorbed in a scene of complete moral depravity, when somebody pretend knocks on the top of my umbrella.

"Knock, knock."

I look up to find a Lana-less Graham in front of me.

"Too many big fish out there?" I air-quote the words with my fingers.

"We have about fifteen minutes before our ride gets here," says Graham, ignoring my remark and sitting down in the sand next to my feet.

"Our ride?" I lower my Kindle onto my lap.

"The shuttle that's going to drive us to the scooter shop."

"Excuse me?"

"We're renting a scooter in Hamilton, and then we're going to ride it all over the island."

Mom's eyebrows hit the stratosphere. Dad looks as if I just drove up to the house with a pack of Hell's Angels. I perk up a bit.

"When did we decide to do this?" I ask.

"Last night, after you went to bed. After Lana and her friends stumbled off into the night." He picks up a handful of sand and sprinkles it on my ankles. "We have a plan, remember?"

My mind is racing. Lana didn't stay the night? Graham stayed up alone researching scooter rentals?

"What plan?" asks Mom, snapping me out of my thoughts. "I don't like the sound of this. Richard, are you hearing this?"

"I keep hoping that you'll forget about the plan," I say.

"Never," says Graham. Then he turns to my parents. "Don't you worry about a thing, Mrs. H. Summer is in good hands. I watched a bunch of YouTube videos last night about how to ride a scooter."

"Oy!" cries Mom. "Richard, I don't feel well!"

"He's joking, Mom." I glare at Graham. "You're joking, right?"

Graham shrugs. "I guess you'll just have to trust me."

I'm about to concoct some sort of high school field hockey injury that prevents me from riding scooters, when Graham holds out his hand.

"Come on, leave your stuff with your parents. You and I are going to meet the shuttle back up at the main road."

Somewhat distracted by the feeling of my hand in his, I allow myself to be pulled out the chair. I can't back out now. We have a deal. And did I not come to the realization last night that Blenderman was right? That doing these kinds of things is my only way to a happy medium? I need to go for it.

"Richard! Stop them!" says Mom. You'd think we were about to leave the country with the Maltese Falcon.

"You can't do this!" pleads Dad, his face twisted with horror. "We need your cell phone!"

"Richard!" Mom smacks Dad in the arm. "Who cares about the cell phone? Summer is going to ride on a *motorcycle*!"

"Here, take mine." Graham casually tosses his phone onto Dad's lap. "Summer still has hers. And it's a scooter, not a motorcycle. She'll be perfectly safe. Don't you worry about a thing!"

He shakes the sand out of his towel and winks at Mom and Dad. Then he drags me off down the beach.

Don't you worry about a thing. A more useless phrase has never been spoken to my parents. I glance back at them over my shoulder and give a helpless shrug; my last ditch effort at proving that this wasn't my idea. Mom looks a bit limp. She may have fainted.

"Sorry to jet like that," says Graham. "But I had to get you out of there quickly. We don't have much time. I wasn't counting on that little walk we took earlier."

"How are they going to get back to the ship?" I ask. "If that same driver is on the reverse route, he's not letting them on."

Graham smiles. "I ordered them a private taxi. In a couple of hours the driver is going to walk down to the beach carrying a sign that says Hartwell across it. He'll even help them with their bags."

"And if they don't see it?"

Graham shrugs. "They'll figure something out."

Good enough for me.

"Hey," I say. "I noticed you've been saying 'scooter' instead of 'scooters.' Is there a reason for that?"

"You're very astute. That would be because I rented one scooter. I thought you'd be more willing to give it a go if we rode together. You don't mind wrapping your arms around all this, right?" He puffs out his chest and struts back and forth in front of the umbrella return. He looks a lot like Larry the Lobster from *SpongeBob*.

"I'll try to contain myself," I laugh. "Lana's not joining us, is she? I don't know if they make scooters big enough for three people and a set of fake boobs. They certainly don't make hot tubs big enough."

"No, wise ass. And I *knew* you were mad about something."

"I'm not mad," I say, as we start the long walk back up to the main road.

"I was just teasing you about the hot tub. Nothing happened out there. If LuLu and Jessica really worked at Hooters, it was in nineteen eighty-seven. They also looked like they've never heard of sunscreen."

"Really?" I ask, brightening up a bit.

Graham nods. "I told you I wanted you out there with me. Why did you leave?"

"Um, let me think. We were about to be joined by two more Hooters waitresses. Do you not see how I might have been uncomfortable?"

"You've got way more to offer than any of them, even if they didn't happen to look like Siegfried and Roy."

"Yeah, right."

"Hey," says Graham, pulling me to a stop on the side of the road. "Don't put yourself down. And I'm sorry. I shouldn't have let them come over. These older women, they just walk all over me." He gives me a helpless Graham face and a shrug.

"No, it's your suite too. You're allowed to do what you want,"

I mutter, angry with myself for being so, well, angry.

"What I wanted to do was go to the comedy show with you, but you took off. Then Lana descended on me like some kind of sexually frustrated Dementor. When you showed up back at the suite, I was happy. I thought you'd get a kick out of Lana and her friends. To be honest, I kind of thought we'd be laughing about it today."

"Ha. Ha."

Graham frowns. "I really wish you'd stayed."

We stare at each other for a bit longer than is comfortable. I can't help noticing that his skin has taken on a lovely golden glow since yesterday. I feel like such a freckly, sticky mess standing next to him. Still, he's staring at me with this *look*. If I weren't so damn sweaty, it might give me goose bumps.

"I was just a little jealous," I say. "You always have this whole smorgasbord of women to choose from, when I can't even find one normal human being to spend time with. I just didn't want it rubbed in my face."

"You've been spending a lot of time with me, haven't you?"

"That just proves my point."

Graham laughs. "Hey, I may have a smorgasbord of women to choose from, but they don't possess a whole lot of substance."

"Silicone is a substance."

Graham laughs again and pushes a stray piece of hair out of my face, tucking it behind my ear. "That's what I was missing last night, Sum. Not a single one of those women knew how to make me laugh."

Sweaty or not, I've suddenly got goose bumps.

19

I know that I've known Graham most of my life, and that wrapping my arms around him should feel as if I'm wrapping my arms around my brother, but it doesn't feel like that at all. Not one bit. To be honest, there haven't been many brotherly/sisterly feelings between us since we set foot on this boat. The second I put my arms around his waist, with my body pressed up against his back, my heart rate picks up and I am hyper-aware of every movement that I make. My hands are clenched together in front of Graham's stomach, and I have this fear that I will move them in such a way that will make it seem as if they are enjoying being where they are. Not that it would be the end of the world if I should accidentally give the impression that maybe later, if he wanted to, we could—

No. Stop it, Douchewell. Don't set yourself up for rejection. Lesson learned, remember?

Rather than risk it, I tense up my body and keep my breathing to a minimum. My hands are rigid and motionless. If we hit a bump I might just fall off the back of the scooter like a two by four. I should mention that we have not even left the parking lot of the rental shop yet. We're just driving in circles, taking the scooter for a little test drive. Finally, Graham gives a thumbs-up to the rental guy, and we head out onto the streets of Hamilton.

The wind blows gently in our faces as we attempt to stay on the left-hand side of the road. At least Graham is attempting to stay on the left-hand side of the road—all I'm doing is freaking out every time we make a turn. I can't believe I'm being such a dope, especially since we're driving about fifteen miles per hour. But fifteen miles per hour on a scooter feels like we're flying, and there is a bit more traffic than I was expecting.

Graham is clearly enjoying my discomfort and keeps saying things like "Uh oh!" and "Whoops!" Then he laughs when he feels my grip tighten around his waist.

"Stop it!" I laugh. "This is terrifying!"

"You realize this is way slower than the Jet Ski you rode yesterday, right?"

"Yes, but yesterday we were in the middle of the ocean. Today there are *cars*!" As if to illustrate my point, a tiny Peugeot starts backing out of a parking space up ahead. I scream.

"Seriously, Summer?"

"I'm sorry. I thought it was going to hit us."

"It was on the other side of the road. Just relax. We'll be out of the city soon."

As we keep riding, the city slowly starts to dissipate and we find ourselves on a winding road running alongside the harbor. On the other side of the road are shops and houses—some tiny, some mansions behind wrought iron gates—all in beautiful pastel shades. Now that we're out of the city, our speed is starting to feel excruciatingly slow.

"I think that was my grandmother," I tease as the third scooter in a row whizzes past us.

"I'm driving slowly for *your* sake, you know. You were screaming just a few minutes ago."

"Well, I'm used to it now," I say. "No more screaming. I promise."

"If you say so." Graham squeezes the throttle and brings us up to twenty-three, possibly twenty-four, miles per hour. "Is that better?"

"Much," I laugh. Then I scream. "Chickens!"

Graham hits the brakes to avoid hitting a flock of chickens crossing the road up ahead. We come to a complete stop to let them pass.

"Sorry," he says. "You alright?"

"Yeah. Good thing I lied about no more screaming." I press my forehead against his back, embarrassed.

"Good thing. So, um, why did the chickens cross the road?"

I lift my head. "Because they saw how slowly we were driving and knew they had plenty of time?"

"Do you want to take over?" He looks at me in the rearview mirror and takes both hands off of the handlebars.

"No! I'm just teasing you. I'm perfectly happy back here. Keep your hands on the wheel!"

"We've stopped for chickens, it's okay to let go."

I loosen my hold around his waist and sit up straighter. Graham looks at me over his shoulder with a crooked smile. "I meant it's okay for me to let go of the handlebars. You didn't have to go anywhere."

"Oh, right." I put my arms back where they were. I feel a bit silly, as we haven't even started moving yet, though not silly enough to take them away again. The chickens are certainly taking their sweet time.

Finally, we get on our way again and ride along in comfortable silence—making only the occasional remark about the scenery or whether or not I can handle our extreme speeds. At one point I find myself looking not at the scenery, but at the back of Graham's neck—analyzing where his hairline ends and how many freckles he has, and how the skin below his collar isn't quite as tanned as the skin above. I'm not doing this in a creepy sort of way—although there probably isn't a non-creepy way to study the back of somebody's neck—I'm just, interested. It's a rare situation to be this close to a person, without them being able to look you in the eye.

We stop a few times along the way for scenic photographs, and then for lunch at a café overlooking the harbor. Sitting across from Graham, sharing appetizers and sipping iced tea in paradise, I almost feel like we're that smiling couple from the cover of the cruise brochure. I have my sunglasses on, so he can't tell how much I've been staring. Instead of studying the back of his neck like I was earlier, I'm drinking in all of him—every movement, every smile, every inch. For someone who constantly pushes me outside of my comfort zone, he sure makes me feel incredibly comfortable.

Of course, I may be enjoying the daily challenges that he's been dreaming up for me, but I must remind myself that that's all they are. Challenges. A game. A way to kill a week on a boat with his best friend's sister. As far as real life goes, Graham has always needed an equal—someone as outgoing, adventurous, and overwhelming as he is. I've seen his parade of girlfriends over the years: models, kayakers, sophisticated world travelers. Not a single librarian who still lives with her parents. It hurts to think it, but maybe we really are like the couple on the cover of the cruise brochure—two people, captured together for a brief moment in time, before moving on with their normal but separate lives.

I force myself to switch gears and think about Logan while we wait for dessert. But honestly, it isn't doing much for me. Still, Dad claims that he waited outside Mom's office with a bouquet of roses every single day for three weeks before she agreed to go out with him. My point being, that these long-term relationships aren't always love at first sight.

We finish our dessert, pay the bill, and are soon back on the scooter heading toward King's Wharf. At least I thought that's where we were headed. I'm a bit surprised when Graham starts to slow down and turns off of the main road.

"Is this where you're going to murder me?" I ask.

"Yes."

"I bet Mom and Dad didn't even consider that possibility."

We drive for a few more minutes before turning into a parking lot. *Gibbs Hill Lighthouse* the sign reads. We find a place to park and Graham turns off the engine.

"I thought you were afraid of heights?" I ask.

"Oh, I am," he says. He takes off his helmet and tosses it to me. "Terrified, actually."

I look at him curiously, but don't ask any further questions. I hang our helmets from the handlebars and follow him across the parking lot, tilting my head back to see to the very top of the lighthouse. Once we're inside, Graham goes to the counter to purchase tickets while I mill around the lobby looking at lighthouse related memorabilia. There are some framed black and white photographs and a lot of ancient looking lamps on display. It's a bit dull, to tell you the truth. I'm not exactly sure why Graham wanted to stop here, being afraid of heights and all. I really hope that it wasn't for my sake. Maybe he's got some secret fascination with maritime history. Or maybe he's just nuts. I'm leaning toward the latter theory as he rejoins me with an informational pamphlet and an enthusiastic smile on his face.

"This place was built in 1844," he says.

"Awesome."

"By the British."

"Even better."

Graham smiles. "Race you to the top?"

"How many steps?"

"One hundred and eighty-five, according to this." He waves the pamphlet at me. "Want me to carry you?"

He starts heading toward me with his arms outstretched, and I run laughing away from him into the stairwell. I take the spiral steps two at a time until I've climbed about twelve of them and am out of breath. Graham blows past me, disappearing around the bend. I hurry after him.

"Ah!"

He's stopped on the narrow staircase, facing backwards, waiting to scare the crap out of me. As I slam into him he grabs me around the waist to make sure that I don't topple back down the stairs. My stomach knots up at the feeling of his hands pulling me into him, and I put my hand on his shoulder to steady myself.

"If I go down, I'm taking you with me," I say.

Graham gives me a crooked smile, eyebrows raised. He doesn't have to say a word for me to know what he's thinking.

"You *know* what I meant, you perv." I punch him in the shoulder and wiggle out of his grip, laughing as I push past him up the stairs. As we ascend the remaining hundred or so steps, I glance back every so often to make sure that he's still behind me. I wouldn't put it past him to let me climb the entire way up while he sneaks back down to the café for a beer. But he's still there, and the higher we get the more I notice his face changing from a look of enthusiasm to a look of extreme nausea.

"You okay?" I ask.

"Yeah. It's just, you know, the height thing." He shrugs it off and we continue to climb.

I stop short in the doorway at the top of the stairs. Unlike the cruise ship that has a nice solid wall all around the perimeter, the top of the lighthouse is enclosed only with an open railing. The viewing platform is only a few feet wide, so even from back here I can see down to the ground. Graham squeezes past me and out the door, but stays close to the center of the lighthouse rather than approach the railing. He looks over at me, wide-eyed.

"Bright idea coming up here," I say, moving out of the doorway to let a few other people through. "Maybe tomorrow we can conquer my fear of man-eating sharks."

Graham gives me a weak smile. He really looks awful. Well, as awful as Graham can look.

"I gave you a whole speech the other night about not being afraid to live your life," he says. "Meanwhile I'm too afraid to climb a rock wall on a cruise ship. I don't want to be a hypocrite."

"Very well. As soon as you unsuction your butt from the side of the building, we'll get started." I stand there looking at him expectantly, waiting for him to take the first step, before I realize that he's going to literally need my help. I move in close and slip my arm around his waist.

"Come on." I start to inch us forward. "I take it you've never been up the Empire State Building?"

"I try to avoid it."

"Smart. You didn't happen to bring a change of underwear, did you?"

"I knew I forgot something."

"My parents have about seventy-five pairs back on the ship if you need some. Though, that won't help either of us on the ride back." I crinkle up my nose and Graham laughs.

Joking around has helped the inching process, and before I know it we've made it to the railing. Graham latches onto it with one hand, and uses the other to pull me tightly into his chest. I know that he's holding onto me merely as a human life preserver, but it still takes me by surprise. He's trembling slightly, so I gently rub his back.

"We're okay," I keep repeating. "Just relax. Try to enjoy the view."

I take a deep breath and try to take my own advice. The view is gorgeous. White rooftops surrounded by lush green trees dot the land in all directions. Hundreds of yachts are moored in the water, awaiting the return of their lucky owners. I take a moment to remind myself that I could be up here right now with Mom and Dad. I mean, obviously I wouldn't be because Mom and Dad would have never walked up two hundred steps for fear of straining themselves. But theoretically, I could be. I could be locked between the two of them, when instead I'm here with this non-hideous, thoughtful person who, for reasons I am still a bit unclear on, wants to improve the quality of my life. Graham has literally, if only for a few hours, whisked me away.

"Thank you for helping me do this," he says. I can feel his lips in my hair, brushing the top of my head. He's no longer shaking, but suddenly I am.

"Thank *you* for making me do this," I say. And I mean it.

"Can we be done now?"

I smile. "Just one more thing." I fish my cell phone out of my pocket and slowly turn the two of us around. Graham never takes his hand off the railing. I hold the phone at arm's length and take a picture. "Lighthouse selfie. Now we can be done."

Graham releases me from his grip and makes a beeline for the safety of the stairwell. I take one last look at the view, before following him through the door and down the stairs.

182

20

It's dinnertime when we get back to the ship. Mom and Dad have left about seventeen voicemails on our phone saying that if they don't hear from me soon, they're calling the police. Their last message says that they are heading to dinner and that it's my own fault if I want to break my neck riding a motorcycle like a lunatic.

Fair enough.

I'm just relieved that I won't have to spend the evening discussing whether or not Dad's steak is undercooked. I really didn't want to recap the excitement of my day only to be met with looks of horror and the question of whether or not I wore a helmet. There will be plenty of time for that tomorrow.

After I delete all of Mom and Dad's voicemails, I find one more. It's from Logan, and he's asking me to meet up for drinks. I watch Graham from across the room as I listen to the message, wondering what he has planned for tonight. Wondering if those plans might have included me. I chew on my lip as I delete Logan's message. I need to do this. I already spent the entire day with Graham. Even if Logan is a complete disappointment, I at least need to know that I tried.

I go into my bedroom to call Logan back in private. He picks up on the first ring and we agree to meet up at nine o'clock for drinks. Apparently he's located an onboard pub that serves organic craft beer. Done and done.

"So, I think I'll just get room service for dinner tonight," I say, coming out of my room. "And watch *Sharknado* on SyFy or something. I don't have any plans until later."

"Is *Sharknado* really on?" asks Graham, looking more interested than he should.

"No, not really. That was just an example."

"Ah, too bad. Wait, did you say you have plans later?"

"Yeah." I turn on the television and pretend to be deeply interested in the Bermuda weather report. Tomorrow will be sunny. As will the next day.

"Not with that hipster moron I saw you talking to this morning?"

My mouth drops open. "How do you know about that?"

"I was taking a walk and I overheard him snarking on Starbucks. You sure that's who you want to spend the rest of your life with?"

"I'm not spending the rest of my life with him. We're just having drinks. And seriously, you need to stop stalking me around the ship."

"I told you, I was taking a walk. You could hear that guy from a mile away."

"Yeah, if a mile away is from behind a potted plant in the corner."

"Very funny."

"He wasn't that bad."

"He wasn't that good."

"Maybe you should just mind your own business," I say. "Not all of us are babe magnets like yourself. Some of us have to take whatever we can get."

"Is that what you think?" asks Graham. "That you have to settle for whatever you can get?"

There's an edge to his voice that makes me look up from the TV, and I'm surprised to find him staring at me in disbelief. What did I say that was so shocking? Embarrassed, I look away again.

"Not really," I lie. "I just mean that I need to give everyone a fair chance."

"Everyone?"

The word feels a bit loaded. I can feel his eyes on me, but I don't dare look up.

"Look, I appreciate the concern," I say, avoiding the question. "But I'm fine, really."

"Maybe I should come with you."

"Are you out of your mind?" Now I've abandoned the television and look at Graham, my eyes blazing. "Look, I'll be extraordinarily aware of any creepy male behavior. Just, please God, do not chaperone me on my date."

"Okay, okay," he says. "I shouldn't have suggested that. I'm sorry. Just keep your creepy male behavior radar turned up, that's all I ask."

"I will. I promise. I'm starting to get some readings on it right now, actually."

Graham laughs. "So I guess I'm on my own for the night then, huh?"

"You could order room service with me," I say, not quite

ready to send him off into the night. "We can watch SyFy until it's time to go out."

"Deal." Graham jumps over the arm of the couch and sits down next to me. He grabs one of the leather binders off the coffee table and flips through until he finds the page for room service.

We eat dinner and watch a movie about dragons living outside a small village that occasionally carry off the townspeople's children. It's not a tornado made up of sharks, but it's entertaining and we have some laughs. When the movie ends I check my watch. 8:15.

"I'd better go shower and get ready," I say, reluctantly turning off the television.

"Me too," says Graham. He stands up and heads toward his bedroom, but stops before going inside. "You did good today."

I nod in agreement. "You too. Especially you, actually. Are you ready for the rock wall tomorrow?"

"Maybe on our next cruise."

I smile and pretend not to have noticed the *our* part of that statement. Fat chance that Graham and I will ever be on a cruise again together.

I take a quick shower and change into a pair of white pants and a yellow sleeveless top. I curl my hair into loose waves and spray on a light perfume that smells like the beach. My skin has a bit of color to it, and a lot more freckles, after my long day in the sun. But it looks good. It looks like I was out in the world, living life. I hope Logan's not too offended that my pants were made in Bangladesh.

I fiddle with my phone the entire time that I'm getting ready, opening and closing blank text messages to Graham. I want to send him something witty, something that will make him laugh while he's getting ready over there in his own bathroom. I know it's lame, but I want to do it. I can't explain why. The problem is that I can't figure out anything quite right to say, or why I should even say anything at all. I mean, I came on this trip to find myself a husband, not Graham. Graham doesn't need finding. He's always been there. He's been in and out of my life for as long as I can remember, never being anything more to me than a celebrity type crush. Pure fantasy. Unattainability. I learned a long time ago to never consider Graham attainable.

I'm also smart enough to know that if one were to ever attain a relationship with their celebrity crush, it most definitely wouldn't work out. You and he would have nothing in common—you with your regular life, and he with his Hollywood life—the two of you would never make it past the first date. Then the fantasy would be over and twenty years of pleasant interaction would be replaced by strained conversation and awkward Thanksgiving dinners.

No thank you. I'm on this boat to find a suitable mate. I'm looking for somebody who complements my personality, not somebody who completely overwhelms it. What Graham's looking for in a relationship is not the same thing that I'm looking for—even if he did say that women dating him for his money was starting to lose its charm. Even if he did squeeze me at the top of a lighthouse.

The lighthouse. I suddenly remember the photo that I took. It actually came out quite good.

Oh, what's the harm?

Nobody can even tell that you just crapped your pants, I type. I attach the photo and laugh to myself as I hit Send.

I smile at the sight of his name on my screen a minute later.

Nobody can even tell that I was grabbing your ass.

Ha!

Oh please. Your hands were too busy hanging on for dear life.

A few seconds later I get a response.

I liked today :)

I stare at the words, my heart beating fast. I liked today too. Very much so. But I've already sorted everything out in my head, and I've got a date to go on. I should never have started this conversation.

I sit down on the edge of the tub and stare at myself in the mirror. I wonder what Lana's wearing tonight. I squish my boobs together, making them pop out the top of my shirt. Yep. That's probably about right. Just multiply by ten. Not that Graham's going out with Lana, but you never know where she might be lurking. I'm sure she'll track him down.

I try out several witty responses, but end up deleting all of them. Finally, I send him back two relatively innocuous, but truthful words—*me too*—before heading back out into the sitting area.

Graham comes out at the exact same moment, wearing a pink button up shirt and skinny jeans. There's a little extra spike to his hair.

"How do I look?" he asks. He twirls around and Moonwalks over to me.

"Like an Alaskan Salmon."

"Is it too much?"

"No, you look good. Come here." He steps closer and I pick a fuzz ball off the back of his shirt. "Now you're perfect."

"Thanks. You look nice too." He's still standing close,

smiling down at me, his salmon colored sleeves rolled up to just below the elbow. He smells good. I glance at his tanned, muscular arms, imagining what might happen if I were to reach over and touch him. If I—

"You'd better get going," I say, a bit too loudly, snapping myself back to reality. I pull open the door to the suite. "Logan's waiting for me."

"Right," says Graham, clearing his throat. He starts to head out the door, but stops and looks back at me. "Text me if you need to make a quick exit, or whatever. Anytime."

"I will," I say. I paste a smile on my face as my heart starts to sink. "Enjoy your night."

***

The pub where I'm meeting Logan is English style, with a long cherry finish bar and lots of high top tables. Cozy booths with porthole windows line one side of the pub and the walls are packed with pictures of mustachioed golfers in plaid pants. I notice with some degree of horror that there is a karaoke machine set up in the corner, and that somebody is already performing a rather poor rendition of *Yellow Submarine.* I double check to make sure it's not Graham. Nope, not him. Not yet at least.

I spot Logan sitting at the bar and slide onto the stool next to him. He's still wearing his Comic Con t-shirt, with a pair of khaki shorts and flip-flops. I don't know what it is, but I don't particularly enjoy looking at a man's feet. I kind of wish he'd stuck with the loafers. I feel a bit overdressed sitting next to him.

"Cheerio!" he says. "Can you believe they haven't got a single thing brewed in Vermont?"

"Do they have Bud Light?"

"Well, yeah. But who wants that?"

"I'll take a Bud Light," I tell the bartender.

"I can't believe you drink that stuff."

I shrug. "My pants were made in Bangladesh."

"Excuse me?"

"Nothing." I stare at the television over the bar for a few seconds, even though I know I should be making conversation. The whole point of this date was to give Logan a chance; I don't know why I'm feeling so hostile. With a nervous smile, I turn my attention back to him. "I don't think I ever asked you who you're traveling with?"

"Just my brother," he says. "He's graduating from college in the spring, so this is kind of an early graduation present."

"That's nice of you." I take a sip of my beer, enjoying the fact that Logan finds Bud Light irritating. "What'd you guys end up doing today?"

"We went to the craft market. Stocked up on Gombey hot pepper jam. You can't find a good Gombey jam back in the States. How about you?"

"Oh, just regular old jam for us," I say, taking another sip of my beer. Honestly, I have no idea what he's talking about.

"No," Logan laughs. "I mean what'd you do today?"

"Oh, right. Nothing much. Just went to Horseshoe Bay Beach with my parents."

Yes, that's a lie. But you can't exactly tell a guy you're on a date with that you spent the day riding around on the back of a scooter with a different guy. Let alone the same guy that you're sharing a suite with. Talk about sending mixed messages.

"That beach is so commercialized," he says. "I don't know how you could stand it."

"Commercialized? They just have a snack bar and umbrella rentals. It's not like there was a McDonald's set up down there."

"Just you wait."

I roll my eyes at the bartender who snorts back a laugh.

"So where is your brother now?" I ask, trying to change the subject.

"Losing all his money in the casino, would be my bet," says Logan. "I was supposed to be down there chaperoning, but then you called." He gives me a wink.

"You can still go down there," I say, brightening up a bit. "I didn't mean to disrupt your plans."

With any luck I could be back in my room within the hour.

"Hmm, hang out with my brother in front of a slot machine or drink with a pretty girl? Tough choice."

Damn it. What'd I have to get so dressed up for?

The conversation flows uncomfortably for the next hour, with Logan educating me on everything from politics to Paleo diets to obscure indie movies and bands. My admission that I never heard of something or someone only makes him more excited by the opportunity to fill me in on all the details. At one point he tries to pressure me into signing up for karaoke—he only wants to do it "ironically" of course—but I politely decline. Even though hearing me screech, "Love is a Battlefield" into a microphone would be a surefire way to end this date, I'm not totally convinced that I should pull the plug. I mean, a whole day has gone down the tubes and this guy is all I have to show for it. Maybe when the clock strikes midnight he'll turn into a normal person.

I do, however, need a break. I excuse myself to make a quick trip to the ladies room, when I spot Graham, my parents, and Angel Cake O'Brien all walking into the pub.

21

They're practically arm in arm, the bunch of them.

On second glance, I see that Angel Cake literally *is* walking arm in arm with my father, talking and laughing and tossing her hair around. Mom looks irate. Graham, as usual, looks amused.

I glance at the time. Ten thirty. I can't even believe that Mom and Dad are still awake. I sit back down at the bar and try to hide behind Logan, but it's too late. Being on this ship is like if your entire family accompanied you to college.

"There she is!" says Graham. He comes up behind me and vigorously rubs my shoulders. Mom, Dad, and Angel Cake hang back to claim a large table. Somehow, a table for six in an extremely busy bar has managed to open up. The Universe is working against me. "I found this motley crew down in the casino." Graham jerks his thumb toward Mom, Dad, and Angel Cake.

"They were all there together?" I ask.

"Graham told us you went to bed!" interrupts Mom, coming up beside me. "You could have been killed being out by yourself, and so late!"

I glance over at Logan. He looks like he's trying not to laugh. He probably finds my family ironic.

"Killed? I'm not roaming the city streets, Mom. I'm here with a friend—this is Logan. Logan, this is my insane family." Logan shakes hands with everybody while Graham leans in close to my ear.

"I told them you were staying in tonight," he says. "So they wouldn't worry. But they insisted on coming here."

I shrug and give him a grateful smile. Then I turn to Mom.

"Mom, what is Angel Cake doing here?"

Mom's face quickly changes back to disgust. "This morning she just happened to turn up behind us at the buffet. She asked your father if she could cut in and grab some *sausage.*"

I choke back a laugh. "Okay, but what is she doing here *now*? Are you guys all on a date or something?"

"Oy, please. We ran into her again at dinner and she latched right onto your father. The three of us ended up eating together, can you imagine? Then she followed us to the casino, and now here. I've had to listen to her go on and on all night about her business."

"What business?"

Mom leans in close and whispers into my ear. "S-e-x toys!"

"What?"

Mom nods solemnly. "I'm thinking about getting a divorce."

"Oh, Mom. Don't you think that's a bit drastic?" I glance over her shoulder to see Dad studying one of Angel Cake's many golden bangle bracelets. They line both of her arms and jingle and shake when she laughs.

He had a broad face and a little round belly, that shook when he laughed like a bowl full of jelly. I stifle a giggle.

"Maybe he's just made a new friend. Dad could use some friends."

"You sound just like him! That's what he told me—that it's about time he made some *friends.* Can you imagine? Friends! This is the type of friend that he chooses? He's too much of a fool to see what she's *really* after."

"What *is* she really after?" I ask. Seriously. I'm not one hundred percent sure I understand what Dad has to offer a woman like that. She's probably got about a thousand sex toys at home.

Mom just shakes her head. "I'm thinking about getting a divorce."

"I know, you already said that." I crinkle up my nose. "I really wouldn't worry though. She's not very attractive."

I glance back over in time to see Angel Cake showing my father a tattoo located deep within her cleavage.

"But maybe you should get back over there. Just in case."

"Oy, please. Your father can go to—"

"Why don't you two join us?" interrupts Graham. He grabs my drink off of the bar and heads to the table. I have no choice but to follow him. I motion to Logan to come with us, and unfortunately he follows too.

Graham takes a seat across from Logan and me. Dad sits to Graham's right, and Mom sits on the end. Angel Cake sits at the other end like some kind of nightmarish Thanksgiving dinner. I glance over at Graham to gauge his reaction to all of this, only to find that he's already staring at me.

Once we make eye contact, his eyes start to roam from my

face down to my neck and my shoulders, and then back up. He's not doing it in a leering, creepy sort of way. To tell you the truth, he looks like he's trying not to laugh. Still, I shift uncomfortably and feel my face growing hot. He continues with the staring until I have to look away. I'm sure that making me uncomfortable is his ultimate goal, so I count to twenty before I allow myself to look at him again. When I do, he's still staring. I kick him under the table and he smiles, then looks away. His eyes land on Angel Cake who has her hands up in the air, lip-synching *I Love Rock and Roll*, and he bursts out laughing. Moment over.

"Don't think I forgot about today," whispers Mom, whacking me on the arm.

"What are you talking about?"

"You know what I'm talking about. I don't like how you took off with that Graham," she says, shooting a dirty look across the table. "You know how we feel about motorcycles."

I can't believe she called him *that Graham*. The simple act of putting the word "that" in front of a person's name is my mother's equivalent of a blacklist. *That* Graham. *That* Angel Cake. *That* Adolf Hitler. It seems that this one little transgression with the scooters made her lose some love for him. He may no longer be the perfect, piano playing gentleman that she always thought he was. For some reason, this idea kind of excites me.

"First of all, it was a scooter," I say. "Second of all, I survived didn't I?"

Mom doesn't answer.

"And did you know," I continue, "that even Dad said he always wanted to ride a motorcycle?"

"Oy, please."

I shrug. "True story."

I glance across the table at Graham. He's no longer staring at me, but is instead looking critically at Logan. He takes a long, deliberate drink from his commercially brewed beer. I can see the wheels in his head turning.

"So, who wants to do karaoke?" I ask, desperate to prevent any sort of conversation starting between the two of them.

"Oh I've been *dying* to sing," says Angel Cake. She grabs the sheet of song selections from the center of the table and starts reading through them in her deep, yet breathy way. "Richard, what do you say?"

At the sound of his name, Dad jumps about a foot in his chair. "Who, me?"

"Yes, *you*," says Angel Cake. "We could do 'I'll Make Love to You,' or Love Shack,' or maybe 'Shake Your Bon-Bon.'"

Dad shoots a few desperate glances at Mom, but she refuses to acknowledge him.

"I, um, I don't think I know those songs," he says, tapping his hands nervously on the table. "Shake your what-what?"

Poor Dad. He's really not cut out for nightlife.

"I'll do it with her," offers Graham, placing a calming hand over Dad's nervous one. "Whatever song she wants."

Angel Cake's eyes light up as she turns her attention from Dad to Graham. She licks her lips and scribbles a number down on a slip of paper.

"Are you nuts?" I ask, as she brings the paper up to the DJ.

"Just helping out Rich," he says, clapping Dad on the back. Dad jumps another foot in the air. "That woman's apt to eat him alive."

"And now she's all yours."

I watch in fascination as Graham and Angel Cake head onstage and pick up their microphones. The opening strains of "Paradise By The Dashboard Light" begin to play and I bury my face in my hands. Then the singing starts. Graham's not bad. Angel Cake sounds like somebody jumping on a sack full of cats, and she keeps invading Graham's personal space. Halfway through the song I ask Logan if he wants to leave, or maybe jump off the back of the boat. But he keeps claiming to be having a good time, which makes me dislike him even more.

By the time Graham and Angel Cake finish their song, Logan has slid down to the end of the table and is flipping through a catalog with a picture of a blow-up doll on the cover. She's wearing a French maid outfit and looks a bit surprised.

Graham slides into the empty seat next to me.

"Amazing job," I say, giving him a high-five. "Truly breathtaking."

"Thanks. So, uh, how come your date is looking at pictures of blow-up dolls?"

I laugh and run my hands through my hair. "It's Angel Cake's. She's a sex toy salesman, did you know?"

"Do you believe me now when I say that guy is a tool?"

"Well it's not *all* blow-up dolls," I say. "There's other stuff in there too." I will never admit to Graham that my date's a tool.

Graham raises his eyebrows. "Okay, if your guy is so great, how about the fact that your *dad* is looking at a catalog full of blow-up dolls?"

I snap my head around to find Dad leaning over, trying to inconspicuously look over Logan's shoulder.

"Dad!" I shriek. "What are you *doing*?" I walk over and rip the catalog out of Logan's hand. Angel Cake looks deeply offended. Mom comes up behind me and starts peering at it through her bifocals.

"Are those mannequins?"

"No, Mom. They're not mannequins. What do you *think* they are?"

Mom clutches her chest as reality sinks in.

"You get the hell away from my husband!" She grabs the catalog out of my hand and slaps Angel Cake across the back of the head with it. A page falls out and gently wafts to the floor.

"Lighten up!" says Angel Cake, retrieving the page from the floor and grabbing the catalog out of Mom's hand. "You'll be sorry if you keep too tight a leash on your man!"

"Are you threatening me?" asks Mom.

"Just a friendly warning," says Angel Cake, with a look that is anything but friendly. "Thank you for the song, Graham. I'll see *you* later, Richard." She gives my father a meaningful look and storms out of the pub.

I'll see you later? Seriously? I glance nervously from Mom to Dad and then back at Mom. She's fuming. Dad looks lost. He's patting her hand and offering up excuses, but the most I hear him say is *'But she said she wanted some sausage'*.

Oh, Dad.

22

"Now that that's out of the way," says Graham, leading me back to my seat, "we're up after these guys." He nods toward the two men in Red Sox shirts that just started yelling "Sweet Caroline."

"Out of the way?" I say. "My parents are about to get divorced, if you haven't noticed!"

"Nah, they'll work it out," says Graham. "Look, I know it's not as wild and crazy as riding scooters, but it's fun and you need to try it."

"Divorce?"

"Karaoke. I'm talking about you and me singing 'Bohemian Rhapsody.'"

Graham is totally straight faced, as if he just told me something mundane like our train for Cincinnati leaves at four o'clock.

"'Bohemian Rhapsody!'" I shriek. Mom looks over at us and I remember her newfound distaste for all things Graham. I lower my voice. "'Bohemian Rhapsody?'"

"You heard me. I know singing karaoke isn't going to push your parents over the edge or anything, but it'll be good for you.

It's definitely outside of your comfort zone."

"You realize I'm on a date, right?"

"I am very much aware."

"You realize that Logan and I are just trying to have a nice, normal, non-embarrassing evening, right?"

"Really? Because if I'm not mistaken, your mom just smacked a sex toy salesman upside the head with a blow-up doll catalog. There is nothing nice and normal about this evening."

"Well, none of that was Logan's fault! For your information, he's very well read and intelligent."

"So are you. That's why I don't understand what you're doing with him."

"That doesn't even make any sense. And how can you say that to me when you've been out with Playmate of the Year Cougar Edition?"

"Touché. I knew you were jealous."

"I am not jealous! And I'm not singing with you."

"Yes you are. I conquered my fear at the lighthouse today, and now it's your turn."

"Making a fool out of myself in front of a bunch of strangers is not a fear that I need to conquer. It's called self respect, and I would like to keep it."

"Why do you care so much what other people think?"

"I don't know." I fold my arms across my chest. "I'm shy, I guess. You know that."

"I don't think you're shy," he says, shaking his head. "I think that you've just never taken any chances."

"And there's a difference?"

"Of course there's a difference. If you got up there with me, and just for five stinking minutes stopped caring if a bunch of strangers think you sing off key, you would discover a whole new side to yourself. You're stuck."

"Stuck?"

"Yeah. You're stuck between being a little girl who was smothered by her parents, and being an adult who never took any chances out of fear of hurting her parents. You rationalize it all by claiming to be shy. I call bullshit."

I open my mouth to argue. Then I close it. He has a point.

"You talk a lot."

"I just want you to have fun." He takes a sip of his drink and narrows his eyes at Logan. Logan has his head buried in his phone and doesn't seem to notice.

"Why are you so concerned about my happiness all of a sudden?" I ask.

Graham rests his arm on the back of my chair and leans in close, looking me in the eyes. I lean back in my seat, feeling his arm across the back of my shoulders.

"I'm just re-evaluating what's important in my life," he says.

"Does this have anything to do with your relationship hiatus?" I air-quote the words.

"Sort of."

I squint one eye at him, skeptically. "Are you dying?"

Graham laughs. "No, not dying. Look, I just owe you for prying my butt off of that lighthouse wall this afternoon. Really, that was huge."

"And you want to repay me by forcing me to sing karaoke?"

"Yes."

"Oh. Well, okay then." My mouth suddenly feels quite dry.

"What was that?"

"I said okay. I'll do it. I'll sing your stupid song. Don't make me say it again." I take a long sip of my drink until there is nothing left but ice. "Bohemian Rhapsody" is only the most difficult song on Earth to perform. So, you know, how hard could it be?

Graham smiles. "Come on, I've got something that will help." He takes me by the hand and leads me to the bar. "Two Redheaded Sluts, please."

I roll my eyes. "You *would* order that."

We down the shots at the same moment that our karaoke number is called. I glance over at Logan, hoping to convey the message that this is entirely Graham's fault, but he's too absorbed by his phone. I feel somewhat bad for singing with Graham when I already said no to Logan. But once he hears me sing he'll probably be glad it's not him up there with me.

The second we get on stage, I start to panic. Scratch that. I start to panic the second we get on stage and I turn around to face the crowd. Sure, it's just a room full of drunken people on a cruise ship, but still. I hate being the center of attention, and now I've got to be Freddie Mercury.

I am *not* Freddie Mercury. Damn it, Graham. I am Summer Eve Douchewell, school librarian, and I'm about to make a complete fool out of myself. I rather enjoyed being stuck in my little world of not taking any chances.

"Who's singing which part?" I say, starting to sweat. "We need time to rehearse!"

Graham just winks at me. "There's no time to rehearse, darling. It's karaoke. We wing it." Then he jumps right into the opening vocals. He sings the entire opening ballad while I just stand there blinking. Occasionally he motions to me to join in, but I'm totally frozen up.

Then Red Headed Slut kicks in.

Suddenly, I'm scaramouching and doing the Fandango all over the place.

This is kind of fun. I don't sound half bad either, screaming at the top of my lungs. The audience is going crazy. Forget school librarian, I should have been a rock star!

For me…for me…for meeeeeee!

And there goes my nicely curled hair, whipping around in circles.

Never in a million years did I think I would be disappointed when my moment in the spotlight was over, but live and learn. Five minutes and fifty-five seconds later, Graham and I are heading back to the table, laughing hysterically, and I'm already thinking of which song we can do next.

Logan gives me a high five as I slide into my seat next to him. Mom is no longer at the table, and I notice that Dad's been eyeing the song list.

"You ready to try one?" I ask, pushing the list across the table to him. "Go ahead!"

Dad smiles sheepishly and picks it up.

"I know some Johnny Cash. Do they have Johnny Cash?"

"Of course they do," says Graham. He grabs the list and flips through the pages. "Right here, 'Folsom Prison Blues.' Do it!"

It seems like we're all about to burst into chants of "Dad! Dad! Dad!" when suddenly Lana is there, wrapping her arms around Graham and turning him around in his seat. And now she's *kissing* him. Where the hell did she come from? My stomach lurches and I look away, smoothing down my hair. Of course Graham's performance would excite her. She was probably in college when Queen was popular. I lean my elbow on the table and rest my head in my hand, turning to look at Logan while simultaneously blocking out my view of Lana and Graham.

"Do you want to get out of here?" I ask, suddenly desperate to be anywhere but here.

"Definitely." Logan gives my thigh a squeeze under the table. Ugh.

I mumble an announcement that Logan and I are going for a walk, and we quickly make our exit, hand in hand. I don't even look in Graham's direction. I can't get the stupid image of him and Lana out of my head. I know that he's kissed countless women over the years. He probably kissed someone the day we boarded the cruise ship. What's the difference?

As soon as we've made it out of the bar, I pull Logan into an alcove and push him up against the wall.

Don't judge me. One must kiss a few frogs before they find their prince, that's how the old saying goes. It's not my fault that I was tasked with finding my prince within the confines of an eight-day cruise. And if Graham's out there testing the waters, after laying all these speeches on me about living life to the fullest and taking chances, why shouldn't I? If anything, it's his fault. So I kiss Logan, and it's okay. It's not like I'm in the throes of ecstasy or anything, and his beard's a little scratchy. And at one point I open my eyes, look down at the floor, and see his flip-flopped hairy feet staring back at me.

"Do you want to go to the pool?" I ask, still riding a bit of a high from the karaoke and the booze. And lucky for Logan, he's the only one I've got around for company.

"Sounds good to me. Do you want to go get changed and meet back here?"

"I've actually already got my swimsuit on." I pull one of the straps out from under my tank top and shrug. "I thought maybe I would need it."

I don't know what I was thinking when I put my swimsuit on after my shower. Well, I sort of know what I was thinking. I was picturing Graham and I somehow winding up alone in a hot tub. I must have had too much sun today. Now I just feel like an idiot.

"Okay, do you want to wait for me in my room?"

I'm already regretting kissing him and asking if he wants to go to the pool. The last thing I should do is go to his room.

"I'll meet you by the elevators on the pool deck," I say.

I leave Logan and make my way to the elevators. I ride up to the pool deck and sit down on a bench right outside the doors. I take out my phone, hoping to see a text from Graham—but there's nothing. I open up the Facebook app and type *Logan Emery* into the search bar. A few different Logan Emerys show up. I scroll down until I find one that looks like him. Scruffy. Smarmy smile. Wearing a Phish t-shirt and standing in front of a statue.

Logan Emery. Studied Political Science at Boston University. Worked at blah blah blah.

Everything he told me at the bar seems to check out. At least I now have proof that he's an adult with a job and not a total fraud like some other people on this ship. That is, if you consider a Facebook profile proof. I move on from the *About* section and over to the part where all of his posts and updates are. The only posts I can see are the ones that he made accessible to the public. But it's enough.

There's a video—a video of a crime that took place in China. Why would he post something like that? I check the time stamp. He only posted it thirty minutes ago. This must have been what he was so absorbed with at the table. He probably had some smart and profound political comment to make about it that just couldn't wait. I click on the comments below the video. That's when my jaw hits the floor.

Hey now.

Suffice to say, Logan was very upset by this video. The problem is that he was so upset by the video that he decided to write off an entire race of people with a few stereotypical adjectives. Stereotypical adjectives mixed with the foulest of references to the human anatomy. Equal opportunity, sustainable rainforest, locally brewed craft beer supporter, Logan, who I envisioned spending the rest of my life with—well, not really—is a complete and utter racist.

Should I just leave? Or should I confront him? I sit there debating with myself about it for so long that the elevator doors finally open and out walks Logan.

"So you don't like the Chinese, huh?" I blurt out. Screw it. If there's one thing I can't stand, it's ignorance.

"Excuse me?"

"Your Facebook post. I saw it. It's right here!" I wave my phone around in the air.

"Oh, that. Well, did you watch the video? They're disgusting!"

"You're repulsed that people still buy non-organic apples, but you're okay with promulgating this kind of hatred on the Internet? We have murderers here in America too, did you know that? And in Canada, and in Brazil, and everywhere!"

"They're stealing all of our jobs too."

"You pretentious ass."

Logan tries to form more of an argument, but I've heard enough. I actually heard enough this morning and should have just trusted my instincts that this guy was a piece of work. But no, I had to go and be all *give him a chance, Summer, he might not be that bad, Summer.* Ugh. And I thought that hooking up with a teenager was bad. Now I go and find myself a racist. You just never can tell with people. I shudder to think of whom I will encounter next. Maybe my mother was right; I could get myself killed hanging around alone on this ship. There seems to be a very high chance that the next man I encounter will be a homicidal maniac.

23

Or, it could be Graham.

I'm surprised to find him alone in our suite, sitting on the couch and watching television. That's not to say that Graham couldn't be a homicidal maniac. God knows my judgment is utter garbage.

"He's a racist," I say, in as plain and calm a voice as I can muster, flinging my key onto the kitchen counter.

"Who?"

"Who do you think? Logan!" I flop down on the couch and rub my temples. "He wrote the most disgusting things I've ever read on his Facebook page."

"That's why you guys left the bar? To go read his Facebook page?" Graham gives me a perplexed look.

"No, he was changing into his swimsuit so we could go to the pool. I looked him up on Facebook."

"So you snooped?"

"It's not snooping. It's Facebook. Isn't it better that I found this out anyway?"

"You sure he wasn't just joking around? You ever hear of

hipster racism? Guys like him will make these blatantly racist remarks as some sort of ironic political statement. Like *only kidding*, but on a larger scale."

"What kind of a moron would do that?" I crinkle up my nose. Graham shrugs. "Beats me. But it's a thing."

I shake my head. "No way. There was zero irony. This was not some sort of commentary on outdated beliefs. Trust me. These are his current, completely fucked-up beliefs."

"Wow," says Graham. "You may have met the world's first authentically racist hipster. You've got some rotten luck, you know that?"

"Thank you, yes. I see that now. What is wrong with me?"

"With you? Nothing. There's something wrong with all the guys you keep picking up, that's for sure. Maybe you're trying too hard."

"But that's the whole point," I say, getting frustrated. "I'm trying to find somebody and I've got hardly any time left to do it. Maybe I should give up. Maybe Poseidon's trying to tell me something."

"You really think Poseidon is trying to communicate with you? With his little trident and all that?" Graham waves the remote control around in the air. "Oooh, look at me and my scary trident! Suuuummer! Stay awaaaay from the loooooosers!"

I laugh. "No not *really*. Duh. I meant, you know, whoever's up there." I point toward the ceiling. "Maybe they're trying to tell me that it's just never going to happen."

"I heard the people up there going at it the other night. You really think they're interested in *your* love life?"

"Not *them*, you idiot. I'm referring to God, or Zeus, or

whoever may be in control of our destinies. Do I have to spell everything out for you?"

"Oh," says Graham. "Well, I think that God, or Zeus, or whoever, has more important things to do than teach you cryptic life lessons. Especially cryptic life lessons that imply you'll be alone forever. Do you really think that's what God, or Zeus, or whoever wants?"

I shrug.

"Look," says Graham. "It's like I said before. You're trying too hard. It's when you stop looking that you find someone."

"That's the worst advice. I hate that advice." I put my feet up on Graham's lap, since he's taking up half the couch. He rests his hands on my shin and rubs it gently with his thumb. A pleasant sensation runs from my shin all the way up to, well, up to everywhere. I take a deep breath. "What makes you the expert anyway? You're not married and you're even older than I am."

"Who said I was handing out marital advice? It's good life advice. I act like myself, and poof, good stuff happens. Sometimes, even women appear." He snaps his fingers over my outstretched body. In all of my Logan rage, I'd almost forgotten the reason that I left the pub in the first place. The image of Lana and Graham kissing reappears in my head.

"Speaking of women, what happened to Lana?"

"Jessica and LuLu showed up shortly after you left, with the entire Brazilian juggling team."

"Brazilian juggling team?"

"From the variety show."

"Oh, right. I've seen the posters. They juggle shirtless, right?"

"Yes, but with bowties. They said they had a bottle of tequila back at their suite and I was welcome to join them."

"Wow. So how come you're here?"

"Because a Brazilian juggling team invited me back to their suite for tequila."

"Fair enough," I laugh.

I roll over onto my side, letting him continue to rub my leg. I'm not finding it as hard to breathe as the last time we were in close contact. I wouldn't say that I'm relaxed, but I'm definitely not the stiff two by four that I was on the back of the scooter. It's like I no longer have that debilitating sense of *I'm going to make a fool out of myself*. I'm just…comfortable.

Except for the fact that my heart is beating rapidly and I'm aware of every single nerve ending in the lower half of my body.

We watch TV in silence for a long time. The SyFy channel is on again. Not *Sharknado*, but a decent film about a swarm of man-eating Monarch butterflies. I try to concentrate on the movie, but my mind is preoccupied. Not only with the feel of Graham's hand on my leg, but with the memory of him and Lana kissing at the karaoke bar. I know I should just let it go, but—

"So, um, that was quite the smoochfest you and Lana had going on earlier." At least I waited until a commercial break to bring it up.

Graham snorts. "Smoochfest?"

"Yeah."

"I had a feeling that was why you left."

"That's not why. I told you, racist Logan and I wanted to go to the pool."

"Right. Well, as you may have noticed, she kind of attacked

me from behind. If you'd stuck around you'd have seen that it ended almost as soon as it started."

"I bet."

"Do you really think I would make-out with a woman in front of your parents?"

I flashback to a few Christmases ago—Graham, sitting in our living room, a blonde Victoria's Secret model on his lap feeding him scallops wrapped in bacon. Granted, they were not smooching.

"I guess not," I mutter.

"I've told you a hundred times that I'm not interested in that train wreck. You could have saved yourself the drama of the racist hipster if only you'd listened to me."

That'd make a great Agatha Christie novel. *The Drama of the Racist Hipster.*

I study Graham's face from the side. In the flicker of the television, he looks tired. Maybe it's the look on his face, or the fact that he was here, alone, watching television when I came in, but I suddenly believe him. Wholeheartedly. A weight that I barely knew was there is lifted from my chest, and I feel more relaxed than I have all week.

The movie comes back on, and we watch again in comfortable silence—the gentle back and forth of Graham's hand on my leg making me smile into my pillow. After a while, he stops. And it's then that I realize how much I don't want him to. It's then that I do the same thing that I did on the Jet Ski— say a little prayer that I don't make a fool out of myself—and I go for it.

Well, in this case, I simply lay my hand on top of Graham's.

I expect him to either pull his hand away—to which I will melt into the couch cushions in a puddle of humiliation—or to turn his hand over and hold mine back. After a few seconds pass with neither of these reactions, I brave a glance in his direction.

He's sound asleep.

Figures. Maybe this is a good thing. Maybe the Universe is allowing me a do-over.

Very carefully, I swing my legs onto the floor. I pull a blanket off the back of the couch and drape it over him, gently tucking the corners behind his shoulders.

"Goodnight, Blenderman," I whisper.

I leave the television on so that he's not awoken by the silence, smiling when I see that the next movie up on the SyFy channel is *Sharknado*. Poor Graham. He's going to have some interesting dreams.

I head into the kitchen before going to bed. I'm dying of thirst. I guess that's what happens when one screams "Bohemian Rhapsody" while whipping one's hair around. I take all the necessary precautions to avoid waking Graham. I remove my shoes before stepping off the carpet and onto the wood floor. I turn all of the lights off. I open the kitchen cabinet ever so quietly and remove a glass. I run the tap very, very gently.

Then I drop the entire glass of water on the floor.

"Shit!"

"Summer?"

"It's me. Yeah. Sorry." I fumble around for the light switch, while trying to smooth down my hair.

"Here, let me help."

Graham walks over, stretching his neck and yawning. He

starts picking up pieces of broken glass.

"Thanks. I was trying to not wake you, actually."

"Nice try."

I crouch down next to him, picking up shards and depositing them into the paper cup that he's holding. The fact that we have paper cups would have been good to know a few minutes ago. Graham stares at me for a few seconds, and then goes back to picking up broken glass.

"How long was I out?"

"Like, two minutes."

He dumps the broken glass into the trash and holds out his hand to help me to my feet.

Up next on SyFy: Sharknado.

The words drift in from the television, and Graham's eyes light up.

"Wanna watch?"

"Right now?"

"Yes, Summer. Right now. Live life on the edge."

I smile. "Okay."

Graham grabs two beers from the fridge, and leads me back over to the couch. It's dark except for the light from the television. We sit close to each other, my hand somehow still in his, and my heart pounding. *Sharknado* is a truly terrible movie, allowing the sarcastic commentary to flow freely. It's nearly one o'clock in the morning, but I'm suddenly not the least bit tired.

"This is what I've been missing, Summer," Graham says softly, tracing his finger around the back of my hand. I glance down at it, and then back up at the television, finding it a bit difficult to swallow.

"What's that?" I ask, curling my hand up into a ball. My chest is starting to burn. Not like heartburn or anything. I mean up higher, like my collarbone. Like, I'm *hot*. I'm hot for *Blenderman*. He's holding my hand and staring at me, and it's sending shivers down my spine. His eyes are burning a hole in me like I'm that idiotic heroine from *Fifty Shades of Grey*. Thoughts of that book are not going to help calm me any. Literary abomination or not, nobody is totally immune to its devices. An intense heat comes over me. Thankfully, we're sitting in the dark, because I'm fairly certain that I've turned bright red.

Before I have the chance to do anything stupid, like stand up, Graham slides to the edge of the couch and puts his other hand on the side of my face, his fingers lacing through my hair. He pulls me toward him and kisses me, gently at first. Then, perhaps when he realizes that there is no resistance coming from my end, he pulls me closer and kisses me harder. I've said before that I find Graham overwhelming. Well, kissing him is nothing short of debilitating. I pull away for a second to catch my breath, and to look into his eyes to make sure he is aware of what he's done. His eyes are still smoldering, and I immediately regret having broken contact. I grab a fistful of his shirt and pull him back onto the couch next to me. He reciprocates by pulling me onto his lap.

All of the feelings I've been trying to suppress since setting foot on this boat have come flooding down the corridor and crashing through the door, drowning all my rationalizations about why I don't want to be with Graham, and why Graham doesn't want to be with me. Maybe this can work. Maybe I've been a complete fool.

I move onto my knees so that I'm straddling him, squeezing his thighs between mine and pinning his shoulders against the back of the couch. I pull back and look into his eyes for the second time. They're a bit hazy.

"Hey, Summer," he whispers.

"Hey, Blenderman."

He combs his fingers through the ends of my hair and pulls me back towards him, crushing me into his chest. I move from his mouth to his ear and down to his neck, the scent of his skin bringing back a thousand memories from my life; memories of Graham always being there in the background—always there, but never this close.

God, he's close.

He gently bites my ear, sending pleasant chills down the entire length of my body. Then his hands are on my back, scratching through my tank top, while his lips move lightly around my neck—the contrast just about driving me mad.

The sounds of *Sharknado* are still going on in the background, and Graham laughs when somebody on the TV starts screaming.

"Mood killer," I mumble.

"Sorry." He kisses me one more time on the neck. "Let's get out of here."

He clicks off the TV and gently rolls me off of his lap and onto the couch. He stands up, and pulls me up next to him. Then he wraps me in his arms and kisses me again—his late night stubble rough on my skin, but I don't mind. I run my hands down his arms to the bottom of his t-shirt, and pull it up over his head. Graham is shirtless once again, except this time I'm not admiring him from afar. This time he's all mine. I press myself into him, and a small

217

moan escapes me. How this is happening, I'm not sure. Nor do I care. He pulls my tank top over my head and flings it into the dark depths of the kitchen.

By the time we get to the bedroom, I've helped him out of his shorts. My own are somehow hanging from the blinds of the sliding glass door. Both of our beer bottles lie spilled on the floor, casualties of this sudden turn of events.

24

The first thing that I think about when I wake up—rather than the fact that there is a boxer-shorts-wearing Graham practically lying on top of me—is that I made plans to hang out with my parents today.

Stupid, stupid, stupid.

It's true. Yesterday, before I met Logan out at the pub, I left a voicemail for Mom and Dad asking if they wanted to go into Hamilton today for lunch, shopping, and assorted tourist attractions. I felt like I owed them some alone time, and I also wanted some space from Graham. At the time it felt like the right thing to do.

Well, no it didn't. To be honest, the thought of it made me want to grind my forehead into a brick wall. But I really did want some space from Graham. Now, space from Graham is the last thing that I want—demonstrated by the fact that we are sharing a bed underneath a cinnamon bun swirl of blankets.

I love this.

"I can't believe I told my parents I'd hang out with them today," I mumble, soaking up the warmth.

"You mean living with them every day of your life wasn't enough?" Graham mumbles back. "Come on, Summer." He rubs my back, pulling me in closer. I sigh, feeling every last inch of him along the length of my body. What I wouldn't give to just stay here all day. But we've already been up half the night, and a promise is a promise.

"I know, I'm sorry." I slide back a couple of inches to start making the transition out of bed a bit easier. "But I promised them some alone time with me. I can't bail, like Eric."

I start inching my way off the bed, when Graham grabs me by the wrist and rolls me back on top of him. His eyes are open now and I self-consciously try to smooth down my hair. He gently grabs my wrist and lowers it down to my side.

"Stop it. I like it that way."

"You're crazy." I lean forward and kiss him on the forehead. "I've got to take a shower, Mom and Dad will be here in an hour. We're catching a bus to Hamilton."

Graham rolls me onto my back and starts playing with my hair, stretching all the sections out into a giant halo around my head.

"I'll come with you then."

"To Hamilton? Why would you do that to yourself?"

He smiles. "No, to the shower."

***

Right. Well, then.

The contrast between showering with Graham, and standing outside of a restroom waiting for my father, is like a bucket of ice water to the face.

My mind is completely consumed with trying to process what happened back at the suite. Various parts of my body are such a hopeless mess of wants and desires that I can barely function, let alone comprehend what my mother has been rambling on about. Is this how men feel all the time? I've been reduced to a bubbling ball of hormones that wants to sit down, stare off into space, and relive the past night—and morning—over and over in my mind. But instead, I've got Mom to deal with.

"Is *that* what you're wearing?" she shrieks for, possibly, the third time.

I meet her confused scowl with a blank stare.

"What's wrong with what I'm wearing?" I ask. I'm wearing a tank top, shorts, and flip-flops.

"You'll get burned!" She starts rifling around in one of her many tote bags. "Here, put this on." She pulls out a long-sleeved cardigan that is two sizes too big, and forty years too old, and tries to cram it over my shoulders.

"Get it off!" I shriek. A woman standing nearby looks over in alarm. I must sound like I just found a scorpion in my purse. I smile apologetically. "Just a cardigan!" I shrug it off and hold it up in the air for her to see. Then I shove it back at Mom.

"It's like ninety degrees outside! And we're just walking around town, going in and out of stores."

"Speaking of walking, how are you going to walk in those things?" She points to my flip-flops as if I'm wearing a pair of six-inch stilettos. "There's no arch support! You need sneakers and socks!" She reaches into another of her tote bags because, of course, she's got an extra pair of sneakers and socks in there. I refrain from making a remark about the fashionability of shorts, sneakers, and socks, since Mom is wearing that exact outfit.

"Mom! Stop it! I'm not wearing sneakers and socks! Let alone *your* sneakers and socks! And I've got sunscreen on, so I'm not going to burn. Please, just relax."

"With skin like yours, it doesn't matter. You need to cover up," says Mom, choosing to ignore scientifically proven evidence that sunscreen actually works.

"I. Am. Wearing. Sunscreen." I annunciate each word.

"What about this?" Ignoring me, she pulls another long-sleeved shirt out of her bag. This one looks like it belongs to my father and says North Conway Scenic Railroad across the front.

"NO!"

More people are starting to stare at us. I feel like I'm about five years old, throwing a tantrum in the middle of Toys R Us.

"I can't take this," says Mom.

"What? What can't you take?"

Before she can answer, Dad emerges from the restroom.

"Richard, look at her. Will you just look at her?"

Dad smiles at me. "She looks cute."

"Oy, please," she says. "I mean, look at how exposed she is!" Mom makes *exposed* motions with her hands.

"Okay *fine*, Mom. I'll wear something. Just stop making a scene!"

"Who's making a scene?" She throws her hands dramatically into the air and tries to hand me the shirt.

"I didn't say I was wearing that thing. I'll go and buy something in the gift shop. At least it will fit."

There's no way I can go back up to the suite to get a sweater, Graham would kill me. Five minutes later I find myself wearing a neon-green, terrycloth hoodie with the cruise line's logo and about a hundred rhinestones emblazoned across the back, and my wallet finds itself fifty dollars lighter. I should have just worn Dad's North Conway shirt.

How spineless am I? If I don't want to wear a cover-up, then I shouldn't have bought a cover-up. Who cares if Mom is freaking out? Did she hold a gun to my head? According to Graham, Eric would have risked the third degree burns and gone without sunscreen for the entire day, just to show Mom who's boss. But I don't have enough gumption for that kind of thing, or maybe I've just got too much awareness of skin cancer. Either way, Graham would not be proud of me right now.

Graham. After a temporary distraction, my thoughts have drifted back to him. Mom and Dad whisked me out of the suite so fast this morning that what happened still feels like a dream. Only it was real.

Graham and I—

About a thousand times.

I feel like Mom and Dad will see it written all over my face. I need to try not to think about it so much, though I doubt if I'll be able to think about anything else for the rest of my life. And why should I? If I cut through all the denial that I've been in over the years, I realize that I want Graham. I always have. Of course I have. Why else would I still be harboring resentment about a stupid high school prom?

Yet here we are again—Graham and I teetering on the edge of possibility—and there's suddenly a warning signal blinking at me from the sidelines. I could have used some warning signals the first time around—when any dreams I had about Graham and I going to the prom together ended in heartbreak and embarrassment.

But there couldn't have been any warning signals. I was too young and inexperienced, and I didn't know Graham the way that I know him now. I didn't even know *myself* the way that I know myself now. Graham and I have lived an entire decade since the prom incident—an entire decade to come to the conclusion that we are completely different people.

Cue the warning signals.

The fact that we are so different didn't matter in the slightest last night. Last night—and this morning—were far, *far*, removed from the real world. My stomach twists at the thought of Graham and I in the real world. Library books and social anxiety and Lord of the Rings make up my real world. Victoria's Secret models and flash mobs and jet skiing in Aruba, that's the real world for Graham. How could that possibly work? Has Graham even thought about it?

Or is this just...*this*? A few last days of fun before heading back to our own, separate worlds? Worlds that occasionally collide during weekends and holidays. For Graham, that's not such a terrible outcome. For me, it means back to living at my parents' house until I'm married. And did Graham not say, only a few days ago, that he was on a relationship hiatus? Did he not say that my idea of finding a husband on this ship was completely ridiculous? Graham isn't looking to whisk me away. He's just...killing time on a boat. That's probably not something I should overlook.

I mean, I want to overlook it. I desperately want to overlook it. Every time I think about what happened between us I feel queasy and jittery and ecstatic. But at the same time I can't help thinking, what's the point?

My head is swimming with conflicting thoughts as we wind back and forth down the gangway. When we finally step off of the ship, Mom and Dad stare into the distance as if they've just stepped off the Mayflower. True, they've already disembarked from the ship twice, but that means absolutely nothing to them. Fear of the unknown has arrived anew. In all fairness, the past two times they had Graham to entrust with their lives. Today they've just got me, and they didn't even trust me enough to drive into Boston, never mind navigate them around a foreign country.

This should be fun.

Our plan is to go into Hamilton where we can do some shopping, have lunch, and then get back on the ship as quickly as possible in order to salvage some actual fun out of this day. Well, that's my plan at least. I suppose Mom and Dad genuinely want to spend time with me, which makes me feel a bit bad. But for God's sake, they've already made me 1) buy a sweater and, 2) promise not to eat from the buffet because this morning, this very morning, they saw a man pick up a piece of toast with his fingers instead of the metal tongs. The *horror*.

Once Mom and Dad are sufficiently acclimated—that is to say, they've wandered about two hundred feet from the ship and sat down on a bench—I walk over to the bus kiosk to purchase tickets. As we wait for the bus I keep my fingers crossed that the driver from the other day isn't on duty. If it turns out that we've been permanently banned from the bus system, there's always a ferry to get us to Hamilton. Although, putting Mom on another seafaring vessel is a definite last resort. Then again, she did ride a Jet Ski a few days ago. I look over at her in her khaki Mom shorts and her straw hat and I think, how the heck did *that* happen?

But I know exactly how that happened—Graham. He does amazing things for my family. He does some amazing things in general.

Anyway, it's our lucky day. The bus pulls up with a different driver behind the wheel, and we file obediently onboard. Mom and Dad remain seated and refrain from screaming and flailing around, resulting in a surprisingly uneventful ride into Hamilton. Before I know it, I'm trudging down the sidewalk, twenty feet ahead of my parents, stopping every so often to let them catch up. To break up the boredom, I check my phone for text messages from Graham, but nothing comes in. I wonder what kind of plans he has for today.

The boredom also allows for my internal debate to pick back up. What to do? Enjoy whatever this is between Graham and I, or continue with my mission? Have a few more of the hottest nights of my life—as I imagine they would be—only to return home just as alone and hopeless as I was at the beginning of the week? Instant or delayed gratification? I came on this vacation to fulfill The Prophecy, not to have a fling. I set foot on this boat in order to find somebody with similar interests, with whom I can envision spending the rest of my life. I'm looking for somebody who is ready and willing to make a commitment— not somebody who is on a relationship hiatus, and might, at any moment, announce that he's signed the both of us up to run a twelve-mile obstacle course through the backwoods of Maine.

After a couple of hours of wandering in and out of stores,

purchasing miscellaneous tchotchke, and searching for restrooms, we all agree that it's time for lunch. I come to a halt in front of a restaurant, and wait for Mom and Dad to catch up. There is a menu posted by the front door that Mom eyes suspiciously.

"Do they have anything that isn't spicy?"

"Why do you think it's spicy?" I ask. The restaurant looks fairly benign to me, which is why I stopped here. Well, that, and because it was the first restaurant that we came to.

"These islands all serve that *jerk* stuff. Your father and I can't handle that kind of a thing. It gives us funny stomachs."

"Jerk is Jamaican, Mom. We're in Bermuda. Fast fact though, even in Jamaica you can get a cheeseburger."

Mom ignores me and continues to peruse the menu through her bifocals, her face turning to a scowl at the mention of garlic, jalapeno, or Cajun spices. Finally, she throws her hands up in defeat, rolls her eyes, and heads into the restaurant. I look at Dad and shrug. We follow her through the doors.

The hostess is leading us over to a table, when a whistle comes from the direction of the bar. I glance behind us and in a split second realize that there's only one person in this country who would choose to wear that shade of purple.

25

Oh, God.

I've still got the stupid hoodie on. Maybe he won't notice.

Graham gives me a little wave and slides off his bar stool. My stomach turns into one huge knot as he approaches. He looks me over and raises his eyebrows.

"You weren't wearing this when you left this morning, were you?" he asks, twirling me around and rubbing a piece of the fabric between his fingers. "Terrycloth, nice."

"Maybe I was." I yank the fabric out of his hand and take a step away. I'm very aware of how close he's standing, and paranoid that my parents will notice something.

"It's got some words on the back. What's that say?" Graham walks around behind me, placing one hand on each of my shoulders. "Ooh, the name of the cruise line. Very nice. Very youthful."

"Shut up."

"I *made* her buy that," says Mom, with pride. "So she wouldn't get burned!"

Graham looks at me, his eyes practically twinkling. "Did you, really? Well, that was very obedient of Summer."

I give him a dirty look. "Come on, the hostess is waiting for us."

"Join us!" says Mom.

"I'd love to." Graham winks at me. He returns to the bar to grab his plate and his beer, and carries them both over to our table.

Five minutes ago I was starving. Now I seem to have lost my appetite. I try to focus on the menu, but keep sneaking sidelong glances at Graham. Despite all of the doubts and warning signals running through my mind, I find myself desperately wanting to get him back into that cruise cabin and out of that purple shirt. Out of everything.

Stop it, Douchewell. I look back down at the menu, trying to concentrate.

Seafood Mixed Grill

Roasted Prime Rib

Graham reaches over and squeezes my thigh under the table. I jump about a foot into the air. Then I brush his hand away, embarrassed that my parents might see.

New York Steak

Fish & Chips

His hand is back, giving my leg another squeeze. This time I let him, my heart racing. The words on the menu are just kind of swimming around in front of me. God knows what I'm going to end up ordering.

"Summer?"

"Yeah?" I jump at the sound of my mother's voice and smack Graham's hand off my leg. He laughs.

"What are you getting?"

229

"Oh, uh, I don't know yet. I was a little distracted."

As I go back to reading my menu, Graham slides something underneath my placemat. I wait until after the waitress takes our order to pull it out. It's a piece of paper with one word written at the top—*Tattoos*—and an address underneath.

My eyes widen and I excuse myself to use the ladies' room. When I come out, Graham is waiting for me outside the door.

"Tattoos?" I ask. "Are you out of your mind? You think I'm getting a tattoo?" I shove the slip of paper into his chest.

"I don't *think* you're getting one. I *know* you're getting one."

"What are you even doing here?"

"I missed you. I thought I'd take a little day trip to Hamilton."

"So you're stalking me?"

"I was here first. Maybe you're stalking *me*."

I guess he has a point. I smile.

"I'm sorry. I'm just a little frazzled after spending so much time with those two." Being alone together, even if it is just standing outside of a restroom, takes me back to the suite this morning. My palms start to sweat. "I'm glad you're here. Strange coincidence or not."

"I'm glad I'm here too."

Graham pulls me into a corner where nobody in the restaurant can see us, and I kiss him. I'm suddenly very aware of why people partake in public displays of affection. Once you get started, it's a bit hard to stop. I force myself to take a step back.

"As happy as I am to see you," I say, "I'm not getting a tattoo. My parents will absolutely murder the both of us."

It's kind of nice to have my parents to blame, when, in all honesty, I don't want to get one either. Last year I passed out after getting my flu shot. This may be the first time that my parents and I have ever wholeheartedly agreed on anything.

"You're overreacting," says Graham. "Besides, I spent five whole minutes researching this place online last night. They do amazing work."

"You really have no idea who you're dealing with, do you? When I was fifteen I asked my mother if I could get a second piercing in my ear. My *ear*. Do you know what she said? She told me that I would look like an asshole."

"That's exactly my point," says Graham. "You need to do this for the shock value. They need to know that you're going to do what you want regardless of what they think. Our little jet skiing excursion was a major success. Now, they need to see that having a tattoo doesn't magically transform you into an asshole either. Nice job buying that sweatshirt, by the way."

"It was a moment of weakness," I say. "Stop trying to change the subject. Let's stick to the fact that I'm supposed to sit calmly in a chair while some dude *stabs me with a needle*?"

Graham smiles. "I'm not asking you to get a map of Bermuda tattooed across your ass. You can get a tiny one."

"A tiny map of Bermuda across my ass?"

"Very funny."

"Okay, so you mean that I can get a 'particle of dust' tattoo?"

"I was thinking more like a heart or a butterfly," says Graham. "And to help you out, I'm going to get one too."

"Oh, yeah?"

"Sure. I wouldn't ask you to do something that I wasn't willing to do myself. Besides, I've been dying to have a butterfly tattooed on my hip."

"I would definitely like to see that," I say. "Or maybe you could get a picture of my parents tattooed across your face."

"Perfect. Then every time you look at me you'll remember what we did here today."

"Or every time I look at you I'll be reminded of how my parents had to be rushed to the hospital having simultaneous coronaries."

Graham tilts his head from side to side, weighing the pros and cons.

"That's another possibility," he says. Then he places a hand on my shoulder, and pushes my hair back behind my ear. "Or maybe every time you look at me you'll be reminded of how I changed your life."

***

I can tell you one thing Graham's going to change about my life—he's going to turn me into an alcoholic. I decide to get myself a bit liquored up before the big moment—the big moment not being when a huge needle full of black ink sinks itself into my tender flesh, but the moment when I announce to my parents that Graham and I are getting tattoos. Yes, I am caving in. But no, I'm not caving in the same way that I caved when I bought the sweatshirt. I'm caving because I know that Graham is right. However little I wish to have a needle stabbed into my flesh, I need to do this.

No pain, no gain.

Mom is studying a mound of yellow mush through her bifocals. She and Dad ordered something called Pan Seared Rockfish as they assumed it was the closest match to the Baked

Haddock they've been ordering at every restaurant they've ever eaten at for the past fifty years. I don't think, however, that their Baked Haddock at Applebee's ever came with a black rum banana chutney, and Mom looks immensely horrified as she nibbles at her fork.

"I hope this doesn't give us funny stomachs," says Dad, as if at any moment their stomachs will either explode into diarrhea or start doing stand up comedy. I don't know why they didn't just order cheeseburgers. I wish I had. Instead, I ended up with some sort of Thai curry dish as it was the first thing I saw on the menu when the waitress came to take our order, and it sounded exotic and spicy enough to freak out Mom and Dad. I will never admit it to them, but it's actually a bit too much for me. I've already mentally retraced the location of all the public restrooms we visited today, just in case.

The matter of telling my parents that Graham and I are getting tattoos must be handled delicately, and with a vast display of tact. That's what we decided earlier, by the restrooms. Graham even offered to tell them for me, which I agreed to quite readily. Obviously, I don't feel comfortable telling them myself. And since this was *his* brilliant idea, it's only fair that he be the one to make the announcement. Still, he seems to be taking his sweet time. I would rather just get it over with than sit here any longer with my stomach in knots. I wait until the plates have been cleared, and Mom and Dad are happily munching on a standard issue brownie sundae, before breaking the news.

"Graham and I are getting tattoos," I announce in the voice of a three hundred pound linebacker. I take a gulp of beer to calm my nerves. "Graham and I are getting tattoos." I repeat the words in my normal voice, looking from Mom to Dad and back again. There, now it's all out in the open. Que Sera, Sera. I glance over at Graham who is staring unhelpfully into his beer.

"Oy, please," says Mom. She waves her hand, brushing me off like a child who has just announced she's going to be a ballerina *and* a firefighter when she grows up.

"What do you mean *oy please*? I wasn't just throwing out ideas. I was making a statement. Graham and I are getting tattoos. Today. After lunch."

I am suddenly quite determined to go through with it.

"Where are you going to get a tattoo in Bermuda?" She waves her arms around like we're dining at an Everest base camp.

"Um, at a tattoo parlor? There's one not too far from here. We're going."

"You can't!" Mom shrieks, suddenly comprehending that I might actually be serious. Several other patrons look in our direction, convinced that I've just informed my parents that I will in fact be having the sex change operation on the twenty-fourth of September.

"It's not as bad as you think," says Graham. "Summer just wants to get a small one. You'll probably never even see it."

Mom narrows her eyes at Graham. "This was all your idea, wasn't it? You used to be such a nice boy."

"It wasn't his idea," I lie. "It was mine. He just helped me to find a place."

"But what do you *need* it for?"

A woman at the next table turns to stare, certain that my mother is referring to the penis I am having surgically attached to my loins. I smile at her and she quickly looks away.

Mom and Dad have both abandoned the brownie sundae, but I find myself suddenly quite hungry. I scoop a piece onto my plate and take a bite before responding. Something about the way Mom brushed off my announcement has hardened my resolve to get the stupid tattoo. I see now, more than ever, that this could be a major turning point in my life. I think if I had facetiously told her that I was joining the Navy, and she had brushed me off with an *oy please,* I would have found myself down at the enlistment center. *Ahoy!*

"I don't *need* one. I've just always wanted one," I lie again. "Eric has one."

Okay, so Eric doesn't have one. At least not that I know of, but I'm dying to see their reaction. And I'm dying for them to kill him as soon as we get back home.

"He does not!" says Mom.

"Sure he does. He got it freshman year of college. It's a picture of a naked girl and it's on his butt." I try to keep a serious face as Graham nonchalantly reaches over and moves my nearly empty, twenty-two ounce beer glass to the end of the table.

"You're kidding!"

"Nope. She's about three inches tall and she's got—" I cup my hands in front of my chest in the universal symbol of huge breasts.

"Really?" asks Dad, suddenly more interested than he's been this entire conversation.

"Yup."

How my parents think I would know if my brother has or doesn't have a tattoo across his butt is beyond me. But I find the direction this conversation has taken quite amusing.

"What the hell would he do that for?" asks Mom. "What would you let him do that for?" She looks accusingly at Graham.

"He's his own man, Mrs. H.," says Graham. "If Eric wants a naked girl tattooed on his butt, he's going to have one. And if Summer wants a naked man tattooed on her butt, or maybe a heart on her ankle, she's going to have one too. You only live once."

"What about when she's an old lady?" asks Mom. "She'll look like an asshole!"

Here we go. I'll look like an asshole if I get my ears double pierced. Boys look like assholes if they wear their baseball hats backwards. Dad looked like an asshole that time he hung his sunglasses from the collar of his shirt. By Mom's calculations, the world will be irreparably consumed by assholes before the next presidential election.

"When Summer is an old lady, she'll look down at that tattoo and be thankful that she lived her life to the fullest. Besides, if anybody wants to judge her based solely on a tiny little tattoo, well then, I think we know who the real asshole is."

Graham drains his beer and motions to the waiter to bring us our check.

Mom and Dad sit in stunned silence for a few moments. Then they return to the brownie sundae, occasionally whispering to each other about needles and skin infections.

"They *are* professionals," mutters Dad. "They must know what they're doing."

I look at him in surprise. Did he just defend my getting a tattoo? I glance over at Graham. He's watching Dad with an amused expression on his face. He looks over at me, his mouth twitching into a crooked smile.

"Almost ready to go?" he asks, rubbing his hands together.

"*So* ready."

The man should totally run for president. Within an hour of proposing this completely insane idea, he's got me one hundred percent sold.

Dad too, I suspect.

26

The sight of Mom and Dad sitting in the waiting area of a tattoo parlor, transferring wads of cash and tissues between their pants pockets, is surreal enough to keep my mind off the pain shooting through my right ankle. Well, almost. At least I haven't passed out yet. The heart that I've chosen as the symbol of my independence is the simplest design in the tattoo catalog. It doesn't even need to be filled in; it's just the outline of two hearts linked together and is about one inch in width.

Graham is in a chair on the other side of the room having his and Eric's corporate logo tattooed on his wrist. I don't claim to be in the running for any awards of bravery, but this is still the bravest thing I've ever done. I lean back in the chair, trying not to hyperventilate. My mind wanders to what Graham and I might be up to later tonight. That doesn't help with the hyperventilation. I try to think about something else.

"Mom, you should get Dad's name tattooed across the back of your neck," I say.

"Oy, please."

I'm pretty sure Mom has written me out of the will. Dad is

keeping busy flipping through a tattoo catalog, occasionally showing something to Mom who rolls her eyes. Eventually she gets up and wanders over to my chair.

"Will that get infected?" she asks the tattoo artist. "The last thing she needs is an infection."

"Mom, nobody needs an infection. They know what they're doing." Normally a comment like that coming from my mother would annoy me to death, but I kind of appreciate the distraction. "I can't believe you guys are actually here. I'm proud of you."

It's true. Mom's only announced twice since lunch that she's having a nervous breakdown, and only one of those times was in relation to my getting tattoo. The other time was when we tried to cross the street and she realized that cars were driving on the left-hand side of the road.

"If you're going to do something this stupid, we want to be here in case you need us." Mom peers at my ankle through her bifocals. "God knows we can't trust *him* anymore." She waves dismissively in Graham's direction.

I smile. "That's actually kind of nice. Thank you."

"When's the last time you shaved your knees?"

"Mom!"

She really doesn't know how to quit while she's ahead. I shrug off the neon-green hoodie, trying not to move the lower half of my body, and lay it across my knees. I miss one hair and she has to make an announcement. The tattoo artist is trying not to laugh. Great. What I need even less than an infection is for this guy's hand to start shaking when he gets the giggles.

I look over at Graham, but he's kindly pretending that he didn't hear anything. He's probably waiting until later to tell me that I should stop shaving my legs and armpits altogether. He'll say that the shock value will do Mom and Dad good. If he had his way he'd have me covered in tattoos and body hair before the week is out.

Well, maybe not.

I close my eyes and try to relax.

"Um, how much…how much would it be for this one?" says a voice that sounds an awful lot like my father's. My eyes fly open. My ears did not deceive me. Dad is standing at the counter, pointing to something in the catalog.

"Richard!" Mom snaps. "Are you crazy?"

"You only live once, Joan."

Oh.

My.

God.

I don't think I've ever in my life heard him stand up to my mother.

"YOLO!" calls out Graham, giving my dad a thumbs-up.

"Dad! Are you crazy?" I laugh. "What are you going to get?"

He brings the catalog over and holds it out in front of me, looking embarrassed and ecstatic all at the same time. I look to where he's pointing, and realize the monster that we've created. I put my hand over my mouth.

Dad's getting a naked lady tattoo.

***

I suppose I should say that Dad *got* a naked lady tattoo. That's right, he did it. Riding on the coattails of Graham's "You Only Live Once" speech, and effortlessly fending off Mom's protests like a champion swordfighter, he took the plunge.

He chose to have it done on his upper arm, amidst the freckles of his pasty-white New England flesh. I can't say that it looks particularly good. I mean the artist did a good job. It's not that. It's just weird to see that kind of thing on my father, the same man who sprays toilet seats with Lysol.

And then there's Mom.

She's been staring out the window for the entire bus ride while Dad chats it up with a young woman across the aisle. This particular young woman has pink hair and a pierced tongue, and I'm pretty sure I heard Dad ask her *if it hurt*. I can only hope he was referring to the piercing and that I wasn't catching the tail end of a *did it hurt when you fell from heaven?* sort of pick-up line. The way Dad's been acting today, who knows.

Mom is most likely daydreaming about asking the cruise staff for a new cabin assignment. I can't say that I blame her. Not only did her husband get a tattoo against her wishes—he got a naked one to boot.

I'm giggling about it to myself for the hundredth time, when I suddenly have the terrible fear that Mom will kick him out of their cabin and he'll have to sleep on the couch in my suite for the rest of the trip.

Shit.

"So, Mom," I say, reaching over the seat and tapping her on the shoulder. "Haven't you always wanted to be with a bad boy type? Tattoos are kind of sexy, no?"

"Bad boys are assholes."

Right.

"But it's still Dad, you know? Dad's not an asshole. Remember that time he surprised you with an entire tray of Italian cookies from Brandano's?"

That's their favorite bakery, and also one of her favorite memories. Those pink and green cookies are like raw oysters to the two of them. I might throw up thinking about what that implies, but I'm in dire straits here.

"Those cookies were stale," she says with the same venom one might expect had Dad brought home a tray full of decapitated rodent carcasses.

Great. Why the heck isn't Dad helping out here? He should be apologizing profusely instead of striking up a relationship with Lolita.

"Dad's a very nice man," I say, glancing at him out of the corner of my eye. "I think he's just gotten a little carried away."

Now the girl's got her shirt hiked halfway up and is showing him her navel piercing. Enough is enough.

"Dad!" I punch him in the shoulder and give the girl the stink eye. He looks at me guiltily over his shoulder. I jerk my head in Mom's direction. It takes him forever, but he finally gets the hint and starts mumbling apologies to her. I'm pretty sure I hear the name Brandano's being tossed around. Good luck with that, Dad. Mom continues to stare out the window.

I leave them to themselves, and look down at my ankle. Tiny as my tattoo is, I feel different knowing that it's there. Knowing that I made a firm decision on something that I will have to live with for the rest of my life, despite all of my mother's arguments, has been quite a confidence booster. Even if Eric does have a tattoo that I don't know about, he certainly didn't have it done right in front of Mom and Dad. That took some serious guts.

Okay fine, it was mostly Graham's guts that made it happen. But still, it's my skin. I'm the one that went through with it.

It is rather red and itchy though. And they told me that I should stay out of the water for the next two weeks. Seriously. I'm on a cruise ship in Bermuda, and I have to stay out of the water. I can't help but feel that maybe Graham should have told me this beforehand. I yelled at him about it on the way back to the bus. At least with his wrist tattoo he can keep one arm out of the water while he holds a Mai Tai. What am I supposed to do? Go in headfirst?

I'm not really mad at him though. I do appreciate everything that he's done for us this week. Mostly I'm just wandering around in a state of angst. I keep bouncing back and forth between wanting to tear off his clothes, and envisioning next Christmas Eve when the family is sitting around the Christmas tree sipping on hot toddies, and I'm still as single as ever. I keep picturing Graham there, with his latest supermodel girlfriend on his lap, winking at me over her shoulder because he's suddenly pictured me naked. I really don't know if I can live like that.

Now that we're seated next to each other on the bus, our shoulders touching and Graham's arm resting on my knee so that I can inspect his tattoo, my hormones continue to stampede all of my rationalizations to death.

"So, um, what are your plans for tonight?" I whisper, not wanting Mom and Dad to hear, and still completely unsure of what I want his response to be.

"I guess that depends on what *your* plans are for tonight," he whispers back, taking my hand and squeezing it into his. "Also, why are we whispering?"

I give him what I hope is a meaningful look, and jerk my head towards the back of Mom and Dad's seat.

Isn't it obvious?

The corner of Graham's mouth twitches as he leans in closer.

"Why do you care so much what other people think?" he whispers.

"They're not other people, they're my parents," I whisper. "I don't want them to get the wrong idea."

"YOU MEAN YOU DON'T WANT YOUR PARENTS TO THINK WE'RE SLEEPING TOGETHER?" he says in literally the loudest voice I've ever heard.

I hate him. I really, truly, hate him. I quickly pull my hand out of his grip as Mom turns around to stare at us. *Oh God.* I'm fairly certain that Mom thinks I'm a virgin. This is going to lead to an extremely awkward *I wish you would wait until you get married* conversation later on tonight, with Mom telling me for the thousandth time about her high school chum that got knocked up and ruined her life. As if a sixteen-year-old girl getting pregnant fifty years ago, and a fully-grown, modern-day woman with a job getting pregnant are even remotely related.

Ugh, I can't do it.

I slide closer to the window and attempt to shrink into the side of the bus.

Amazingly, Mom was having enough of a nervous breakdown over Dad's tattoo, that despite Graham screaming into the back of her skull, she seems to have no clue what he was talking about. Instead of chastising me for a life of sin, she asks me how a man who had promised to love and cherish her, 'til death do they part, has managed to destroy any chance they had of a normal retirement, by permanently stamping such a horrid image on his arm. I honestly think that when she looks at Dad's tattoo, she sees a swastika.

As I try to reassure her that Dad very rarely even wears short-sleeves, I become freshly awash with thoughts of what it will be like when we return home—the bickering, the neuroses, each of them trying to pull me into their side of an argument that I care absolutely nothing about. And what if they really are going to get a divorce? Dad will move out and then I'll be expected to split my time between the two of them, relaying messages back and forth and teaching Dad how to iron clothes and scramble eggs. No, I can't do it. I need to get out of that house. The Prophecy must be fulfilled.

"I think maybe I'm going to check out one of the singles' events tonight," I say, barely believing that I spoke those words.

"Oh," says Graham.

I can't even look at him. "We had a deal, remember? My nights are my own, and all that."

The words feel wrong coming out, and when I finally do glance over at him, he looks sadly perplexed. But I don't bother trying to take them back.

"I remember," he says coolly, looking down at the floor and nodding slowly. "I suppose that means *my* nights are my own as well."

I know I have no right to be jealous, but try telling that to my stomach. While I will be out searching for a man to spend the rest of my life with—a man with whom I want to have my future children—Graham will probably be tracking down Lana and bending her over the back of our couch. It doesn't seem fair. But it is fair, because I am voluntarily passing Graham up for the sake of my future. If I'm jealous, all I have to do is give the word and it will be me he's bending over the back of the couch. Or, you know, having a very romantic evening with.

But I have to do what I came here to do. I can't just throw away this opportunity in order to have a fling with my brother's best friend. We had a deal and he knows it.

I just wish he didn't have to look so sad about it.

27

Once we return to the ship, Graham and Dad take off to the Internet café to Skype with Eric and show off their tattoos. Graham didn't even invite me. It's okay though, I'm still too angry with Eric to want to speak to him. And I'm sure Graham doesn't want to pay by the minute to watch me yell at a computer screen. Not to mention that I don't want to be around when Dad finds out Eric doesn't actually have a tattoo of his own.

Awkward.

Instead, I'm sitting by the pool, reading *Fifty Shades of Grey*, and debating what the heck I'm going to do with myself this evening.

"Have we got any singles in the area?"

I look up at the sound of a nearby crewmember. He's wearing the classic uniform of white polo shirt and khaki shorts. He looks a lot like Zack Morris when he worked that summer at the Malibu Sands. Earlier in the week, I made eye contact with a crewmember and nearly ended up in a game of water polo. Lesson learned. Today, I keep my sunglasses on and my head buried inside my Kindle.

Have we got any singles in the area. Who's going to shoot their hand up in the air at that question, anyway? *Ooh ooh! Me! Nobody loves me! Over here!* Yes, I know that I told Graham I was going to a singles' event tonight, and that one is currently being handed to me on a silver platter, but the thought of standing around like a piece of meat and getting hit on by the likes of Logan and Jackson sounds absolutely appalling. I was secretly hoping that there wouldn't be any singles' events tonight, and that I could meet any further men organically, like in the gift shop when we both happen to reach for the same coffee mug.

No such luck. The Zack Morris lookalike is heading toward me, swinging his arms and clapping his hands.

"Tonight!" he yells. "Eight o'clock!"

Who is he even yelling at? I glance around the pool. There are like four people here. Okay, tonight? Tonight what? Get on with it. Oh no, he's coming my way. I look desperately back at my Kindle, wishing I could just disappear into it. Why is there never a time vortex around when you need one?

"Singles' Night at the champagne bar! Eight o'clock!" With his job duties complete, he sits down in the lounge chair next to me.

"Single?" he asks.

"Why would you assume that?" I ask, not removing my head from my book.

"Wishful thinking? My name's Colin." He sticks out a hand. "Will you be joining us tonight?"

"Summer." I reluctantly shake his hand. "Isn't it a little late in the week for a meet and greet?"

"It's never too late to meet new people. We've still got two full days left. Might be nice to meet someone to shack up with."

"Shack up with?" I raise my eyebrows. "Is that what they taught you at activities director training?"

"Poor choice of words," he laughs. "Spend time with. Is that better?"

"Slightly."

"So, what are you reading?"

Ugh.

I've read hundreds of works of literary genius in my life. And now, the only time that I'm reading an absolute piece of garbage, everybody wants to know what I'm reading. Now he's going to think I'm single *and* horny. I close the cover.

"Just an old classic," I say. "You've probably never heard of it."

"*Fifty Shades?*"

"Oh, come on!" I laugh. "There's no fooling anyone on this ship, is there?"

"There are at least two hundred copies of that book onboard. The odds were in my favor. So, what do you say, Miss Summer? Will I be seeing you at Singles' Night?"

"I don't know," I shrug. "Maybe."

"You're killing me. Do I have to beg?"

"I just have a touch of social anxiety," I say. "Don't take it personally."

Colin reaches over and rubs my shoulder. "You've got nothing to worry about. If you come by tonight, I'll take good care of you."

He gives me a semi-creepy wink before standing up and heading toward a couple of single-looking girls at the pool bar. I wonder if he'll say the same exact lines to them.

I let out a long sigh. I did tell Graham that I was going to a singles' event tonight. And if there's any chance left of fulfilling The Prophecy, I'm going to have to push aside my social anxiety. Besides, Graham is probably going to track down Lana tonight. The thought of it turns my stomach. Well, if he does he does. He's got every right. I had my chance, and I let him go.

You made your bed, Douchewell. Now lie in it.

***

Mom is joining me for Singles' Night.

You heard me right. Just as I was putting the finishing touches on my hair and makeup, there was an angry knocking at the door. I opened it to find Mom practically in tears. She and Dad—dressed against his will in a long-sleeve shirt—had gone to dinner in the main dining room, where they had been seated with two similarly aged couples. All was going well until one of the other husbands mentioned having spent the day at the Bermuda Perfumery. Then the other husband chimed in to say that he and his wife had eaten a lovely lunch at the Lighthouse Tea Room. What I gathered from Mom's side of the story, and from my own educated guessing, is that Dad could no longer contain his excitement at having beaten the system—the system being the collar that Mom and the other women at the table keep fastened tightly around their husbands' necks. Before Mom knew what was happening, Dad had unbuttoned his shirt, stripped down to his Hanes cotton undershirt, and was showing off his new tattoo.

"Her bosoms were everywhere!" cried Mom. "I don't know what's gotten into him. He's not the same man that I married."

She seemed so utterly devastated that I felt bad ushering her back to her own room for the night. So when she calmed down enough to ask me what I was all dressed up for, I told her the truth. And then I invited her along.

"I suppose I'll be single soon enough," she declared, rifling through her pocketbook for tissues, and reapplying her lipstick. "Your father took off to the casino after dinner anyway. He's probably meeting *that one* again."

I'm guessing *that one* is Angel Cake O'Brien, but who knows. From Mom's tone it sounds like he's meeting Bugsy Siegel.

And so here I am, sitting at the champagne bar in a tank top and four-inch heels, with my mother by my side. She didn't exactly have any sexy attire packed in her suitcase, so she's wearing a pair of khaki Capri pants, white sneakers, and a seahorse-bedazzled t-shirt. Needless to say, I'm drinking rather heavily.

Colin from the pool deck is here as well, moving from group to group, attempting to get people to mingle. He spots me at the bar and waves. I reluctantly wave back. He's changed from his khaki shorts into a pair of khaki pants, still with a white polo shirt. He walks over, smiling at my mother like he's Mr. Burt Reynolds.

"And who is this lovely young lady?" he asks, sidling up to her.

"This is my mom. Mom, this is Colin. His job is to force people into talking to each other."

Colin laughs. "My job is to make sure everybody has a good time. Are you having a good time?"

"I was," says Mom. "Until my husband went and ruined both of our lives."

"My father got a tattoo in Hamilton today," I explain.

"A naked woman!" says Mom, clamping her hand onto Colin's arm. "And he's run off with another woman!"

"Wow," says Colin. "Well, there are quite a few mature singles here tonight as well, if that's what you're in the mood for."

"She's not interested in any mature singles! My father did not *run off* with another woman! He just made a new friend, that's all."

"Her name is Angel Cake!" says Mom, clutching Colin's arm even tighter. "What kind of a name is that? What kind of a mother names her child Angel Cake?"

"Angel Cake O'Brien?" asks Colin.

"You *know* her?" Mom and I ask in unison.

"Who doesn't? She comes on these cruises all the time. She's quite the gold-digger, actually."

"You mean she's after his money?" Mom lets out a delighted laugh. "What money?"

I snort. "Well, you guys are staying in a luxury suite. And if she was lurking around at the terminal, she probably saw us step out of Graham's Camaro. Oh, and the other night at the karaoke bar, Graham ordered that bottle of expensive vodka."

"Oh, that's right!" laughs Mom. "Boy, is she in for a disappointment. Wait until she finds out he drives a ten-year-old Hyundai!"

"Or that he buys his socks at the dollar store."

"And his shoes!"

Mom and I are dying laughing.

"So," says Colin, clearly starting to lose interest in the both of us. "Are either of you ready to mingle?"

"Oy, please," says Mom, pulling herself together and waving her hand dismissively in the air. "It seems my husband won't be going anywhere. This is the one we need to worry about." She points to me, and Colin nods in agreement.

"I think we can find something for this one," he says. "I've got to go make the rounds for a bit, but don't worry. I'll be back with some candidates."

Something for this one? Candidates?

Colin gives me a wink and heads straight toward a couple of desperate looking men with comb overs at the other end of the bar.

Great.

"So, do you forgive Dad?" I ask, once we're alone again. I take a long sip of champagne. This stuff goes straight to my head. Mom must have been really upset, because she's drinking a glass as well.

"I don't know," she says. "Thirty years of marriage, down the drain."

"What do you mean? We were just laughing about Angel Cake only wanting him for his money. I thought everything was okay?"

"Now I'm talking about the tattoo."

"Oh, give him a break, Mom. It's just a tattoo. You're being a little dramatic." She gives me a dirty look. "Well you *are*. Dad just wanted to do something for himself. He wanted to make his own decision for once. I'm sure he wasn't trying to ruin your marriage."

"You wouldn't understand," she says. "You got one too."

"You're right," I say. "But I do understand, because I did it for the same reason. Don't take this the wrong way, but you can be a little suffocating at times." I take another long sip of champagne. I'm not exactly sure where this conversation is going, or how someone could possibly not take *you can be a little suffocating at times* the wrong way.

"You think I'm suffocating?" she asks.

"I just meant that you have very strong personal opinions."

"What's wrong with having personal opinions?"

"Nothing, Mom. You just need to let other people have them too. Sometimes you make it seem like yours is the only one that's valid. Especially when it comes to Dad."

"Your father can never make up his own mind."

"There," I say. "Right there. You just did it. You assume that he's incapable of making his own decisions, so you force your opinions on him. All he did today was rebel a little bit. For once in his life he knew exactly what he wanted, and he got it. I'm proud of him." Okay, maybe I'm not literally *proud* of him for tattooing a naked woman on his arm, but I am in theory.

"So, what are you saying? Everybody hates me?" asks Mom, always the optimist.

"Did I say that everybody hates you? Everybody loves you. I'm just trying to explain why Dad did what he did, and sometimes the truth hurts. Luckily, we have champagne. Drink up."

I hold my glass up in the air and swivel around on the stool, facing outward into the bar, shoe dangling off my foot. *Okay, fellas. Come and rescue me.*

"So you *do* think I'm suffocating," says Mom, her voice uncharacteristically quiet.

I put my glass down on the bar and swivel back around to face her.

"No, Mom. You're not. I swear." I reach over and squeeze her hand, gritting my teeth against the white lie. "You love me and you want me to be safe, that's all. It's up to me to choose how I handle that. I know that now."

"You and Graham sure gave me a scare this week, with the jet skiing, and the scooters, and the tattoos. Graham used to be such a nice boy."

"He still is, Mom. And everything turned out okay, didn't it?"

"I suppose it did," she says, studying my face. "So tell me, did you have fun?"

I take a sip of champagne and slowly nod my head. "I had a blast."

"I never even knew you wanted to try any of those things. You certainly don't get that from me."

"Mom."

"What?"

"You rode a fucking Jet Ski."

"Summer!"

"I'm sorry. But you rode a *Jet Ski*, Mom! Don't sell yourself short."

"Not bad for an old lady, huh?" Mom wiggles her shoulders back and forth in her tough-old-broad-from-the-nineteen-thirties impersonation.

I laugh. "Not bad at all."

"So tell me," says Mom, suddenly serious again. "Why exactly are we here?"

"What do you mean?"

"I mean, what are we doing at a singles' night? You're not trying to meet men on a *cruise ship* are you?"

"Of course I'm trying to meet men on a cruise ship! I'm not getting any younger!"

"So what? You'll live with us until you get married. There's no rush."

"I know, Mom." It's funny how she views The Prophecy as something comforting and wonderful, while I view it as the equivalent of being locked away in prison with only a very slight chance of parole.

"So, what's the problem?"

I sigh. "You say that I'll live with you until I get married, but I'm never going to get married if I never meet anybody. It's hard to meet people back home, you know? I thought that this trip would be a good opportunity. But, the further we get in the week, the more hopeless it seems."

Mom doesn't say anything for a few seconds. Then she reaches over and squeezes my hand.

"Look at that one," she says, tipping her head in the direction of an attractive man in his early thirties. He's wearing jeans, a t-shirt, and a sport coat. He's cute.

"What?"

"Look at what he's wearing!"

"What's wrong with what he's wearing?"

"Oy, please."

"Okay. How about that one?" I point to another man, slightly older, but with greying hair. Not out of the question.

"What do you want an old man for?"

"He's not old, he's just got grey hair. I like it." Mom looks like she might pass out, which is funny because Dad's had grey hair since he was thirty-five.

"How about that one?" she asks, pointing toward a guy wearing tapered leg jeans and sneakers so white they can be seen from space.

"Um, no. How about that one?" I point to a man who is clearly homosexual.

"He's cute."

I laugh.

"What?"

"Nothing. Just don't ever leave Dad."

28

My night has turned into *The Dating Game*.

No, I mean it. My night has literally turned into *The Dating Game*. Colin wasn't just being cute when he said he would return with a few candidates. When he returned to the bar he informed me that there were three eager men waiting for me backstage—backstage being the corridor outside the champagne bar—and that I was to be the lucky bachelorette in the cruise ship's version of the game show. He must have been wired remotely, because as soon as he told me the news the lights came on in a darkened corner of the bar to reveal four folding chairs and a privacy screen.

Normally under such circumstances I would have run for the exit and not stopped running until I was treading water in the Atlantic. But Mom and I have been having quite a good time drinking champagne and making fun of people, and we are both pretty giggly by the time Colin tells us his plan. Mom is all for it, and I do very little to resist. Like many fools before me, the idea of playing *The Dating Game* on a cruise ship somehow seems like a good idea. I decide that it must be fate. I want to meet men, and now I am going to have three of them to personally select from. I can't turn this down. Especially since I'm tipsy enough that the thought of being the center of attention doesn't completely freak me out.

"This wasn't on *Cruise Notes*," I point out. "I checked the schedule before I came out tonight so there wouldn't be any surprises. This isn't fair."

"No, it wasn't on the schedule," admits Colin. "Sometimes we like to keep these things small. We don't want a bunch of hecklers turning up."

"You get *hecklers*?"

"Occasionally." Colin smiles. "But trust me, Summer. Nobody is going to heckle *you*." He rubs my shoulder for a few seconds and I get the distinct impression that he's hitting on me. Are cruise staff allowed to do that? Not that I'm complaining. If you don't mind the Malibu Ken type, Colin's not half bad. Maybe the man I've been searching for is right here under my nose. He's a lot like Graham actually, minus the colorful wardrobe and the potential for awkward family get-togethers. The thought of Graham out somewhere tonight without me makes the champagne feel a bit sloshy in my stomach.

I turn my attention back to Colin. I look at his nametag, and for the first time notice that the word Alaska is printed underneath his name.

"Are you really from Alaska?" I ask, hoping that he says he's from the little-known town of Alaska, New Hampshire.

"Sure am. I started my career on an Alaskan cruise line."

"So, when you're not working, you go back to Alaska?"

"That's right. My family lives in Juneau. You ever been?"

Have I ever been to Juneau, Alaska? I try not to laugh.

"No, but I've always wanted to go."

Yeah, right. Bears, five hours of daylight, dogsleds—why wouldn't I want to go to Alaska? I'm sure it's lovely. You know what would be lovelier? If Colin didn't live five thousand freakin' miles away.

"Do you have a closet full of these things?" I ask, tugging on the sleeve of his white polo shirt."

"Yeah. It's my uniform."

"What about when you're not on duty? What do you wear?"

"I don't know. Other stuff."

"Like, colorful stuff? Or is everything just white?"

"What are you getting at?"

"Nothing. It's just that sometimes a man looks nice in bright colors."

"Yeah. Right." He gives me an odd look and glances at his watch. "It's just about time, are you ready?"

"Ready."

I nervously head towards the stage with Colin bounding after me asking a few personal questions to include in his introduction speech. He hands me a pile of cards containing the questions I'm supposed to ask the guys. I hope there are a few questions in there about literature, and maybe opinions on the origin of the Universe.

Awful music blasts out of the sound system as Colin grabs a microphone and struts around the stage like Chuck Barris. On second thought, maybe it's a good thing that he lives in Alaska.

"Let's welcome our beautiful bachelorette—Summer Hartwell from Massachusetts!"

A small titter of applause goes around the crowd. This is actually pretty embarrassing. I shift nervously in my seat while a barrage of judgmental eyes look me over.

"Summer enjoys French cooking, parasailing, and long walks on the beach with that special someone."

I glare at Colin. That is absolutely *not* what I told him about myself. I said that I was into science fiction, alternate universes, and long walks *alone*, by myself. What a nerve.

Mom is still sitting at the bar, smiling at me as if I'm truly on a television show and not just some lame last minute time-filler on a cruise ship. The crowd starts to clap as the three bachelors take their seats on the other side of the screen. I wonder if tapered-leg-jeans guy is over there. I catch a glimpse of him standing in the corner by a ficus tree, and breathe a bit easier.

"Alright, Summer," says Colin, handing me a microphone. "Let's start with the first round of questions."

I pull a card out at random.

"Bachelor Number One," I read. "If you were an animal, which animal would you be and why?"

What the hell kind of a question is that? Who cares what kind of animal he would be? I'm trying to find a man to spend eternity with, and I'm supposed to base it off of *this*?

Relax Douchewell. You're turning into an angry drunk. It's just a game. You never have to talk to any of these men again if you don't want to.

The only problem is that I do want to. I really want to. This may be just a stupid cruise ship game, but it also might be destiny. My future husband might very well be on the other side of that screen, and if he decides to say that he would rather be a naked mole rat than a Bengal tiger, I might easily pass him over. My future children might never be born.

I start to flip through the rest of the cards when I realize that the audience is clapping. I missed Bachelor Number One's reply. Crap.

"I'm sorry, could you repeat that?" I ask.

"Um, I said I would be an octopus. Because of all the arms and stuff."

Wow, disturbing.

"Okay, thanks. Bachelor Number Two." I continue flipping through the stack of cards. God these are stupid. "If you were a circus performer, which act would you be?"

"I would be a clown because I love making people laugh."

Real original.

"And what would you do to make *me* laugh?"

"I'd, like, pull a rabbit out of a hat."

"That would be the work of a magician, but nice try. Okay, Bachelor Number Three. If you could invite anybody to dinner, living or dead, who would it be and why?"

"You mean like there would be a dead body at the dinner table?"

The audience laughs, but I'm not so sure he was joking.

"No, like anybody from history," I say. "Even if they are currently dead."

"Oh, well then, I think I would have to go with Anna Nicole Smith."

"Are you fucking kidding me?"

The audience erupts into laughter. I glance over at Mom who's got kind of a scandalized expression on her face.

Oops.

That's the second time tonight that she's heard that word come out of my mouth. But seriously, *Anna Nicole Smith*?

"Why not?" says Bachelor Number Three, sounding offended. "She was hot."

"Um, I don't know. Maybe because it should be someone you can actually have a conversation with? Like Carl Sagan or Abraham Lincoln? Hell, I would have accepted Britney Spears as a better answer than *Anna Nicole Smith*."

"Okay!" says Colin, bounding back onto the stage. "Why don't we just move along to Round Two?"

"No, I don't think so," I say. "Can I choose you instead?" Compared to the other three morons onstage, he's not looking too bad.

Colin smiles and raises his eyebrows. "I'm flattered, Summer. But I'm afraid that would be against cruise line policy." He turns and gives the audience a wink.

"Okay, fine. I'll take Bachelor Number Two then, the rabbit out of the hat guy. I don't need any more rounds."

"Um, alright," says Colin, looking a bit thrown. Apparently nobody's ever cut short one of his activities before. "It looks like we've made an instant love connection! Come on out Bachelor Number Two, and meet your date for tomorrow night!" The strains of *Sugar Sugar* start playing as sixteen-year-old Jackson walks out from behind the screen, smiling at me smugly.

All I can do is laugh.

"You didn't check his I.D., did you?" I whisper into Colin's ear. He shakes his head, confused. "Why don't you go ahead and check it. Check it real close. Then shred it. I'm going to get the hell out of here now."

I grab Mom from the bar and drag her toward the exit.

***

I'm just getting into bed when there's a knock at the door to our suite. It can't possibly be Mom again. I deposited her back in her cabin where she most likely passed out from all the champagne. She's going to hate me tomorrow. Maybe it's Graham. He might have forgotten his key. Although, if Lana's out there with him, he can just forget about it. I'm not letting the two of them in here. Although, if Lana were with him, wouldn't they have just gone back to her room? I suppose if her gaggle of girlfriends are all sharing one cabin then they would have had to come here. *Good old Summer won't mind. Summer's probably been in bed since eight-thirty. Summer ditched me to attend a singles' event after we slept together.*

A stab of regret sears me right in the chest.

Did I really, honestly, do that to him?

The knocking starts up again. I'd better go see who it is. Maybe the ship is going down and this is the only warning I'm going to get.

I drag myself to the door and look through the peephole. It's Colin, and he's looking nervously back and forth down the hallway. He starts to knock again.

What the hell is he doing here?

I've already washed off all my makeup, and I'm wearing one of my brother's promotional t-shirts that say *Fart Attack* on it. That's the name of the app that made Eric rich. *Fart Attack.* Those are the words currently emblazoned across my chest while a good-looking guy is knocking on my door. Not that I'm interested in Colin, but still.

"Just a minute!" I call out. I run into the bathroom and rake a brush through my hair. Then I grab the neon-green hoodie off the foot of the bed, and zip it up to my neck.

"Hey," I say, pulling open the door.

Colin practically leaps over the threshold.

"Sorry. I didn't mean to barge in," he says. "It's just that I'll get into trouble if anyone sees me outside a passenger's room at this hour."

For someone apologizing for barging in, he marches quite forwardly over to the couch and sits down.

"So, what *are* you doing at a passenger's room at this hour?" I ask, closing the door and following him to the couch.

"What do you *think* I'm doing at a passenger's room at this hour?"

I raise my eyebrows. "Um, apologizing for the morons you selected for *The Dating Game*?"

"Never," Colin laughs. "Let's just say I had no intention of setting you up with one of those guys tonight." He pats the seat next to him.

"So you selected three jerks on purpose?" I sit down on the opposite end of the couch. "Thanks a lot."

"Guilty," says Colin. "I know I said that I'm not supposed to get involved with passengers, but I couldn't let you slip away. You're different." He again pats the seat next to him. I don't budge.

"What's so different about me?" I ask, skeptically. "You don't even know me."

"True. But I'd like to. I've been intrigued ever since I saw you on the pool deck."

"That was like four hours ago," I point out.

Colin shrugs. "Just imagine the torture I've been going through these past four hours." He slides down to my end of the couch, and without any warning, he kisses me.

I let him.

The next thing I know, he's unzipping my hoodie and sliding it off of my shoulders. Still kissing me, he runs his hand down the front of my *Fart Attack* shirt, most likely expecting the feel of lacy lingerie beneath his hands rather than the cotton of a size large men's t-shirt. He leans back and opens his eyes.

"Fart Attack?"

"I wasn't expecting company."

Colin smiles. "It won't be a problem for long." He's trying to pull the t-shirt up over my head, when I stop him and yank it back down.

"What's wrong?" he asks.

I shrug his hands off of me and stand up.

If this situation doesn't have *meaningless fling* written all over it, I don't know what does. I mean, I could be with the real Graham right now—not some dime-store impersonation of him. That familiar feeling of regret stabs me once again in the chest. The thought of Graham brings up the thought of Lana, which in turn brings up the thought of both of them together, which threatens to bring up my dinner.

"I don't usually move this fast," I admit, pulling my hoodie back on.

"You're on vacation. It's excusable." Colin stands up and grabs my hand, kissing it like some sort of pushy Prince Charming. I yank my hand away. Sure, I'm upset at the thought of Graham possibly being out with Lana. But if he is, it's only because I told him I was going to a singles event to meet my future husband. Colin is far from my future husband. There is no point to any of this.

"I think you should leave," I say, walking over to the door and opening it. Colin follows me, but pushes the door shut. He leans his back against it, staring at me. I'm starting to get a bit nervous. I glance around the suite, looking for anything I can possibly use as a weapon. Our two beer bottles from last night are still lying on the floor. Nice job, housekeeping.

Colin takes a step towards me as I take a step back.

"You got any E?" he asks.

"Excuse me?"

"Ecstasy."

Oh for Christ's sake.

"No, there are no drugs here."

"Just wondering," he says, still coming at me. "It makes for a much better experience."

I don't think that I'll be able to reach for the beer bottle without Colin pushing me to the floor, so instead I turn and start making my way back toward the door.

"Look, I don't think there's going to be any *experiences* happening here tonight, okay? I'm pretty tired." I've made it to the door and am about to pull it open when Colin pins me up against the wall, his hands once again groping around my *Fart Attack* shirt.

"Get off of me!" I yell. Then I knee him in the groin, just like Mom always told me to do.

Although quite satisfying, it turns out to be unnecessary. At the very moment that Colin crumples to the floor, the door to the suite opens and in walks a very angry, very determined looking Graham Blenderman.

29

He lunges at Colin like he's Captain America.

I jump out of the way, and watch wide-eyed from the safety of the kitchen counter. I'm not quite sure that Graham knows I've already kneed Colin in the nuts, because he yanks him up off the floor without an iota of sympathy.

"Who the hell are you?" asks Graham.

"Who the hell are *you*?" asks Colin.

They really are quite similar, now that I see them standing across from each other.

"I asked you first," says Graham.

"This is Colin," I interrupt. "I met him at the singles' event tonight."

"Oh you did, did you?" asks Graham. Turning his attention back to Colin, he flicks at the plastic nametag on his chest.

"Cruise staff?"

"Who's this guy?" Colin narrows his eyes at me.

"This is Graham." I clear my throat. "Family friend."

"Nice shirt," says Colin, eyeing Graham's magenta polo. "It's very *bright*. What'd you and your boyfriend have a fight or something?"

269

"He's not my boyfriend," I say. "We're just sharing a suite."

No, he's not my boyfriend. He's just a guy that I slept with who swings in and rescues me from creepy prospective date-rapists. Why can't I just shut up and be grateful?

"Isn't there some sort of rule against seducing the passengers?" asks Graham, grabbing Colin around the back of the neck and guiding him to the door.

"Hey, man," says Colin. "You should know that she was flirting with me all night. And she was looking for men on *The Dating Game*. You and your girlfriend should probably have a nice long—"

His words are cut off as Graham opens the door and shoves him roughly into the hallway.

"He's got a gun!" Graham shouts before slamming the door.

I clamp a hand over my mouth, trying not to laugh as I hear a scuffle start in the corridor. Graham and I look at each other in silence for a few seconds.

"You didn't have to rescue me," I say. "But thank you. I don't think I would have been able to drag his body into the hall by myself."

"Are you okay?" Graham asks. He's not laughing.

"Yeah. I'm fine." I chew on my bottom lip, suddenly ashamed. "I never should have let him in here. That was dumb."

A deep voice echoes through the corridor outside our door. *Is that him? Get him!*

"Don't you think you should go out there?" I ask. "Explain that you were just kidding?"

"Nope. I'm more interested in knowing how you could think *that* guy is more worthy of your time than I am?" Graham is looking at me like I've lost my mind. Maybe I have.

"I didn't initiate that," I say, twirling a spoon around on the counter like a propeller. "He just showed up here, I told you."

"He said you were a contestant on *The Dating Game.*"

Oh right.

The spoon shoots across the kitchen. I pick it up off the floor and put it in the sink. I've never seen Graham looking so serious. So pained. Not even the time I dropped a bowling ball on his foot in the seventh grade. This is different. He looks so...abandoned.

I swallow around the lump forming in my throat.

"You knew the plan, Graham," I say. "Your job was to make me ride motorcycles and get tattoos. My job was to find myself a husband. I know you were hoping that one might cancel out the other, but I never said that I was quitting."

"Do you hear yourself?" asks Graham. Actually, he's almost yelling. "You could have been...I don't even want to say what could have happened to you if I hadn't come in just now. How can you still think that traipsing around this ship, meeting idiot after idiot, is the right thing to do? What about last night, Summer? Huh? Was last night really not good enough for you?"

"Of course it was *good*, Graham. God. It was more than good. But come on, you know that I'm looking for someone to spend my *life* with. Not just someone to have a meaningless vacation fling!"

The look of pain and abandonment on his face increases tenfold. "Is that what you think last night was? A meaningless vacation fling?"

"Well, wasn't it?"

"I spent the entire day looking forward to spending tonight with you, Summer. And then you tell me on that bus that you're going to Singles' Night instead. Why don't you tell me which one of us thinks it was a meaningless fling?"

"It's not like that," I say. "I only went because…" I trail off, unsure of how to word this.

"Because *what*?" He takes a step toward me and cups the side of my face in his hand. "Enlighten me."

I look blankly up at him, unable to think of a single reason why I would abandon him to go to a stupid Singles' Night. It was complete lunacy. All I want to do is pull him to me and tell him that I'm sorry, and forget about every moronic thing I did this week. But I can't. Not yet. He's waiting for a reason. He deserves a reason. I take a step away so that I can think clearly, without his hands on me.

"I went tonight because you're *you*," I say carefully. "You're Graham Blenderman and you've got this roulette wheel of women that you spin every couple of months. The ball always lands on either some cougar that can't keep her hands off you, or some girl that I could never even dream of looking like. You intimidate me, Graham, and our lives couldn't possibly be more different. Last night was amazing. But—"

"But what?"

"But on that bus today, hearing Mom and Dad bickering. I realized that I've got to think long-term. I realized that as soon as you decide it's time to spin the wheel again, I'm going to be back to square one of living alone in my parents' basement. And it's going to crush me, just like it crushed me back in high school."

Oops.

"High school?"

"Never mind."

"No, tell me. Did I do something to hurt you back in high school?" He looks troubled, but also like he's trying really hard to remember, which makes it even worse because it was such a defining moment in my own life.

"It's stupid."

"I don't care. Tell me."

"Do you remember offering to take me to the prom?" I feel so stupid even saying the words out loud. *So* stupid.

"Of course I do."

His lack of hesitation takes me by surprise. So he does remember.

"Well, then you must remember me calling a few weeks later to take you up on the offer, only to be informed that you'd started dating someone else." I shrug. "That's when I realized it was only a pity offer. You were only being nice."

Graham frowns. "It wasn't out of pity, Sum. I meant what I said. I wanted to take you to your prom."

"Then why'd you start dating someone else?"

"Because you turned me down, and I was hurt, and I had to move on with my life."

"You were...hurt?"

God, I'm confused. All I ever picture about that day is me lying face down on my bed, humiliated, and Graham hanging up the phone and going on his merry way. Sometimes I picture him whistling.

"Of course I was hurt. Half the time I came over to the house, it was just to see you."

What in the world is he talking about? He's standing close to me again, with the back of his hand against my cheek. I can hardly believe the things that he's saying. But someway, somehow, they must be true. Graham, he doesn't lie. Not to me.

"I...I always thought you were just killing time, waiting for Eric," I stammer.

"I was, at first," admits Graham. "But not for long. At one point I even started paying him to stay in his room an extra fifteen minutes."

My jaw drops open. I try to say something, but I just end up closing it again.

"At some point you transformed from Eric's little sister into this insightful, adorable, amazing person who talked a hell of a lot less than most of the girls at my school, but who had a hell of a lot more to say. And it happened to be prom season when I realized that I couldn't stop thinking about you. When you didn't appear to have a date, it seemed like the Universe was offering me this grand opportunity. So I offered to take you...and within a matter of seconds, it was over. You made this *face*. I'll never forget it. It was disbelief mixed with, I don't know, nausea? Revulsion? Like you couldn't believe that someone who didn't like *The Catcher in the Rye* could possibly make for a decent prom date. Like, I had some sort of *nerve*."

I made a face? I didn't make a face! At least, not the kind of face he thinks I made. And all these years—

"If I made a face, it was because I was embarrassed that you thought I was a loser who couldn't find her own date! I never once meant to come off like I thought I was too good for you, Graham. Never!"

"It's okay if you did," he says. "You had every right to think that way. You *were* too good for me. You still are. Only this time, even if we are unevenly matched, we need each other. This time I'm not willing to let you slip away for an entire decade."

I look up at him, my heart pounding.

"I do have one more little confession to make," he continues. "And you may want to sit down."

***

He's pacing back and forth in front of the television while I perch myself on the edge of the couch.

"You're making me nervous," I say. "I've already thought of a thousand horrible things you're about to tell me."

"It's not horrible. But you might find it a bit creepy."

"Do you attend My Little Pony conventions?"

He laughs. "Yes, I do. But that's not it."

"Okay, just tell me."

He takes a deep breath and sits down across from me, on the coffee table.

"Eric didn't bail on this vacation."

"What are you talking about?"

"Eric didn't bail, because Eric was never coming. This whole thing—me and you and your parents—it was all my idea." He leans away from me, bracing as if I'm going to hit him.

"What?"

"This wasn't a trip to celebrate our success with the app," he says, choosing his words carefully. "This was a trip so that I could get you alone."

I raise my eyebrows, not quite able to wrap my head around

what he's just said. Eric was never coming on this trip with us? Eric was *in* on this?

"Are you creeped out?"

"A little," I say. "But keep talking."

"Okay, well, I had this crazy idea that if I could grab your attention from day one, maybe you would come to see me as more than just a dumb jerk with a *roulette wheel* of women." He air-quotes the words.

"I never saw you as a dumb jerk," I say, shaking my head. "I thought you were out of my league."

"And all this time," he says. "I thought you were out of mine."

"But why *now*?" I ask. "My prom was ten years ago. Why didn't you say something sooner?"

"Well, you know. Life happened. You've had the occasional boyfriend. Eric and I made a bunch of money. Maybe I dated a Victoria's Secret model. *Maybe* I've been living in the fast lane for the past few years."

"I knew you weren't just playing kickball at the YMCA."

Graham gives me a crooked half-smile.

"Ever since Sarah took off with my money and my landlord, I've felt like I needed to come back down to Earth. I feel like this surreal life I've been handed is starting to drain me. You think *money can't buy happiness* is a bunch of bullshit, until you see it for yourself." Graham leans forward and takes my hands in his. "I've spent a lot of time thinking about what would really make me happy, Summer. And my thoughts always come back to you. I don't think they ever really left you."

I stare down at our hands and give his a squeeze. They feel so warm.

"You know, Blenderman," I say. "You could have *just asked me out on a date.*"

He shakes his head. "No, not you. You've got too much going on in that mind. Too many rationalizations and fears and what-ifs. Too many worries about what everybody else will think and feel about your life. No, *you* I had to get out of your normal surroundings and onto a cruise ship. As creepy as that may have made me, it's what I had to do."

Graham was willing to spend a week, trapped on a cruise ship with my parents, just to get me alone.

That might just be the most romantic thing I've ever heard in my life.

I mean, I know that I should feel creeped out about it. But I don't. I feel like this is the kind of story we'll be able to tell our future grandchildren. It's like one step above *I untied your grandmother from the tracks just before the speeding train came through* on the romance scale. For him to do such a thing, he must be genuinely enamored.

Oh my God.

I clamp a hand over my mouth. "And I went and told you that I came on this cruise to find myself a husband."

Graham laughs and looks at the floor. "Yeah, that was a bit unexpected."

"But that's when you decided to make me do all these crazy stunts so that I'd see that I didn't need a man to rescue me from my parents. You were screwing yourself over!"

"No, I wasn't," he says. "Do you think I want you to use me as a means of getting away from your parents?"

"Well, no. But it wouldn't be like that with you." I pull him towards me until he's off the coffee table and hovering over me on the couch. I put my hands on the back of his neck and I kiss him. "This is real, Blenderman. I see that now."

He kisses me back, and then reluctantly pulls away. He sits down on the coffee table again, still holding my hands.

"It's very real, Summer. But even so, I don't want you using me as an excuse for moving out of your parents' house. I don't want you to tell them that it's all going to be okay because Graham is going to take care of you."

"You wouldn't take care of me?"

"Of course I would. But you don't *need* me to. And you don't want them to think that you need me to. If you move out of your parents' house, I want you to own that decision. You're not moving out because you're moving in with me. You're moving out because you're strong, and you don't live your life in fear of what other people are going to think. Your parents can handle it, Summer. I know that you see that now. I know that I said I was going to change your life this week, but I was wrong. I started it, but you're going to finish it. You're going to change your own life."

I nod along with everything that he's saying. He's right. It might have snuck up on me little by little over the course of the week, but he's right. Mom and Dad have ridden on Jet Skis. Dad got a *tattoo*.

The Prophecy, as it turns out, was a false one.

"Okay," I say, still nodding. Still transfixed. "I'm going to do it. I'm going to move out on my own."

Graham smiles and pushes my hair behind my ears.

"At least for a short time."

"And then what?" I ask, pulling him onto the couch next to me.

"Then we see what happens. An eight-day cruise is a bit short to make any major life decisions, don't you think? Maybe we'll move in together. Maybe we'll get married. Maybe you'll dump me for a mature businessman who didn't make his fortune off of fart sounds."

"Or maybe *you'll* dump *me* for some spray-tanned, mimosa-drinking cougar. Then what happens? I'll still have to see you all the time. You're so entangled in my life. At least if I made a mistake with Colin, he lives in Alaska."

"Should I move to Alaska?"

"Be serious."

Graham puts his arm around me. "There are no guarantees in life, Sum. We just have to do what we feel is right and hope for the best. And right now, and for all of my foreseeable days, all I want is you."

"Me too." I smile and tuck my head into his chest. I stay like that for a while, just listening to his heartbeat.

"So your little plan for the week...it's off now, right?" asks Graham. "You're not going to, like, audition for *The Bachelor* or anything as soon as we get home?"

"Oh, Graham," I laugh. "It is *so* off."

Smooth move, Douchewell.

30

Okay, so I'm not allowed to refer to myself as *Douchewell* ever again. Early this morning, during a bit of pillow talk, I let it slip that I've internalized the old moniker. Graham was more upset than I expected. He thinks that the nickname is the root of all my self-esteem issues, and said that if he ever finds this Alex Sanderson person, he's going to, well…it wasn't very nice. I asked him what makes him such an expert on the effects of name-calling, to which he very calmly replied *My last name is Blenderman.* Fair enough. Anyway, I tried to tell him that middle school gym class was enough to destroy anybody's self-esteem, with or without a derogatory nickname, but he wasn't having it. So, goodbye Summer Eve Douchewell.

I'm a new woman.

Oh, and Dad's missing.

It's been a long morning.

Graham and I were summoned from bed, much earlier than we would have liked, by the sound of Mom pounding on the door. She'd been searching the ship for Dad since seven o'clock this morning, going so far as to checking the fitness center, but to no avail. That's when she decided it was time to call in the reinforcements. It's now half past eleven and Graham and I are sitting in their cabin, brainstorming as to where he could have gone.

"Do you think he went ashore?" I ask. "I mean, if he's not on the boat, he's got to be on the island. Are you sure he didn't mention anything to you last night?"

"Last night?" says Mom. "You mean, when I was unconscious from all the champagne you poured down my throat? Your father could have been murdered and thrown overboard right in our own cabin for all I know!"

I roll my eyes. So we're jumping straight to murdered and thrown overboard. Good to know. I knew any fun Mom and I had last night would come back to haunt me.

"I'm sure there would be some sort of evidence if he'd been murdered and thrown overboard," I say, looking around the vicinity of the sliding glass door. Everything looks normal, at least without any sort of forensic equipment. "He'll turn up. Let's not panic."

"Why don't we ask somebody down at the gangway?" asks Graham. "I'm sure if he left the ship they would remember."

"But there are thousands of people onboard!" says Mom. "How would they remember *one* person?"

"Wild white hair. Nervous wreck. I think he's pretty memorable," I say. "Let's go." As I stand up to leave, I notice Dad's bottle of anxiety pills sitting on the desk. I pick it up.

"Look, he left his anxiety pills behi—" I stop talking and read the bottle again. "Um, Mom? Who's Thomas Magasaki?"

"Who?"

"Thomas Magasaki. His name is on Dad's pill bottle."

"He must be the pharmacist."

"No, I don't think so," I say, turning the bottle around in my hand. "I think these are his pills."

Graham walks over and takes the bottle out of my hand.

"Marinol," he reads.

"What the hell is Marinol?" asks Mom. "He's supposed to be taking Xanax!"

"Marinol, if I'm not mistaken, is medical marijuana." Graham bites his lip and looks at me.

I choke back a laugh. "Dad's been taking *marijuana* all week?"

"Oy, God!" Mom shrieks, sinking onto the bed. If I could see into her mind, I would find *Reefer Madness* playing on a high-speed loop.

"That actually explains quite a bit," I say.

"It's alright, Joan. Everything's going to be alright." Graham sits down next to Mom and puts his arm around her shoulders. "Richard's perfectly fine. If anything, he's been enjoying himself immensely. The pills seem to have relaxed him. It could have been much worse. Imagine if he was taking some random woman's estrogen pills."

The humor escapes Mom as visions of drug dealers and orange jumpsuits continue weaving their way around her mind.

"I'm going to go ask around the gangway, like we planned. You two stay here." I smile apologetically at Graham and head for the door, when the phone rings. The three of us exchange glances and then Mom jumps up to answer it.

"Hello? Yes. What? Oy, God! King who? Edward? The Seventh?

Where is that?" She scribbles words down on a notepad. I rush over and read what she's written. It's the name of a hospital.

"What happened?" I whisper, my stomach suddenly in knots. Mom shushes me.

"Okay," she says. "Yes. We'll be there! Thank you!"

She slams down the phone and turns to me. I'm shaking. We both are.

"It's your father. He's been in an accident."

***

The taxi ride from the ship to the hospital in Paget Parish is a nightmare. They wouldn't give Mom any details over the phone, other than that Dad had been in some sort of accident and had sustained minor injuries.

What kind of accident? Was he hit by a bus? Was he mugged? If he had been injured onboard the ship, he would have been brought to the infirmary and we'd have been notified by cruise staff. No, he must have been injured somewhere on the island, early in the morning. All by himself.

Poor Dad. He hasn't been himself all week. He's been wandering around in some kind of drug-induced stupor, and now he's probably gone and jumped off the roof of a building thinking he could fly or something. Or do people only do that when they drop acid?

Either way, this taxi ride is taking forever. We told the driver that we're going to the *hospital*. Doesn't he realize this is an emergency? People don't just take taxis from a cruise ship to a hospital for fun. It's not somewhere that families normally go for sightseeing. One glance in the rearview mirror at the expression on Mom's face should be enough to make him put the pedal to the metal, but he seems to be in his own little carefree world.

I'm considering leaning through the seats and asking him to pick up the pace, when I realize that we've finally come to a stop in front of the emergency room. Graham pays the driver, and the three of us rush inside to the information desk.

"Hartwell. Richard Hartwell," says Mom. "That's my husband. He's here. He's been in an accident!"

We're instructed to follow a nurse through a set of double doors and into the area where patients are treated. Most of the beds are curtained off for privacy, but occasionally I catch a glimpse of someone with a bloody face or with tubes coming out of their nose. It's all so morbid; I'm terrified to think of what condition Dad might be in. We finally come to a stop in front of a pink curtain and I take a deep breath.

Then I sneeze.

It smells a bit odd over here. Not like a sterile, hospital smell, but like a heavy, spicy, oriental kind of a thing. As the nurse pulls the curtain back, I brace myself for the worst. I'm holding onto Graham's arm with one hand, and my mother's elbow with the other.

And there's Dad. He's not in traction or a coma or anything. He's just sitting up in bed, with a miniscule bandage on his forehead.

And there's Angel Cake O'Brien, sitting in the chair next to him reading a copy of *Us Weekly*. I knew that smell was familiar.

"What the *hell* happened to you?" yells Mom.

Wow. Ten seconds earlier Mom was in the throes of despair thinking something terrible had happened to her husband. I guess now that she knows he's alive, it's back to business as usual.

"And what are you doing with *her*?" she continues. "Have you lost your *mind*?"

"Mom," I hiss, grabbing her by the arm and pulling her off to the side. "Go easy on him. He's been taking Marinol all week, remember? *Marijuana*. He's not himself."

"Excuse me? Mrs. Hartwell?" A soft voice interrupts from outside the curtains. We turn to find a tall woman in a lab coat, holding a clipboard.

"I'm Dr. Holland," says the woman. "I treated Richard this morning. Are you his family?"

"Yes," says Mom, clearing her throat. "We've come for him." She makes it sound like we've got the UFO parked outside.

"How is he, Doctor?" I ask.

"He and his, um, lady friend here, were in a minor scooter accident. He was brought in with some lacerations to the head. This type of thing is quite common, I assure you. He's going to be just fine."

"You were riding a scooter with *her*?" shrieks Mom.

Dr. Holland takes a step back, toward the safety of the opposite side of the pink curtain. "Why don't I give you a few moments alone?" she says. "I'll be back shortly with some more information."

"You were on a *scooter*?" I ask, in a bit more kindly manner than my mother. I sit down on the edge of the bed. "That's so cool!"

Dad smiles. "I was just like James Dean!"

"I'm so proud of you!" I take his hand and squeeze it.

"Are you out of your mind?" asks Mom. "A man your age, on a scooter? You could have been killed!"

I want to argue that she's being ridiculous, but it's kind of hard to when you are, in fact, sitting in an emergency room.

"I just really wanted to try it," says Dad. "I knew *you* would never go with me," he looks at Mom, "so I went down early this morning to the rental shop. While I was waiting at the counter, Angel Cake came in behind me."

"You *followed* him?" I ask.

Angel shrugs and continues flipping through her magazine.

"Anyway," continues Dad, "Angel Cake was riding on the back of my scooter and, um, she had her hands around my waist."

"*And*," says Mom. God, she looks foreboding. Poor Dad.

"And, um," Dad glances nervously at Angel Cake, but she's started rifling nervously through her pocketbook and won't meet his eyes.

"She, um, she had her hands around my waist," he continues. "And then, suddenly they were, um, *below my belt*." He says the last three words almost in a whisper.

"*Below your belt?*" Mom and I say in unison.

"You know what that means, don't you?" Dad looks directly at me.

"Yes, Dad. I get it."

This is so disturbing.

"Well, that's when I must have squeezed the throttle a bit too hard because I was, um…distracted. Then I swerved to avoid some chickens, and I hit a fire hydrant."

All of us turn to look accusingly at Angel Cake.

"You were grabbing my husband's privates?" shrieks Mom.

"You were grabbing my *father's* privates?"

"What?" says Dad, turning a bit red. "No! She was just feeling around inside my fanny pack."

I breathe a sigh of relief—although, to be honest, a woman feeling around inside my father's fanny pack isn't any less revolting.

"I think that I should go," says Angel, gathering up her pocketbook and her magazine and swishing towards the door.

"Wait a minute," I say. "Why have you been stalking my father all week?"

"He's a very attractive man," she says, tossing her hair over her shoulder. "He looked like he needed to be shown a good time."

"He has a *wife*," I say. "And a daughter. He doesn't need *you*. He especially doesn't need you rooting around inside his fanny pack."

"My mistake," says Angel.

"Only, it wasn't a mistake, was it? You think he's got money. That's why you were in his fanny pack. You were looking for money, weren't you? Or maybe his watch?"

Angel looks offended for about half a second, and then she narrows her eyes at me.

"Well, what about the Camaro?" she asks.

"Mine," says Graham.

"And the luxury suite?"

"Also mine," says Graham.

"And all of the expensive alcohol?"

"Me," says Graham.

Angel Cake's eyes light up. She sidles up to Graham and slaps her meaty paw against his butt. "What are *you* up to tonight?"

"Get away from him!" I yank the curtain back and hold it open until she takes the hint.

"Never met a duller bunch in my life," she mutters as she passes through the curtain and heads down the hall. The smell of her spicy perfume lingers in my nostrils. I sneeze again.

"Bless you," says Dad.

"Thanks."

"Angel Cake thought I was rich?"

"Yeah, Mom and I figured that out last night. Sorry."

Dad just shrugs. "She seemed like a nice girl."

"A nice girl?" yells Mom. "What is *wrong* with you? Taking that floozy out on a scooter? Flirting with young girls on a bus? Getting a *tattoo?*"

She's picked up a copy of *Internal Medicine Today* and is waving it around in Dad's face. I pluck it out of her hand and guide her away from the bed.

"Mom!" I whisper. "Remember, the *drugs.*"

A light bulb seems to goes off in her head. She walks back to the bed and sits down. She takes Dad's hand in both of hers, and holds it to her chest.

"Oh, Richard, we're going to get you all the help that you need. I just want you to remember that none of this was your fault."

"They already bandaged me up," says Dad, looking a bit flummoxed at her sudden change in behavior, and not at all comprehending her meaning.

Mom looks to Graham for assistance.

"You've been accidentally taking medical marijuana all week," he says bluntly, and with a shrug. "It happens."

Dad looks at us blankly for a few seconds, then he smiles.

"You know, I always wanted to try that."

31

Before Dad can elaborate, Dr. Holland comes back in. She flips through her chart and smiles warmly at us.

"Richard should be just fine," she says. "But because he sustained a head injury, we would like to keep him overnight for observation. Just to be safe. He'll be discharged early tomorrow morning."

"But our ship is leaving tonight!" says Mom. "I'm having a nervous breakdown!"

"I understand," says Dr. Holland. "But it's very important that we keep an eye on him." She looks at Mom with concern. "Bermuda has an excellent mental health facility in Devonshire Parish. If you're truly having a nervous breakdown, perhaps you should be transported for evaluation? Of course, they might have to hold you for a few days…"

"What?" shrieks Mom. "No, I'm fine! I just meant that…that I could use a drink!"

Ha, I knew it.

Mom looks helplessly at Graham and me. I may be a new woman, but I've still got to be a good daughter. This might be the worst possible time to cut my vacation short, but Graham and I will just have to pick up where we left off when we get home. Back home in the real world.

Breathe, Summer. The real world is good now.

"Don't worry, Dr. Holland," I say. "My mother's just a bit dramatic. She doesn't need to be institutionalized. Not today, at least."

I turn to Mom. "Graham and I can go pack up your stuff from the ship, and then I'll find us a hotel for the night. Graham, you can take the ship back home if you'd like. There's no reason for you to have to cut your trip short too."

"No, I'm coming with you," says Graham, slipping his arm around my waist. I hope that Mom's mind is too consumed with nerves to register what he's doing. I'm not quite ready for her to know about us. She sinks down onto the bed.

"No," she says, her eyes clearly focused on Graham's hand around my waist. "You two take the ship home. I'll stay the night here with your father, and we'll fly out in the morning."

"Are you sure?" I ask. "Isn't that a lot for you to handle on your own?"

Mom looks at me and smiles. "I rode a Jet Ski, Summer. Your father got a tattoo of a naked woman." She shoots him a look. She's never going to let him live that down. "We're in our sixties. I think we can manage a simple flight. Isn't that right, Richard?"

"Right," says Dad.

I'm fairly certain he has no idea what he just agreed to. Dad's been terrified of flying for his entire life. But right now, he looks happy. I don't know if it's the marijuana pills, or the fact that he rode a scooter, or the fact that Angel Cake O'Brien felt around inside his fanny pack. But he looks happy.

Then there's Mom, sitting on the edge of the bed, smiling up at Graham who still has his arm around my waist. She's got to be thrilled that Graham and I have finally *gotten together*. Maybe she'd seen it all along, when I was too down on myself to see it on my own. I'll wait until we're home to break the news about moving out. For now, I'll let her have her moment. Just like Dad, she looks happy.

Mom and Dad, looking the happiest I've ever seen them…in the emergency room of a foreign country.

The world is a very strange place.

***

Four jackets of varying weights, enough socks for the entire Confederate Army, three umbrellas, most of the antacid aisle from the local pharmacy, and six pairs of old people sneakers that all look exactly the same—back into the suitcases, and back into The Duffle.

Graham and I quickly pack up Mom and Dad's belongings and lug everything back to the hospital where Dad has been transferred to a regular room for the night. We say our goodbyes and then race back to the ship in another exceedingly slow taxi. Normally, we should have been back onboard two hours before leaving port, but cruise staff had been made aware of our situation. That's why they didn't yell at us when we arrived at the gangway with only twenty minutes to spare, but nobody else onboard seems to have gotten the message.

"That was humiliating," I say, as we stumble into an elevator. We're both out of breath from the long run from the taxi to the ship. There were people leaning over the railings, literally booing us for being late. Booing us! The Captain was kind enough to come over the loudspeaker and explain that the two passengers who were late had been dealing with a family emergency at the local hospital. It helped a bit, but still. They *booed* us. What is wrong with people?

Once we return to the safety of our suite, Graham wants to immediately head back out and watch from the top deck as we pull away from Bermuda. All I want to do is hide in my room until we get back to Boston.

"Did you not hear them booing us?" I ask. "Or is that just a normal day for you?"

"It was like three people, and they should be ashamed of themselves," says Graham. "We were at the *hospital*. We didn't do anything wrong."

"I know. But still, I feel like everyone's going to be staring at us and whispering—*Look, it's the two idiots that were late for the boat.*"

"You'd better get used to being referred to as *the two idiots*, if you're going to be dating *me*."

"True," I laugh. "Okay, fine. Let's go." I jam a baseball hat on my head so nobody will recognize me, and grab the neon-green, terrycloth hoodie off the back of a chair.

"You're wearing that?" asks Graham.

"Not exactly."

As we make our way through the crowd on the top deck, I realize that nobody is staring at us the way I thought they would. Everybody seems to have already forgotten about it. Graham gets the occasional look from an older woman, but that's normal. We find an open spot along one of the railings, and I casually slide my hand—the one holding the hideous hoodie—over the side of the ship. I nudge Graham with my elbow to make sure that he's watching.

Then I open my hand, and down it goes. I'm like the old lady from *Titanic*.

"Oh, what a shame!" cries a woman standing next to me. "Oh gosh, what a shame."

"A damn, damn shame," I say, smiling.

Graham puts his arm around my shoulders as I watch the hoodie bobbing around in the froth of the ship, symbolically headed towards its final resting place at the bottom of the Atlantic. Very slowly the ship starts to pull away from the island, and the pastel houses become smaller and smaller as we head towards home. It's funny to think that Mom and Dad are still over there.

It's funny to think that I'm on vacation, alone with a boy.

Maybe tonight we'll dine on the prow of the ship, with dolphins leaping gleefully in the background. Maybe we'll put on white linen shirts and sip champagne with the Captain. The possibilities are endless out here on the sea.

Maybe Graham and I will get married. Maybe we won't. An eight-day cruise is much too short to make any major life decisions. But an eight-day cruise is an amazing place to start.

For now, we just sail into the sunset.

The End

Join Beth on Facebook:
www.facebook.com/bethlabontebooks

And Twitter:
@Beth_Labonte

You may also visit Beth's website and sign up for her newsletter:
www.bethlabonte.com

Other books by Beth Labonte:

What Stays in Vegas
Summer at Sunset
Down, Then Up (A Novella)

Beth Labonte was born in Salem, Massachusetts and received a B.A. in Sociology from the University of Massachusetts Amherst. She worked as an administrative assistant for fourteen years, turning to writing as her creative outlet in an excruciatingly mundane corporate world. Beth now writes full-time, and resides in Massachusetts with her husband and son.